# MURDER AT THE TEA ROOMS

A 1920s Cozy Mystery

A Lady Felicity Quick Mystery
Book 3

ROSIE HUNT

ISBN: 9789083290621

Editing by Effie Wilson

Cover art by DLR Cover Designs

*For my godmother.*

*Can you spot your word?*

# A Note on Language

This book is written in British English. There are two reasons for this:

- the story is set in England, and
- I, the author, am British.

Part of my British writing style is the use of s where z is used in American English. For example: alphabetised instead of alphabetized, and revitalise instead of revitalize.

However, you may have noticed that in the blurbs and marketing for this book, it's called a cozy mystery and not a cosy mystery.

This is because the American spelling is standard for the genre. Spelling it this way helps people (and algorithms) recognise my book more easily.

But outside of book genres, it's cosy all the way.

# Cast of Characters

## Quick family

Lady Felicity Quick, journalist

Lord Jasper Quick, Earl of Denbury, editor-in-chief of the Western Daily News and Felicity's brother

Lady Henrietta Quick, Dowager Countess of Denbury, grandmother to Felicity and Jasper

Pip, Felicity's Yorkshire Terrier

## Green Ginger Tea Rooms

Mrs Vera Monroe, owner and manageress of the Green Ginger Tea Rooms

Miss Zoe Monroe, Vera's daughter

Mrs Katherine Evans, Vera's sister

Mr Luca Carli, patisserie chef

Miss Frances Lee, waitress

Miss May Pettigrew, waitress

## Residents of Ippleford village

Mr Ernest Biggs, landlord of the Blue Lady Inn

Mrs Gertrude Biggs, landlady of the Blue Lady Inn

Mr Philip Heard, actor

Mrs Ernestine Heard, actress

Doctor Bartholomew Grant, general practitioner (retired)

Colonel Ebenezer Norrington, army officer (retired)

Mrs Prudence Norrington, wife of Colonel Norrington

Mrs Maunder, housekeeper at the Norrington household

Mr Harold Stanton, post master

Mr Lewis Viner, gardener

Mrs Emily Waverley, widow

Miss Millicent Waverley, Mrs Waverley's daughter

## Others

Mr Alexander Cooper, reporter for the Western Daily News

Detective Inspector Robert Daniels, police detective

Sergeant Mervyn Hewitt, police officer

Mr James Kitson, butler for the Quicks

Mr Liam Finnegan, driver for the Quicks

# Extract from the Western Daily News, 1921

**Dramatic Conclusion for Ippleford Enigma**

*Our own journalists were there for the startling finale!*

IPPLEFORD, 23 October — Legends haunt the castle ruins that loom above the usually peaceful village of Ippleford, but recent events eclipse the drama of any ancient story.

Central to the fateful incidents were the Green Ginger Tea Rooms. How this successful yet unassuming establishment became entangled in an intrigue worthy of its own folklore is explained for you in precise detail in this very newspaper.

Our coverage is not only exclusive, it is unique because our reporters were not simply on the spot when matters unravelled. They played a pivotal role in the outcome.

# Chapter One

## THE VILLAGE OF IPPLEFORD, SOUTH DEVON, 19 OCTOBER 1921

Could Lady Felicity Quick have avoided the situation in which she found herself?

Her surroundings weren't the problem. The table in the window of the Green Ginger Tea Rooms offered a splendid view of Ippleford's picturesque, cottage-lined high street, and the easeful bustle of the establishment was like a warm blanket over one's knees.

Waitresses in frilly headbands and white aprons wove between happy, chatty customers seated under the tea rooms' low, wood-beamed ceiling. Behind a glass-topped counter, steaming pots of tea and coffee were prepared, and freshly baked scones, buns, and all manner of sweets still fragrant from the oven were placed onto paper doilies spread on china plates.

All orders were delivered promptly and with a smile.

A slice of dark, silky chocolate tart topped with a generous layer of chocolate shavings lay on the table before Felicity. It was a delicate, handsome confection, befitting of an elegant patisserie on the Champs-Élysées. But Felicity had yet to taste it.

She stroked Pip, her three-year-old Yorkshire Terrier and constant companion, whose presence — usually on her lap whenever Felicity was seated, as was now the case — offered reassurance in most circumstances, although not this one.

"Vera is so very relieved that you agreed to come to Ippleford, Felicity dear."

Lady Henrietta Quick, Dowager Countess of Denbury and Felicity's grandmother, was seated beside Felicity at the Green Ginger's best table, dressed in a typically Victorian smoke-grey high-necked dress, a cameo brooch at her throat.

The dowager dabbed crumbs from her mouth with the point of an embroidered napkin. She'd done her best to conceal her intense enjoyment of a Devonshire cream tea, the clotted cream spread thickly on warm scones, then slathered with bright red strawberry jam.

"So very relieved," continued Lady Henrietta, using hushed tones suited to a delicate matter that ought not to reach prying ears. "To think the police would do nothing about it. The anguish it's been causing poor Vera is unfathomable. Absolutely unfathomable."

Mrs Vera Monroe was, according to Lady Henrietta, the best of domestics ever to have worked at Bradley Court, the Quick family's ancestral home. Vera had amicably departed from her position as the dowager's lady's maid before the war. Lady Henrietta continued to dote on her, and Vera was now the proprietor and manageress of the Green Ginger Tea Rooms, which opened in Ippleford a year ago with support from the dowager.

"And after such a run of awful luck," continued Lady Henrietta, shaking her head sadly. "A war widow left to raise her young daughter alone, only to have her business afflicted by criminal behaviour."

The criminal behaviour in question was a series of rather trifling acts of sabotage, none of which had so far caused harm to anyone or significant losses for the tea rooms. Felicity wouldn't say so to Lady Henrietta, but it was understandable the police hadn't become involved. The whole affair seemed rather domestic.

"Vera has been through an awful lot," offered Felicity with genuine sympathy between sips of milky English Breakfast tea. Trifling or not, it was no fun to be a victim of crime.

Lady Henrietta continued. "When I told Vera about the cases

already under your belt and how keen you are to root out her saboteur, oh! She was enormously relieved."

That Felicity's grandmother thought so highly of her sleuthing skills was misguided — any past successes could be attributed to luck rather than skill — and also a turnaround, considering Lady Henrietta's earlier concerns about her granddaughter pursuing too masculine a career as a reporter.

And here began Felicity's discomfort with the situation.

*You're a journalist, Cici, not a blasted detective.*

It was something Felicity's brother, Lord Jasper Quick, Earl of Denbury, had said to her more than once. As editor-in-chief of Southwest England's most-read newspaper, the Western Daily News, Jasper wasn't just her older sibling. He was also Felicity's boss.

Lady Henrietta's influence as the household matriarch swayed Jasper when he conceded Felicity time away from her normal newspaper duties for the case in Ippleford. That he made no protest at Felicity's engagement as a very amateur private detective had been startling. But it wasn't just Jasper's underlying disapproval and her own lack of professional standing as a sleuth making Felicity uncomfortable.

"I'm glad we can give Vera hope," said Felicity, caressing Pip's soft tan-and-blue ears. "As long as it only takes a day or two to wrap things up."

The main problem with the case in Ippleford was that it threatened to jeopardise Felicity's reputation with fellow journalist, occasional lifesaver, and erstwhile professional rival, Alex Cooper.

When Lady Henrietta made her inescapable request on Vera's behalf, Felicity and Alex had been scheduled to interview Devon's most senior district judge, Chief Magistrate Lucius Hawkins. Not only was it an important scoop for the Western Daily News, it was an open door to closer collaboration between the newspaper and the courts. As Alex specialised in crime reporting and had arrived in Devon only a few months ago, the connection with Judge Hawkins was especially important to him.

The interview now had to be delayed.

Felicity would admit only to Pip that the prospect of interviewing a judge was a trifle boring. Still, she was keen to work with Alex, who had superior experience as a Fleet Street journalist.

Lady Henrietta waved a dismissive hand. "Jasper has it all arranged, my dear girl. You shan't miss anything. And neither shall that pleasant young man Jasper has you working with."

The dowager's knowledge of newspaper business wasn't exhaustive, but she at least had a vague idea of what was at stake. Felicity and Alex had been yoked together as punishment after the two of them — in Jasper's opinion — became over-involved in what admittedly had been a rather dangerous case at Langton Manor. While there were obvious advantages for Felicity as the junior reporter, Alex stood to gain little from being saddled with a sidekick.

Jasper had nevertheless been firm. They would interview Judge Hawkins together or not at all.

Felicity hadn't informed Alex of the Ippleford sleuth assignment herself, so hadn't seen his reaction. The idea of him being at all disappointed was somewhat agonising.

Again, Felicity stroked Pip's ears. "The situation is rather unfair on Mr Cooper."

"You really mustn't worry, my dear," said Lady Henrietta. "Jasper promises to have something very worthwhile for Mr Cooper in the meantime."

Whenever she saw him next, Felicity would explain to Alex how there'd been no way to refuse the dowager's request to help the former lady's maid. Alex was an incredibly reasonable man. The most reasonable Felicity had met. He'd surely understand.

For now, all Felicity could do was focus on the task before her. Perhaps she'd surprise everyone — including herself — and identify the saboteur before the day was out.

A red-cheeked woman of middling age in a floral-print dress and an apron dusted with flour emerged from the glossy green swing doors at the side of the tea rooms. She hurried between the tables towards Felicity, Pip, and Lady Henrietta, tentatively patting her straw-yellow hair, which was set in close waves.

"Vera, my dear," exclaimed Lady Henrietta with ostentatious sympathy. "There you are, you poor, poor thing."

Felicity had barely entered her teens when Vera gently defied Lady Henrietta's pleading and left her position at Bradley Court to seek work in London's hospitality industry. While Vera was no longer the slim, spritely girl she'd once been, her broad cheekbones and the warmth behind her cornflower-blue eyes were unmistakable.

"Lady Henrietta. Lady Felicity. I'm so very sorry." Vera's gentle voice bore a Westcountry lilt. "I had to get a tray of pasties in the oven. We've been terribly busy. I hope Kathy, May, and Frances took good care of you in the meantime." Vera nodded towards the waitresses.

There were, in fact, only three of them — a woman of similar age to Vera and two younger girls — though they did the work of twice their number, moving non-stop between tables and under the arched doorways connecting the tea rooms' seating areas.

"Oh, your girls have been wonderful," gushed Lady Henrietta. "Isn't that so, Felicity?"

"Your waitresses have looked after us extremely well," agreed Felicity.

Pip chose that moment to lift his little black nose above the table and sniff the untouched slice of chocolate tart on Felicity's plate.

Vera blinked. "If our chocolate tart's not to your liking, Lady Felicity, I can fetch you something else. It wouldn't be any trouble at all, my lady. Really, it wouldn't."

Despite the years having changed her, Vera's presence was familiar and comforting. Felicity was transported to when she was still a child, before any talk of war, before the influenza that had claimed her father.

"That shan't be necessary, Vera," assured Felicity, urging Pip to withdraw his nose. "I'm certain the tart is delicious. I'm simply not hungry. In fact—" Felicity lifted her head to watch the waitresses whirling between customers "—I was wondering if I might not start things off by meeting everyone."

Vera cast a gaze over the busy tea rooms, then glanced nervously at Lady Henrietta. "Meeting everyone?"

Felicity offered a persuasive smile. She'd come to Ippleford to investigate, had she not? "Your staff here at the tea rooms, Vera. If you wouldn't mind." It was all Felicity could offer by way of clarification, for there was yet another twist to the assignment.

No one in Ippleford except Vera, the local sergeant who failed to show interest in the case, and the culprit him- or herself was aware of the sabotage.

When Vera came downstairs one morning to a jar of glacé cherries smashed across the floorboards, she considered it an accident and cleaned up before anyone noticed. And when a batch of Chelsea buns left overnight to cool were found to be dusted with salt instead of sugar, Vera held no one to blame, putting it down to an honest mistake.

But a Victoria sponge doused with green food dye couldn't have been an accident. Nor could a Battenberg cake squashed completely flat in the middle.

Vera glanced again at Lady Henrietta for reassurance. She was concerned about scaring away customers if word got out. Not even her staff knew, unless one of them was the saboteur.

The tea rooms' owner returned her gaze to Felicity. "You'd like to speak to my staff for your article about Ippleford, my lady?"

While a thoroughly amateur sleuth, Felicity wasn't inexpert to the point of not having a cover story for her presence in Ippleford. She was reviewing the village as a destination for day-trippers, including visits to the tea rooms and the local inn. She might even trot up to the castle ruins overlooking the village, if time allowed.

It was the simple sort of article Felicity could whip up in no time, and there was always room for extra content in the Western Daily News' well-read fortnightly leisure supplement. If she were to write the piece, Jasper would no doubt publish it. But essentially, Felicity was undercover.

"That's it exactly, Vera." Felicity offered another reassuring smile. "I'd like to gather insight from the local people, starting with your employees, if I may." Like the police, Felicity suspected the sabotage was an in-house affair, the random acts of lunatics being far less common than sensational newspapers would have the public believe.

Vera nodded, still looking uneasy. "We're nearing closing time and still rather busy. The play's final rehearsal is tonight, and Luca has a train to catch." Her face brightened. "But I'm sure we'll manage it, my lady. I'm ever so thankful you're here." Vera looked at Lady Henrietta. "I'm so very grateful to you both."

The dowager tapped Felicity's hand. "My granddaughter will do everything in her power to help. Isn't that right, Felicity dear?"

Felicity stroked Pip and gave a brief nod that she hoped conveyed confidence and capability. "With which of your fine staff members may I speak first?"

# Chapter Two

Lady Henrietta was collected from the front of the tea rooms by the Quick family's chauffeur-driven Rolls-Royce for the punctual delivery of a rousing speech on pleached fruit trees for the Lower Diddleton Plant and Floral Society. Vera had to attend to a table of giggly young tourists wanting to settle their bill, and then another table desiring a booking for the following week.

This left Felicity alone at the Green Ginger's best table, Pip still on her lap, sipping her tea and watching as the activities in the tea rooms wound down for the evening. Cakes were boxed up and tables cleared as the bell above the door tinkled and customers exited onto the high street. Closing time was a busy moment, but Felicity was impatient to begin her investigation.

From a distance, the three waitresses seemed equally friendly and efficient. The oldest had blonde hair much like Vera's, and of the two younger girls, one was red-headed and rather stout, while the other had brown hair and a willowy frame.

The waitresses would surely have had the means and the opportunities to sabotage the tea rooms. Might one of them have a motive?

The green swing doors of the kitchen flew open. A dark-haired, pale-skinned man in a white chef's smock, the sleeves rolled above his elbows, emerged into the main dining area. Setting an intense brown gaze on Felicity, he made his way liquidly like a cat through the tables towards her, a smile dancing on his lips.

Mildly surprised by the suddenness and vigour of his approach, Felicity stood politely to greet the man, tucking Pip under her arm.

The man was older than Felicity, perhaps around twenty-five, and he shook her hand with a powerful grip. "Lady Felicity Quick, no?" His accent was foreign. "So very pleased to meet you."

"Likewise, I'm certain," said Felicity politely, "except I'm terribly sorry. Mrs Monroe hadn't the time to inform me of your name."

"Luca Carli. Patisserie chef *straordinario*." Luca's smile oozed charm. "And may I say that your outfit is ravishing?"

Felicity glanced down at her clothes. Devon's autumn climate being unpredictable and her trip to Ippleford being an occasion where practicality trumped style, Felicity had on a skirt that reached slightly below mid-calf and a drop-waisted jacket in thick, bluish-brown tweed. Her shoes were an eminently comfortable pair of worn-in Oxfords, chosen primarily for their ability to withstand rain.

"That's kind of you to say, Mr Carli, but—"

The patisserie chef held up a hand. "I don't say such things to amuse myself, and our time is short. I must finish my work and make my train. Please—" Luca gestured towards Felicity's chair "—let us sit. You are from Devon, yes?"

As Felicity retook her seat, she shifted Pip aside and fished her trusty notebook and pencil out of her skirt pocket. It was her first interview in Ippleford, and she already risked losing the upper hand.

"Yes, Mr Carli. I was born in Devon and still live in the county. Where are you from, if you don't mind me asking? And how did you come to work at the Green Ginger?" Alex had taught Felicity that sharper questioning sometimes had merits.

"Switzerland," replied Luca, leaning his powerful forearms on the table. "I come here to make cakes, of course. And you come here to make an article? You are a journalist, no? But as an *aristocratica*, you must already have money. Maybe even a castle. Is this not correct?"

Felicity didn't look up from making notes in her brisk Pitman shorthand. She wasn't keen on the patisserie chef's manner, nor did she want to waste time being interviewed herself.

"I'm sorry to disappoint you, Mr Carli, but my family's home is a former monastery, not a castle. May I ask how you find life here in Devon and in Ippleford in particular? Assuming you live here, of course. Please correct me if I'm wrong."

Luca removed his arms from the table and shrugged. "I live upstairs. It is acceptable. Nothing special. Small tea rooms, small village. Tonight, I go to London. There, a man can be a great patisserie chef. A famous one, even."

While Luca's lack of enthusiasm for Ippleford and the Green Ginger was noteworthy, it didn't yet constitute a motive for sabotage. "Are you visiting London for business or pleasure?"

The patisserie chef looked distractedly over his shoulder. "I go for passport matters. It is... How do you say? Bothersome. Before the war, it was not like this."

"What brought you to England, if I may ask?"

Luca drew a sharp breath. "Lady Felicity. Please." He gestured towards her plate. "You have not tasted my creation."

This second round of awkwardness sparked by the untouched slice of chocolate tart could not be blamed on Pip, who was nearly asleep on Felicity's lap.

"I'm sure it's heavenly," insisted Felicity, "but I'm not at all hungry."

Luca continued to gesture, his broad palms upturned. "But you must. I really insist. Otherwise, what does my work count for? What am I doing here if I cannot create wonder?"

The chef's vivid disappointment caught Felicity off-guard. She cleared her throat. "Very well."

With her fork, she carved off the point of the slice and popped it in her mouth. Eating under Luca's keen gaze was uncomfortable, but the blend of rich chocolate ganache, dark cocoa-infused pastry, and the generous curls of chocolate decorating the surface melted exquisitely on her tongue.

Felicity had to be honest. "It's utterly delectable, Mr Carli."

Luca slapped a big hand on the edge of the table. "There. See. Now you have no doubt about my talent." He glanced over his shoulder again. "I must go." With no further note of farewell, he stood up and abruptly left Felicity at the table.

Pip lifted his head and looked around, as if to say, *Did I miss anything?*

"What a peculiar fellow," said Felicity for no one to hear but Pip, who whined thinly upon noticing he'd slept through a start being made on the chocolate slice.

Felicity considered another bite of the tart, including a dropped crumb or two for the Yorkie on her lap, but the patisserie chef's progress through the almost-empty tea rooms distracted her from the thought.

Despite his rush to catch the London train, and his demonstrated ability to behave without common courtesy, Luca slid behind the glass counter to attend to a customer, an elegant woman of around sixty, with a broad-brimmed hat and a wire-haired Dachshund on a lead.

The woman pointed to a shelf behind the counter. Luca smiled as he echoed the gesture, lifting a large hand towards a row of colourful boxes shelved high up. *Oh, you mean this?* he seemed to say with a playful quirk of his eyebrows.

"Sorry for the delay, my lady." Vera had approached without Felicity noticing. "Frances and May are waiting for you upstairs. They're keen to get up to the castle for the rehearsal, but I've told them to expect you."

Felicity wasn't sure what to make of the patisserie chef, but further speculation would have to wait.

"Oh, Vera. How kind of them. And by Frances and May, you mean..."

Vera smiled proudly. "They're my very best girls, my lady."

It was time to interview the waitresses.

# Chapter Three

The stairs to the accommodation above the tea rooms were narrow and steep, as was typical of Devonian cottages. The landing, like the stairs, was thickly carpeted. A single electric light in a simple brass fitting glowed dully against reddish wallpaper. It was quite a contrast to the tea rooms' bright, whitewashed interior. A hint of jasmine perfume hung in the air.

Pip remained alert in Felicity's arms, his nose twitching.

Laughter rang out from behind the second door on the left, which was where Vera had said two of the waitresses, Frances and May, would be waiting to speak to Felicity.

She knocked.

"Come in." The response was bright and immediate.

Frances and May stood between neatly made beds in a small room papered with pale floral wallpaper and nothing for decoration but a posy of dried flowers atop a tall wooden chest of drawers. A window leaded in crisscross fashion offered a view of the castle ruins against a darkening sky.

The waitresses, both smiling politely, no longer wore their white headwear or aprons, although they still had on their black dresses.

"Miss Lee, Miss Pettigrew." Felicity closed the bedroom door behind her. She wasn't yet sure which of the girls was which. "I do hope I'm not disturbing you. Mrs Monroe said you would be expecting me."

Ought she to have been less eager to interview everyone so quickly? To be in the bedroom was oddly intimate, yet she had to press on. Time was of the essence.

"Mrs Monroe said you're a journalist."

The older of the two girls spoke first. She was about eighteen and had square shoulders, freckles, and orange-red hair scraped back from her face. A brown overcoat hung from her arm, and her green eyes flashed warily.

"Will you be writing up the play?" She spoke with a Midlands accent.

Felicity blinked. "The play?"

The other waitress fidgeted uncomfortably, her gaze flitting to Pip. Taller than the redhead and slight of frame, she was perhaps sixteen years of age. Her mousy-coloured hair was tucked behind her ears, and she had on an unbuttoned grey overcoat. In her hands, she gripped a dark green tam o'shanter-style hat.

The red-headed girl frowned, as though ignorance on this point wasn't possible. "The play at the castle, of course. Our last rehearsal is tonight. Are you not coming to the performance tomorrow?"

Regardless of her opinions on amateur theatre, Felicity was unlikely to have the time. However, announcing as much wouldn't make for a favourable introduction.

She stroked Pip. "I'm terribly sorry. I'm being quite rude. I didn't yet introduce myself."

"You're Lady Felicity Quick, aren't you?" said the red-haired girl.

"That's correct. And you—"

"Frances Lee," said the redhead. "And this here's May."

"May Pettigrew, your ladyship." The mousy-haired girl gave an awkward curtsey. She had a thin voice and something like a London accent. "Very pleased to meet you."

Felicity smiled warmly. "It's certainly a pleasure to meet you both, Miss Lee and Miss Pettigrew. I presume Mrs Monroe already informed you of the article I'm writing about Ippleford? Would you mind if I took notes as we speak?"

Frances shrugged. May shook her head.

Felicity took the girls' reaction as consent and removed her notepad and pencil from her pocket, a mildly resistant Pip kept under her elbow.

"Do you both have parts in the play?" enquired Felicity as she positioned herself to write.

Another look of disbelief came from Frances. "I'm the lead, my lady."

"How wonderful." It was an unkind thought, but the abrupt, stocky waitress wasn't typical star material. "And you, Miss Pettigrew?"

The younger waitress shook her head. "But I'm helping, your ladyship. Almost everyone in the village is assisting with the production in some way or another."

"And we can't be late for the rehearsal, can we, May?" Frances lifted her pale eyebrows at the other waitress.

May shook her head meekly, avoiding Felicity's gaze.

"Of course not," assured Felicity, as she weighed how best to use the peculiar little interview. "Allow me to come to the point. May I ask what you enjoy most about living in Ippleford?"

"We're just so thankful to Mrs Monroe for all she's done for us," said Frances, without hesitation. "Aren't we, May? She's made the world of difference to us both. So you'll give the Green Ginger a good write up, won't you, my lady?"

Was the red-headed waitress a little too eager to sing her employer's praises? "What do you mean by that, Miss Lee?"

Frances frowned slightly. "Ippleford's a bit on the small side, if you catch my meaning, my lady. But I'm grateful for the opportunities I've been given. It could have been Ippleford or anywhere else. It wouldn't matter to me."

Felicity nodded while continuing to write in her notebook. Were waitressing jobs really so scarce? "Is there anything you'd like to add, Miss Pettigrew?"

May thought for a moment, tugging at the hat in her hands. "I'd like to help you, your ladyship, but I can't think of anything you'd want to write in the papers." She bit her lip. "I'm sorry. But I am awfully grateful to Mrs Monroe. She knows we'd do anything for her."

"That's abundantly clear," confirmed Felicity. *Perhaps even too clear*, she thought.

"Where will you be visiting while you're here, my lady?" Frances pulled on her overcoat.

Felicity's time was up. Balancing operating undercover with such brief interviews was tremendously tricky. "My agenda's not yet settled, but I'm planning a trip to the inn."

Frances grimaced. "Oh, no. The Blue Lady's nothing like as charming as the Green Ginger. Why would you waste your time in there?"

Felicity raised her eyebrows. "Is there much rivalry between the tea rooms and the inn?"

May grimaced. It was her strongest show of emotion yet. "There's no rivalry, your ladyship. Mrs Monroe is friends with everyone."

"You can't be rivals if you're not on the same level," added Frances. "The Green Ginger has a patisserie chef from the continent, and Mrs Monroe only uses the finest ingredients. You won't find anything like that at the—"

*CRASH!*

A cacophony of breaking china came from downstairs.

Pip barked, startled by the noise. May winced, twisting the hat in her hands.

"Not this again." Frances surged towards the bedroom door. "I'm sorry, my lady. We're needed downstairs."

---

Broken china littered the tea rooms' floor. A tray laden with empty cups, saucers, and plates had been dropped on the way to the kitchen. Thankfully, the last of the customers had departed, and the *Closed* sign had been turned in the window ahead of the mishap.

As Vera stooped over the mess, Frances and May flew in with dustpans and brushes, demonstrating their claims of unerring dedication to the tea rooms' owner.

The oldest of the three waitresses stood by, unhooking her headdress from her jaw-length gold-blonde hair.

"What happened?" enquired Felicity, holding tightly to Pip as he craned his neck, sniffing for any edibles that might have fallen with the tray.

The blonde waitress sighed, as though watching Vera and the girls at work made her weary. She was slender and attractive, with bright blue eyes and broad cheekbones not unlike Vera's. Over her uniform she wore a grass-green topcoat in a fashionable cut.

"It slipped out of my hands," she said.

The dropped tray wasn't exactly the saboteur's style, but so far, it was the closest Felicity had to a clue. Was there any way to find out if it had been deliberate?

Perking up, the blonde waitress turned a smile on Felicity. "I'm Katherine Evans, by the way. Pleased to meet you." Katherine's handshake was firm. Her accent was South of England but of no discernible region.

Felicity introduced herself.

"Vera mentioned your wanting to speak to me, but I'm afraid I haven't the time. I can't be late to collect my niece from school, and it's over in the next village."

A puzzle piece fell into place. "You're Vera's sister, are you not?" Felicity hadn't recognised Katherine's surname. Vera Monroe had been Vera Hood when she'd worked at Bradley Court, before she married. "And it's Mrs Evans, is it?" Felicity wondered if Mr Evans was also in Ippleford, but it was too soon after introductions to make enquiries of a personal nature.

Katherine's smile waned. "I suppose a woman must be twice as smart as any man in a profession like yours."

Felicity ignored the compliment, which was perhaps facetious. "Could we speak later?"

"Tomorrow would be better. I've been roped into helping with that blooming rehearsal up at the castle."

Katherine wished Felicity a pleasant evening, pulled a well-made green cloche over her ears, and disappeared onto the high street. The bell above the door continued to tinkle as Luca followed Katherine outside. He'd been upstairs to change and was going for his train in a tan overcoat and a dark brown Homburg hat, a small leather valise at his side.

Felicity sighed deeply, stroking Pip's silky ears. It had, of course, been utterly ridiculous to imagine she'd solve the case before the day was out.

The remaining two waitresses and Vera dashed about the tea rooms with buckets and brooms, working to undo the mess created by the dropped tray. Felicity might have offered her help, but the interruption combined with her lack of experience would have been more of a setback than a benefit.

Swapping a slightly squirmy Pip to her other arm, Felicity loitered by the cake counter, idly scanning the sweets in colourful packaging arranged on the shelves beyond.

Not being able to mention the acts of sabotage was already hampering the investigation. Enquiring after means or opportunity was rendered almost impossible, making the identification of motive absolutely critical, and even that had to be explored in a circumlocutory manner.

Vera would hopefully be without a prior engagement this evening, as it might already be time for a frank conversation. Felicity wanted to help, but with so many restrictions, how could she?

An extended tinkling of the brass bell above the door marked the hurried departure of Frances and May, leaving Felicity, Pip, and Vera alone in the tea rooms.

Vera approached, a broom still in her hand and a weary smile on her face. "Shall I show you to your cottage, my lady?"

Despite there not being an enormous distance between Ippleford and Lower Diddleton, Lady Henrietta had insisted Felicity stay over, both to dig more thoroughly into local matters and to fit with her cover story. Her motor still being out of service, Felicity had agreed to the approach.

Precise details of the accommodation, however, had been lacking.

Felicity's eyebrows drew together. "Am I not to sleep above the tea rooms?"

Vera chuckled. "That won't do, my lady. You saw how Frances and May share a room. Zoe's in with me, and Katherine's bedding down in the sitting room, which is temporary, of course. Luca's the only one of us with a room to call his own. No, my lady, we can't squeeze you in upstairs. It wouldn't be proper. You'll have the cottage all to yourself. It's small, but it's usually rented to tourists. They find it comfortable enough. And we'll take special care of you, of course."

As she dressed herself most days, Felicity hadn't thought of bringing a maid with her. The idea of staying in accommodation without staff present was mildly unsettling, but with women advancing in so many areas, one had to be open to trying new things.

"Thank you. I'm sure I'll sleep very well in the cottage." It was time to speak frankly. "Before we go, might I ask you a question or two?"

Vera sighed. "I suppose there's rather a lot I should explain, my lady, only Kathy will be back shortly with my Zoe. Might we speak on the way to the cottage?"

For someone in need of help, Vera wasn't making things easy.

Felicity gave a polite nod. "Let's do that."

# Chapter Four

It was a bright, chilly evening in Ippleford village, and rather fine weather for October, with a pale blue sky fading to umber at the edges and the hint of wood smoke in the air. A gentle breeze hissed through tall trees that dotted the edges of the high street, their leaves resplendent in shades of buttercup yellow, log fire orange, and holly berry red. The brook that edged the high street babbled contentedly as a workman's van motored by at a leisurely pace and a horse and cart clopped steadily along, the driver lifting his cap as he passed.

Felicity set a grateful Pip on the ground and turned up the collar of her tweed jacket. The thick woollen fabric was hardly glamorous, but it was warm and hid muddy paw prints well. She pulled a densely felted cloche, which matched the blue fibres in the tweed's weave, tightly over her auburn curls.

Above the village's thatched rooftops, lights twinkled atop the hill where the ivy-covered ruins of the castle stood. A stream of people flowed gently along the high street towards it, carrying theatre props and lanterns, children dashing back and forth. An undercurrent of excitement filled the air.

Vera stepped out of the Green Ginger's front door. A grey overcoat and a purple hat with a lime-green silk flower had replaced her apron, and in the crook of her arm hung a small tooled-leather handbag. Based on fashion choice alone, Vera appeared to be the older of the two sisters.

A young couple on the opposite side of the street waved to Vera as they passed. The man wore glasses and carried a wooden crate stuffed with all manner of items. His female companion had unruly hair and a pile of colourful, medieval-style dresses slung over her arm.

Vera returned a jolly wave. “You’re very lucky with the weather. Let’s hope it stays for tomorrow.”

The couple smiled in acknowledgement. The man held up crossed fingers.

“That’s the Heards,” said Vera as she walked with Felicity along the high street in the opposite direction, Pip already far ahead and making the most of his first opportunity to know Ippleford by nose. “They’re organising the play. Rather daring of them to do it in the autumn. There’s usually so much rain. Then again, it would be daring in any season. I don’t believe Ippleford’s ever known a theatre production before.”

“Your young waitresses seem rather excited about the whole affair,” said Felicity, slowing her pace. She wanted as much time to talk to Vera as possible.

“Frances is over the moon to have the lead role,” said Vera as she slowed her pace to match Felicity’s. “May’s quite happy to tag along with anything Frances does. Don’t let them force you into attending the spectacle, my lady. You’re already doing so much for us just by being here. And there’s already enough enthusiasm for the play. Just about.”

“I didn’t have long to speak to your workers, of course,” said Felicity, as a little girl in a princess costume skipped past. “But I’m rather curious to hear your opinions on your staff members.”

Vera chuckled. “I’d always dreamed of having my own establishment, my lady. It’s thanks to your grandmother I managed it. Lady Henrietta has been very generous towards me. I’d like to support my staff with their dreams, if I can.”

It wasn’t the level of detail for which Felicity had hoped.

She tried a different tack. "How did you meet Frances, May, and Luca? None of them are from Devon, are they?"

Vera's demeanour shifted. Her smile disappeared.

A tall lean man of around forty was approaching. He wore a checked shirt with battered corduroy trousers and no jacket. His tanned, lined face and the highlights in his wavy brown hair implied he was accustomed to outdoor work. A handsome red Border Collie trotted at his side.

As they passed one another, the man eyed Felicity and Vera carefully. He seemed angry, as though repressing the urge to speak out.

Pip stopped to watch the Collie pass, his tufted ears alert. The sheepdog paid the Yorkie no mind.

An aversion to newcomers wasn't uncommon in small, rural communities, especially when growing numbers of tourists threatened traditional ways of life. Might there have been resistance to the tea rooms in the village?

"Who was that?" asked Felicity quietly.

"Never mind him," said Vera, her upbeat air returning. "You put a question to me, didn't you, my lady? I'm afraid my mind is so busy these days. I'm becoming quite forgetful. What was it you asked?"

The unfriendly man catching Vera's attention had been a curious incident, but there were enough equally intriguing alternatives to explore. "I was wondering where you'd found your staff."

"Here we are," said Vera, gesturing to a compact, white-washed cottage with a bright blue door on the opposite side of the high street to the stream. "This is where you'll be staying, my lady."

The cottage was a detached one-storey dwelling with a dense roof in wheat-reed thatch. There was no front garden to speak of, its doorstep opening straight onto the street, but a trellis mounted beside the door was covered in shiny orange rose hips, and dark green ivy and purple pansies protruded from small window boxes on the sills.

"How pretty," said Felicity with some enthusiasm, although she was still not accustomed to the idea of having a dwelling to herself.

Vera smiled warmly. "Let's get you inside, my lady."

The door with its black ironwork latch opened directly onto a sitting room containing two high-backed chairs beside a fireplace in which flames already danced, offering welcome respite from the autumnal chill outside. A modest dresser had a fat, inexpensive clock on top of it, and its ticking joined the snapping of the fire.

Pip trotted across the floorboards, jumped onto a chair, and snuggled into a pillow with a yellow-and-green crocheted cover.

Felicity sighed. "Pip, please. We're guests here."

Vera chuckled. "It's quite all right, my lady. You and Master Pip may make yourselves at home however you like. The bedroom's through here."

A simple wooden door opened onto a room just large enough for a single bed, a big unadorned wardrobe, and a tiny table with a stool tucked underneath it. Atop the table, Felicity's typewriter sat in its case, a glass vase holding sprigs of dried honesty positioned next to it. The handle of Felicity's valise peeked out from under the bed, which was covered in a hand-stitched patchwork quilt. A small window provided a glimpse of the high street.

"And through here is the kitchen."

Vera backtracked into the sitting room and ducked through an archway, leading Felicity into a room just big enough for two people to stand in. There was a pale wooden table pushed against the wall, a small stove upon which stood a shiny kettle, and a stable-style door, presumably leading into some kind of backyard.

Felicity had never been in such a small dwelling before. It was cosy in a most charming manner.

"I'd be happy to do anything for you during your stay, my lady. You need only ask."

"I shall be very comfortable here," Felicity said with a confident nod, a honey-coloured wicker basket on the kitchen table catching her eye.

The basket contained produce ranging from cheese and butter wrapped in paper to a round of bread accompanied by pots of honey and jam. Felicity's stomach rumbled, but Vera made no effort to remove her hat or put down her bag. Their time alone together was limited.

"Vera, I do appreciate how exceedingly busy you are, but there are questions I'd like to ask, if I may."

"My apologies, my lady." Vera swapped her little handbag from one wrist to another. Her face turned serious. "Please, ask away. I shall do my best to answer."

Felicity went straight for the core of the matter. "Can you think of any reason someone in your household would want to sabotage the Green Ginger?"

Vera's mouth fell open. "Oh, goodness, my lady. No. Absolutely not. Why would any of them do such a thing?"

"Everyone is innocent until proven guilty, of course," reassured Felicity. Accustomed to the darker side of human nature as she regrettably was, she could easily imagine myriad reasons. "But living above the tea rooms, your staff and your sister surely had the means and opportunity to carry out the sabotage. Might one of them not also have a motive?"

Vera gripped her handbag. "My staff members are like family, and there is no animosity between Kathy and me. I'm sorry my lady, but I just can't see it."

*Can't or won't*, wondered Felicity. "How did you meet Luca, Frances, and May?"

Vera rubbed her forehead. "I've still got so much to do this evening, my lady. Kathy will be back soon with Zoe, then Kathy has to get up to the rehearsal herself. We can talk again tomorrow. But please, my lady, you won't mention the sabotage to my staff, will you? I don't want them upset. They've been through enough. Kathy, too."

Felicity reluctantly agreed. Combined with how busy everyone was, it was an obstacle to solving the crime, not to mention rather frustrating. There was so little to work with.

Felicity remembered the mean-looking man with the red Border Collie. "Before you go, Vera, might you tell me of anyone outside of the tea rooms with reason to hurt you or your business?"

Vera bit her lip. "Not that I know of, my lady. That's what makes the whole thing so maddening." She looked through the archway to the sitting room. "Dear me, is that the time already? Kathy and Zoe will be back at any moment now. And to think I came back to Devon to give Zoe a quiet life." She bustled towards the cottage's front door. "Not that I'm ungrateful for what I have, but to put an end to these silly acts of destruction would be a load off my shoulders."

Felicity remained full of sympathy for Vera's plight. "I just hope I can help," she said. *And that you'll let me*, she thought.

Reaching the front door, Vera stopped. "Oh, yes. I almost forgot. Your dinner, my lady. I'm not cooking a meal for tonight, seeing as everyone is out, but I'd be happy to warm you up some soup and a piece of pie and bring it over."

Felicity withheld a sigh. The day's sleuthing had all but dried up. "I was thinking of dining at the inn. It would fit with my cover story."

"What a lovely idea," said Vera, in stark contrast to Frances' reaction. "Mr Biggs, the landlord, and his wife are a hardworking couple and very kind. Such a terrible shame they lost their only son in the war."

"It is tragic how commonplace such grave losses have become," Felicity said sadly, mindful that Vera lost her husband in similar circumstances.

"Indeed, my lady," said Vera with barely a hint of emotion. Some people were keen to remember the loved ones they'd lost. Others preferred to forget. "Come, I'll point out the inn. It's not far."

Outside, the light was fading quickly. The cold air was invigorating, although Pip was loath to leave the warmth of the fire and had to be lifted across the cottage's threshold. Beside the stream, a small group of children played with hoops and sticks, eking the most out of the day.

"Here we go, my lady." Vera tucked her bag into the crook of her arm. "The sign for the Blue Lady Inn is just past where that gentleman with the valise is walking now. Oh, I say. He's waving. Do you know him? I can't say I've seen him around here before."

"I know him," said Felicity, an anxious shiver sweeping through her. "But I never expected to see him here."

# Chapter Five

Looking both relaxed and dashing in a slim-fitting grey flannel suit, Alex Cooper crossed Ippleford's high street and approached Felicity, Pip, and Vera, a wide smile on his frustratingly handsome face.

"Mr Cooper." Felicity forced herself to return his smile. Was this what Lady Henrietta had meant by Jasper keeping Alex busy while Felicity worked the sabotage case? Was she trusted to do nothing by herself?

Inexplicably, Felicity's thoughts jumped to her clothing. She'd been more than happy with her decision to wear tweeds. Now she wished she'd chosen something more flattering.

"Lady Felicity. Exactly the person I was hoping to find." Alex stopped outside the cottage and put down his case. "You must be Mrs Vera Monroe?"

Vera melted a little as Alex turned his dark blue eyes on her. "Please, do call me Vera. Any friend of Lady Felicity's is a friend of mine."

Pip approached to give Alex's shoes, a pair of mahogany brown cap-toe Oxfords, a customary sniffing.

"This is Mr Alexander Cooper." Felicity worked hard to keep her tone free of paranoia. "He's the top crime reporter at the Western Daily News."

Vera's eyes widened. She flashed a worried look at Felicity. "What crime are you here to report on? I've not heard of anything occurring locally."

Alex beamed. "Fear not, Mrs Monroe. I'm here to assist Lady Felicity with her piece on Ippleford. And what an attractive village it is, even with autumn's chill in the air." Alex wasn't beyond currying favour through charm, but as a recent arrival from London, his praise was likely genuine.

Vera sighed with relief. "Oh, I see. How wonderful." She glanced briefly at the cottage's blue door. "I've arranged only for Lady Felicity's accommodation. The cottage has just one bedroom."

Felicity's heart leapt into her throat at the idea that she and Alex might sleep under the same roof.

"Thank you, Vera," said Alex quickly, "but I've a room at the inn."

Vera's forehead creased as she stared down at the valise. "But you've your luggage with you, Mr Cooper."

It was Felicity's turn to promptly explain. "It's a camera case, Vera. Which means Mr Cooper is here to..." She raised her eyebrows quizzically at her colleague.

"I'm here as Lady Felicity's photographer," confirmed Alex. "You can't publish an article about how pretty a village is without images to prove it. Words alone aren't enough these days. Although I misjudged the light. It's getting rather dark. Oh, well. There's always tomorrow."

Vera chuckled. "If you're both settled, I'll get back to the tea rooms. I'm happy you won't be dining on your own, my lady."

After Vera's departure, Alex raised a thick, dark blond eyebrow and voiced the query on Felicity's mind.

"Are we indeed dining together this evening?"

Felicity's stomach growled ferociously. Thankfully, the babbling of the stream, combined with Pip's enthusiastic sniffing of any discernible foliage, hid the sound.

"Jasper sent you, did he not?" She needed to know, but she regretted the accusatory tone.

Alex's lips twitched into a half smile. "I realise we've a habit of running into one another unexpectedly, but it's an absolute pleasure to see you again, too."

"Of course, it's good to see you. It's just..." Felicity's feelings were a jumble. Her courteousness, usually effortless, failed her. "What exactly are you doing here?"

Alex's forehead creased, the scar he received in the war becoming visible. "I'm here to help, just as I said. And yes, Jasper approves, but I'm not his spy. Never have been. Never will be."

Alex had a knack for uncovering Felicity's inner workings quite without her wanting him to. He was also more deserving than most of polite and respectable treatment.

Felicity sighed. "I'm sorry. It's a surprise to see you, that's all. You're here as my photographer, you say?"

"Yes, and..." He leaned in a little, lowering his voice. "Your grandmother had a word with me."

Felicity lifted her eyebrows. The situation at the tea rooms was delicate, and Alex could be something of a sledgehammer in making people talk.

"I'm grateful you're here to help," she began. Then she remembered something, and her chest tightened. "Do you not resent the delay to the interview with Judge Hawkins?"

Alex shrugged. "Your grandmother's friend seems a worthy cause. And we'll be back to our normal work in a day or two, whatever happens. Jasper made that abundantly clear."

A weight lifted from Felicity. "You're quite right, on all counts."

"It's also your first official job as a private detective," added Alex playfully. "I couldn't miss that."

"But I'm not a private detective."

"So, dinner at the Blue Lady?" Alex reached down for his camera case.

Pip was already sniffing along the high street in the inn's direction. When Alex set off behind the little Yorkie, it left Felicity little choice but to follow. A chilly breeze rattled fallen leaves alongside them and set the inn's sign swinging.

"And it's not an official job," continued Felicity, catching up with Alex.

"Mr Cooper! Oh, Mr Cooper!"

A tall woman of around forty-five with shining brown curls, a lipsticked smile, and broad hips squeezed into a teal dress stood beside the inn's sign.

Behind her, a generous front garden with neatly clipped hedges and rows of unoccupied tables and chairs separated the inn from the street, its pale blue walls nestled under a roof of dark brown thatch. Leaded windows provided a view of a handful of patrons under glass lamps at the bar.

Pip paused, paw lifted, and sniffed the air. The scent of cooked meat and rich gravy drifted by. The inn's kitchen was busy preparing dinner.

"Yes. I'm Mr Cooper." Alex threw a confused glance towards Felicity.

With relief, the woman with the brown curls dropped a hand on her generously proportioned chest. "Well, when your motor pulled up, I said to Mr Biggs, that'll be Mr Cooper. Smart young man. Looks the journalist sort. Then, when I looked again, you'd gone. Only we'd started getting your evening meal ready. I've got to get up to the castle, you see. Help with that play." The woman gave a rich, throaty chuckle. "Not your fault, of course, Mr Cooper. Not your fault at all. But might you be ready for your supper now?"

Alex nodded, surer of himself. "Thank you. Mrs Biggs, is it?"

The woman laughed again. "Oh, please, call me Gertie. At the Blue Lady, our patrons are as dear to us as friends. Shall I have someone take your luggage to your room?" She nodded towards Alex's camera case.

"Actually, Gertie, I happen to have run into a colleague," said Alex. "This is Lady Felicity Quick, another reporter at the Western Daily News. Lady Felicity has accommodation elsewhere in the village." Alex turned to Felicity. "But I believe it'll be dinner for two?"

"Certainly," said Mrs Biggs. "Our customers' wishes can always be accommodated. Welcome to you, your ladyship. I shan't say anything as crude as I hope you give the village a good write up, although I do hope that, of course. And not just about the inn. But anyway." Mrs Biggs flapped a hand. "I'm getting ahead of myself. Tonight, we have a choice between beef stew and dumplings or venison."

Felicity's mouth watered at the suggestions.

"And rice pudding for dessert," continued the landlady.

Pip looked at his mistress longingly and licked his lips.

Alex looked to Felicity. "That all sounds rather good, doesn't it?"

It did indeed. Yet something tugged within Felicity.

She looked from Alex to the landlady. "I'm sorry, but on this occasion, I shan't join you. Although your menu sounds exceedingly tasty." She turned to Alex. "And my colleague here is, naturally, fine company."

Alex's mouth hung open for a moment. Felicity immediately felt regret, but it was too late.

"Perhaps on another occasion, your ladyship," said Mrs Biggs with an obsequious nod. "You're welcome at the Blue Lady any time."

"As you wish," said Alex, already recovered from his surprise at Felicity's decision. "Shall we meet tomorrow morning at the tea rooms?"

Felicity swept Pip off the ground before he could follow the dinner smell any further. "Splendid idea," she said, smiling uncomfortably.

After farewells, Felicity hurried back along the high street, darkness closing in and Pip whimpering under her arm.

"There's a tremendous amount of food at the cottage," said Felicity as brightly as possible. "Not to mention that wonderful fire. We shall have a thoroughly cosy evening together."

Neither Felicity nor Pip were convinced by her words.

Why had she turned her back on dining with Alex? She couldn't put her finger on it. Had he been mocking her about her 'first official job' as a sleuth? Even if he had, was it reason enough to be as unmannered as Felicity had been?

On the hill from where the crumbling castle overlooked the village, flaming torches had been lit, giving the onset of darkness an ominous feeling.

Finding the fire still alight in the cottage was a relief. Felicity had only to throw on an extra log to get it roaring.

Supper for both herself and Pip was fashioned from the simple, though delicious, supplies left in the kitchen. The cheese scones, once warmed and spread thickly with butter, were extremely filling. A slice of moist fruitcake proved an irresistible dessert.

Seated comfortably in a high-backed chair in the tiny sitting room, Pip in the seat opposite, and the fire crackling between them, Felicity opened her faithful notebook.

In Pitman shorthand, she wrote the names of the tea rooms' residents — Luca, Frances, May, and Katherine — and created a column headed *Motive* alongside. Felicity tapped her pencil on the page. The column remained blank.

*Sibling rivalry?* She pencilled this alongside Katherine's name. The dropping of the tray and Katherine's lack of effort to clear things up had been odd at the very least.

There came another twinge of regret at having walked away from dinner with Alex. Felicity enjoyed discussing precisely this kind of matter with him. She would tell him everything in the morning.

Giving up on her notebook, Felicity went to bed, snuggling down under the layers of blankets as Pip joined her, climbing atop the patchwork quilt. By the light of an old-fashioned oil lamp, Felicity read a few pages of a detective novel she'd brought with her, but when she was dozing off, chatter and footsteps outside woke her up.

The villagers were returning from the rehearsal at the castle. It was a gentle hubbub of light footsteps and hushed but excited discussions, which went on for rather a while.

When Felicity finally fell asleep, she did so with the detective book open on her chest and the oil lamp still burning.

However, it wasn't long before her sleep was once again interrupted.

## Chapter Six

Upon waking, Felicity felt mildly startled.

It was still dark outside, which was confusing. The oil lamp burned dully on the bedside table.

What time was it?

Heavy footsteps ran past the cottage. Muffled voices came from further along the high street.

Pip's ears twitched as Felicity tugged on the patchwork quilt, pulling it towards her chin. If people were still returning home from the rehearsal at the castle, it was perhaps not that late. She would go back to sleep.

*Tick!*

The sound was at her bedroom window.

Pip sat up straight at the bottom of the bed. He didn't growl, which was reassuring.

*Tick!*

The sound came again. Something was striking the windowpane.

Felicity got out of bed, went to the bedroom's small window, and parted the thin, checked curtains. Her breath steamed the glass, but there was enough moonlight to recognise the pebble-throwing culprit.

Undoubtedly mindful of the impropriety of staring into a

woman's bedroom, Alex stood with his hands in his pockets and his gaze directed away from the cottage.

It was the middle of the night. What could he possibly want?

Closing the bedroom curtains, Felicity fetched her floor-length silver-grey silk robe and tied it at the waist over her chemise.

The wood fire had gone out in the sitting room. The cottage's thick cob walls kept some of the warmth, but when Felicity cracked open the cottage's front door, the chill of the night air rushed into the cottage, chasing an inquisitive Pip away from the front door and causing Felicity to shiver.

Alex turned as the cottage door opened. His shoulders dropped with relief. "So, you're all right."

Felicity blinked, bewildered. "Any reason I shouldn't be?"

Pip bravely put his nose back around the door, sniffing in Alex's direction. Silvery clouds sped across the inky sky, and a chilly wind hissed through the branches of tall trees.

Alex swept an errant lock of dark blonde hair from his forehead. "There's rather a to-do, by all accounts," he said, nodding up the high street.

Felicity strained her neck to follow Alex's gaze. The climbing rose on its trellis blocked the view, and it wouldn't have been proper to expose any more of herself to the outside world in her current state of dress.

"A to-do about what?" she enquired. "And where, exactly?"

Alex squinted down the street. "Not sure yet. The police are in attendance."

Felicity's stomach clenched. The to-do was in the direction of the tea rooms.

Alex returned his gaze to Felicity. "Did you not hear anything?"

"Wait there just one moment, please."

Felicity closed the cottage door and hurried back to the bedroom, where she quickly changed out of her chemise and into her tweeds, pulling her hat down over her hair and wasting hardly any time with her hand mirror checking for errant curls.

"Pip," she said to the Yorkie, who sat expectantly in front of the unlit log fire. “I’d prefer you to stay here. I’m afraid we don’t know quite what’s ahead.”

After glancing at the clock — it was almost two in the morning — and closing the front door to the cottage with Pip safely inside, Felicity joined Alex in the chilly night air.

---

The tightness in Felicity’s stomach continued as she and Alex approached the tea rooms.

An ambulance was parked at an awkward angle across the street, and some figures moving about wore police helmets.

Felicity felt the colour drain from her cheeks. “Oh, dear.”

Alex raised his eyebrows. “We have a duty to investigate. Do you not agree?”

Felicity nodded, although her chief concern wasn’t her responsibilities as a journalist.

A police motor car passed them as they drew closer to the Green Ginger. Relief washed over Felicity when she saw Vera on the street in front of the tea rooms. Pale and in her dressing gown, Vera had her hands on the shoulders of a little red-cheeked girl with the same straw-coloured hair.

“Vera.” Felicity hurried towards her, with Alex close behind. “What’s going on?”

A tear rolled down Vera’s cheek. “Oh, it’s horrible, my lady. Too, too horrible. Kathy found her.”

Vera looked to her sister, who was standing close by. Katherine had on her grass-green topcoat but no hat, and she hugged herself tightly.

“Found who?” asked Felicity of the two women.

The little girl, who Felicity presumed to be Vera’s daughter Zoe, clung to her mother.

Katherine’s eyes were wide. “I only wanted a glass of water. Almost tripped over her.”

“Tripped over who?” pressed Alex.

Ambulance men appeared in the doorway of the tea rooms bearing a stretcher. A pristine white sheet covered the body atop it, including the face.

It was a ghastly sight.

May stood sobbing beside the tea rooms' entrance, a handkerchief bunched hard in her hand. Frances was with her, her arm reassuringly around her friend's shoulders. Both were wearing overcoats on top of dressing gowns, everyone having been roused unexpectedly from bed.

Vera, Zoe, Katherine, May, and Frances were evidently alive and well. Who lay under the sheet?

A tall, thin man of around sixty carrying a doctor's case followed the stretcher out of the tea rooms. He approached Vera, tucking a silver pince-nez into the top pocket of his brown jacket.

"I'm afraid it's as we expected," he said. "Quite a blow to the back of the head that did for her, although I doubt she would have known anything about it. Time of death was a couple of hours ago, at least."

Vera brought a hand to her mouth. Katherine tightened her arms over her chest. Felicity hoped the situation was beyond Zoe's comprehension, but from the anguish on the child's face, she clearly knew something was very wrong.

"I expect the police will want to speak to you all." The doctor said this rather stiffly, casting a glance at Katherine, May, and Frances. "I suppose I ought to wake Colonel Norrington and tell him the awful news. The man's my neighbour, after all. Poor blighter." He sighed. "And to think I came down here to get away from precisely this sort of thing."

"Thank you for rushing to our aid, Doctor Grant." Vera's voice trembled.

The doctor grimaced. "I'm only sorry there wasn't more I could do for the poor woman."

As the doctor strode off, the ambulance men loaded the stretcher into their van. Two uniformed officers, their notebooks at the ready, approached Frances and May, the latter dropping her handkerchief and looking the most shaken of anyone.

Felicity spoke gently. "Vera, I don't wish to be any kind of nuisance, but might you tell us what has happened? And is there anything Mr Cooper and I can do to assist?"

Vera shook her head, more tears escaping down her wide cheeks as she stroked her daughter's hair.

"Oh, my lady," she said between sobs. "I hardly know what's happened myself. Mrs Norrington is dead."

"Mrs Norrington?" asked Alex.

Vera dabbed at her eyes. "She was a customer. I didn't really know the woman, yet she died in my tea rooms this very night."

Katherine put a reassuring hand on her sister's arm.

"Well." Felicity did her best to remain composed. "This rather complicates things."

She glanced towards Alex, but he was approaching a uniformed officer, seemingly the most senior at the scene, with a dark grey moustache and a military uprightness about him.

"I'm a reporter with the Western Daily News," Alex told the policeman. "Is this a murder investigation?"

The policeman looked at Alex through wary, hooded eyes. "You made it here rather sharpish. I'm afraid there won't be any statements to the press till the detectives arrive from Exeter."

"So, it is a murder you're investigating?" pressed Alex.

The policeman narrowed his eyes further. "It seems highly unlikely to have been an accident."

# Chapter Seven

Soon after Felicity and Alex's arrival outside the tea rooms, Vera, Katherine, Zoe, Frances, and May were ushered towards Ippleford's church.

Ippleford's vicar had not long retired. While the search for his replacement continued, the vicar from the neighbouring parish of Star Torrington oversaw church matters in Ippleford. The police had to send for the key to the church hall, which was to become the hub of their activities in the village.

Felicity, Alex and the rest of the onlookers, many of whom had come onto the street in house clothes and hastily pulled on overcoats, were ordered politely by the police to return to their dwellings.

Nobody made a fuss except the rather unfriendly man who'd crossed Vera and Felicity in the street the day before. He argued with a fresh-faced policeman about his right to remain present on the high street, his Collie alert at his side and his checked shirt only halfway tucked into his trousers, but gave up when more officers went to the aid of their colleague.

With nothing further to be done, and the moon still casting its silvery light on a smattering of fast-moving clouds, Felicity and Alex bade farewell to one another before her cottage, agreeing to meet for an early breakfast at the inn.

But after a fitful sleep of what felt like a couple of hours, Felicity awoke to a banging on her front door.

Bleary-eyed and putting her silk gown to good use, Felicity opened the door to grey daylight and Katherine on the doorstep in her grass-green topcoat with a wicker basket over her arm. Underneath the powder on her cheeks and colour on her lips was a pallor confirming that the prior night's happenings, although nightmarish, hadn't been imagined.

"Sorry, it's late," Katherine said rather flatly. "Mind if I step in?"

Felicity requested a moment to get dressed properly. She was barely awake, but her mind was already racing with questions. Tea and breakfast were required before sense could be made of anything, and that meant joining Alex at the Blue Lady Inn, just as soon as whatever business there was with Katherine was completed.

Her tweeds on — including the jacket, as the fire hadn't yet been lit — and her Oxfords laced, Felicity welcomed Katherine into the tiny sitting room. Pip was curled in a high-backed chair, his tail touching his nose, clearly hoping someone would soon light the fire.

The clock read nine, which was by no means early for breakfast at the inn. Felicity hoped Alex had also needed extra sleep.

Katherine went straight to the kitchen where she unpacked crusty bread rolls, a bottle of fresh milk, and a small pot of honey.

"Vera asked me to apologise to you," she said, her eyes fixed on her hands as she filled the kettle and fetched a plate and cutlery. "The tea rooms won't be opening today, so I'm afraid this is all we can offer for breakfast. Not that you'll be writing your article about Ippleford now, I suppose." Katherine caught Felicity with a serious glance. "But then you know what my sister's like. Vera wouldn't want you going off on an empty stomach."

Pip trotted into the kitchen, his black nose twitching. The sound of cutlery on china was more effective for seizing the Yorkie's attention than calling his name.

"I believe you're right about the article," said Felicity, standing in the arched doorway.

Her mind was sliding into gear. With her cover story gone and sabotage having escalated to murder, why should Felicity stay in Ippleford? The interview with Judge Hawkins could proceed without delay. Alex would be pleased.

"But after everything you've been through," she continued, "I would expect waiting on me to be low on your list of priorities. I hadn't expected anyone to bring me breakfast. You even found the poor woman, did you not, Mrs Evans?"

Katherine stopped, a bread knife in her hand. She nodded. Her expression was hard, as if she resented being reminded of what she'd seen.

"Did you know her?" asked Felicity gently. "If you'd rather not talk about it, I quite understand."

"Her name was Prudence Norrington." Katherine's voice was flat. "She was a customer of the tea rooms. Lived up at Rose Cottages with her husband. I didn't know her, really. None of us did."

"What happened to her?"

"A blow to the back of the head." Katherine grimaced. "Horrible, isn't it?"

"What business did Mrs Norrington have in the tea rooms in the middle of the night?" The murder wasn't within Felicity's remit to investigate, and Alex was likely waiting to place his breakfast order, but she couldn't fight her curiosity.

"That's the mystery of it. No one should have been there except us residents."

"And how might Mrs Norrington have gained access? The tea rooms must have been locked up for the night."

Katherine gripped the bread knife's handle. "The door in the kitchen. It was hardly ever locked."

Felicity raised an eyebrow. While unlocked doors were common in the countryside, Vera might have been more careful considering the sabotage.

Katherine sighed. She put the bread knife on the kitchen table. "I suppose that's the end of the smashed jars and that salt-instead-of-sugar business."

Felicity blinked. "You knew about the sabotage?"

"There are no secrets between sisters. Besides, it's all over the village by now. The police haven't been too subtle in investigating the link."

"Do they assume Mrs Norrington to have been the saboteur?" Murder wasn't how Felicity imagined her investigation would end.

Katherine folded her arms over her chest. "The police found a pile of lace-edged napkins cut to ribbons. They were in perfect condition when I folded them yesterday, before we all went dashing off for that blooming rehearsal at the castle."

Felicity swallowed. Lady Henrietta would need to be informed of the developments at the Green Ginger. Had the motive for the murder been to stop the sabotage?

"There's no need for you to make my breakfast, Mrs Evans," said Felicity.

Her face relaxing, Katherine stepped away from the kitchen table. "Thank you. I'll get back to Vera and Zoe."

Katherine having departed, Felicity forewent the time needed to boil the kettle but ate a quick slice of bread and creamy honey to quell her growling stomach and in anticipation of a wait till her breakfast would be served at the inn. Then she hurried onto the high street, Pip at her ankles.

---

The temperature outside was warmer than the day before. A blanket of soft grey clouds emitted a fine steady drizzle, and Felicity's tweeds and Pip's blue-and-tan fur were soon covered in a light coating of tiny rain droplets.

Felicity turned towards the Blue Lady Inn, but the little Yorkie trotted in the opposite direction. And he was right to do so.

Alex was standing not far from the tea rooms, speaking to the uniformed officer with the steel-grey moustache from the night before and a young detective, the latter recognisable as such thanks to his trilby, overcoat, and stern face.

"That's all we can share with you for now, Mr Cooper," said the detective as Felicity and Pip approached, and after a round of polite nods, the two policemen departed.

"Did I interrupt?" asked Felicity, feeling mildly guilty.

Alex looked down at his notes as Pip sniffed his shoes. He tapped his pencil on an open page. "The murder weapon was a teapot. Can you believe it? The blow was so hard the handle came off. Only they can't find the handle."

Felicity blinked. "Are you writing this up?"

Alex frowned. "*We're* writing this up. Jasper telephoned the inn. The interview with Judge Hawkins has gone to someone else. You and I are covering the tea rooms murder."

Felicity felt almost nauseous. Alex had lost his story. "Can't we give the Ippleford article to someone else and interview Judge Hawkins ourselves?"

Alex shook his head as he returned his notebook to the inside jacket pocket of his grey flannel suit. "We were in the village when it happened and on the scene moments after the police arrived. No editor in his right mind would allow such a scoop to slip through his fingers."

A horse and cart rattled by, the flat-capped driver craning his neck to watch the police knocking at doors and speaking to passers-by.

"Are they certain it's murder?" Felicity persisted. "Could it not have been an accident? Might the teapot have fallen from a shelf?"

Alex sighed stiffly. "Accident's been ruled out. Quite a brutal attack, by all accounts."

Felicity winced. She'd had the misfortune to be in the vicinity of violent death before, but nothing as confronting as a bludgeoning.

A fast-moving motor rushed by. Felicity swept a befuddled Pip from the ground just in time. The vehicle was packed with men easily recognisable as news journalists, their eyes sharp with keenness to gather the details of the story and their photography equipment strapped to the motor's rear.

The situation threatened to tumble even further out of control.

"If you wouldn't mind giving me a minute or two." Felicity

addressed Alex, but she was already moving past the tea rooms. "I'd like to speak to my brother myself."

---

Protected from the drizzle by the canopy of a large oak with orange-brown leaves, a shining white telephone box stood at the edge of the village on the hill leading up to the castle. To Felicity's relief, she found it vacant.

With Pip inspecting the booth's exterior, Felicity lifted the receiver, dropped a coin into the slot — she was always sure to have coins about her person — and asked the operator for a connection to Bradley Court.

The Quicks' butler, Kitson, responded to Felicity's request to speak to Jasper promptly. She didn't want to leave Alex alone for too long. After a moment's waiting, a voice came through on the line.

"Felicity, dear?" It was Lady Henrietta.

"Hello, Grandmama." Felicity did her best not to sound vexed. She wasn't ready to explain matters to the dowager, not while the interview with Judge Hawkins hung in the balance. "I was hoping to speak to Jasper."

"Oh, Felicity." Lady Henrietta's voice was almost a wail. "Your brother told me what has happened."

Felicity should have guessed. As a well-connected newspaperman, Jasper knew about most goings-on before they'd even happened.

Lady Henrietta went on. "It's absolutely terrible. I've sent a telegram to poor Vera. I've reassured her you'll be assisting with the investigation."

Felicity blinked. Her grandmother's confidence in her was encouraging, but this was a step too far. "The police have control of the situation. I'm sure they won't appreciate my meddling."

"But you'll be reporting on the matter for the paper, won't you? It shan't take much extra effort. And the police must have their suspicions about poor, dear Vera. They'll suppose she's taken matters into her own hands. Oh—" Lady Henrietta's voice was full of distress "—and she's been through such a lot already."

The idea of Vera as a suspect was far-fetched. Murder to put an end to the sabotage wasn't exactly good for business. Yet pooh-poohing Lady Henrietta's ideas was never conducive to settling the dowager's nerves.

"That's precisely what I wanted to speak to Jasper about." After a little more coaxing, Felicity finally persuaded her grandmother to pass the telephone to her brother.

As Felicity waited for Jasper to come on the line, Pip pawed at the door of the telephone booth, tired of the damp outdoor air. Felicity let him in, and the Yorkie inconsiderately shook himself, dampening Felicity's ankles. It wasn't the weather for an outdoor play, but the performance at the castle would surely be cancelled now, anyway.

Jasper arrived on the line. "I don't like to be brusque, Cici, but I'd appreciate it if you kept to the point. I've a meeting at our Exeter office with an important advertiser. You know how it is."

Felicity slid another coin into the slot. She wasn't quite sure where it came from, but a hot flush of indignation rose in her chest. "Very well. Here's my point. Is it essential that Alex and I cover the story here in Ippleford?"

Jasper huffed. "You usually can't be prevented from getting yourself mixed up in grisly happenings. And didn't you find the prospect of the interview rather dull?"

Had Alex also noticed Felicity's lack of enthusiasm for speaking to Judge Hawkins? She hoped not, but it didn't matter now.

"You make me sound exceptionally gruesome, Jasper. I don't appreciate it." The days when Felicity was highly fearful of her brother's opinion felt long ago. "And as you well know, the interview with the judge was important to Alex."

"Oh, I see." Jasper's tone changed. "This is a call for Alex's sake, is it?"

Felicity almost stamped her foot in frustration. "It wasn't my idea to come to Ippleford."

Jasper sighed. "Very well, old girl. If your taste for murder is finally waning, I shan't stand in the way of it, but I can't promise anything. The judge's secretary has been extremely accommodating so far. I can't keep pushing it."

"I'm grateful for your efforts," said Felicity stiffly.

"And in case you didn't notice," continued Jasper, "the Ippleford story's a big one. There's national interest. It's not every day a retired colonel's wife is knocked dead with a teapot. So, until we get someone else out to Ippleford, you and Coop are to stay on the story. Is that understood?"

# Chapter Eight

The stream alongside the village high street babbled apace as Felicity hurried from the telephone box to find Alex, Pip darting ahead.

That there was still a chance they would interview Judge Hawkins was good news. The situation was, nevertheless, peculiar. Being asked to report on a crime with Alex would normally have been an ideal outcome.

Alex was still outside the tea rooms, talking to some recently arrived journalists. Felicity recognised a couple of them from the affair in Lower Diddleton, but she didn't feel comfortable approaching. The tone of their conversation was imbued with masculine energy and verged on raucous. Thankfully, Pip was too busy drinking from the stream to sniff any of their shoes.

Upon seeing Felicity, Alex broke away from the group. He looked hopeful. "What did Jasper say?"

"There are no guarantees, but we're still in with a chance to interview Judge Hawkins. Jasper's looking for someone to replace us. In the meantime, we're to report on events here."

Alex tucked his jacket back and put his hands on his hips. "I suppose a chance is better than nothing." He didn't quite sound relieved. "The police are still speaking to the tea rooms folk. Any ideas on how we should approach this? There's not long before the deadline for the next edition."

There was no point relaying what Lady Henrietta had said about Felicity contributing to the investigation. Flattering though the suggestion was, it was also fantastical. "I suggest we split up. We'll cover more ground that way. You have your contacts with the police and the other journalists. You can leave the softer side of things to me."

Alex's forehead creased, his scar becoming visible. "The 'softer side'?"

Felicity immediately regretted her use of the expression. "I'll interview Vera and her staff as soon as the police are finished with them. In the meantime, I can research the victim. Even if the family won't speak to me, I might get an impression of Mrs Norrington from her fellow villagers."

Alex smiled. "Splendid plan."

---

Having agreed to meet Alex at the inn ahead of the deadline, to combine notes and call in their story, Felicity called Pip to heel as Alex dashed off towards the church hall.

Pip responded to the command by bounding towards the tea rooms' front door. If he hoped for a cosy lap and some cake crumbs, he was out of luck.

Beyond the closed sign hanging in the Green Ginger's window, policemen were holding up items for inspection and tapping out clouds of fingerprint dust.

"Your ladyship."

May, the youngest of the three waitresses, stood under a small, black umbrella. She had on her grey overcoat and a simple black hat. There were red rings around her eyes. Nearby, Zoe played with a rag doll in a solitary game of make-believe, her straw-blonde hair frizzy in the damp.

"Miss Pettigrew," began Felicity. "I'd imagined the police would still be busy with you."

The waitress swallowed. "They finished with me rather quickly, your ladyship. And someone had to keep a watch on Mrs Monroe's daughter."

Pip whined and scratched at the Green Ginger's door. Felicity ignored him.

She looked with sympathy at the two girls. "It's a rather beastly situation to find oneself in, isn't it?"

May's bottom lip quivered. "The policemen find it hard to believe we heard nothing, but we didn't, your ladyship. Really, we didn't. Mr Carli got back this morning, and the police are speaking to him, too, when he wasn't even there. It's all so awful."

The waitress was more loquacious than when Felicity first met her, yet it didn't feel entirely right to ask for a quote for the paper. She seemed overwhelmed with emotion. Vera's daughter being present also made it hard to talk about the violent death.

"The police sometimes repeat their questions, just to make sure they missed nothing." Felicity spoke from experience. "It doesn't mean they don't believe you, Miss Pettigrew."

Zoe dropped her doll to the ground and ran to May, sniffing as she hid her face in the waitress' coat.

May stroked the little girl's yellow hair. "Your mum will be back soon. There's no need to cry."

Zoe said something that got lost in the folds of May's overcoat.

It was painful to see Vera's daughter so upset. "What did she say?" enquired Felicity.

May sighed sadly. "Zoe's worried she and Mrs Monroe will have to move on again. Mrs Monroe has already said she's determined to carry on with things here in Ippleford, but it doesn't look good, does it?" The waitress continued to stroke Zoe's hair, as much to comfort herself as the little girl.

Felicity was curious to know why Mrs Monroe and the Green Ginger meant so much to its young waitresses, but it wasn't the time to press May for her history.

Zoe uncovered an eye and looked at Felicity.

Felicity smiled at her. "I say, do you happen to like dogs?"

The little girl hesitated before nodding.

Felicity scooped Pip from the tea rooms' doorstep and presented him to the little girl. "This is my friend, Pip. Would you like to stroke him? I'm certain he wouldn't mind."

The little Yorkie wriggled in Felicity's hands but made no further protest.

Yes, there was a deadline. But if there was an opportunity to help Vera and her family, then Felicity would take it.

"Zoe loves animals, your ladyship," said May, daring to smile.

Pip was patience itself as the little girl slowly and awkwardly flattened the blue-and-tan fur on the top of his head with unexpectedly earnest affection.

Zoe smiled. Then giggled.

"He's ever so friendly, isn't he?" said May to Zoe.

Pleased with her canine companion's performance, Felicity put Pip on the ground. Instead of retreating, the Yorkie sat before the little girl and allowed himself to be stroked in her awkward manner from nose to tail. Felicity's heart swelled with pride.

She turned to the waitress. It was a pity to ruin the mood, but there was work to do. "Miss Pettigrew, do you perhaps know where Mrs Norrington lived?"

May's smile disappeared. Her hand tightened on the handle of her umbrella. "Rose Cottages, your ladyship. Just up past the church. The Norringtons are in the cottage at the end. I can't remember the name. They've all got such funny names."

"That's extremely helpful, thank you."

"Are you reporting on the murder?" May's eyes were hopeful.

"For the time being, yes. Until another journalist comes to replace my colleague and I."

"Mrs Monroe will be so pleased you're doing the reporting, your ladyship. She has a good deal of trust in you. We all do."

"I shall do my best for you." Felicity meant what she said, but her best would likely not be enough to change Vera's fortunes.

As Felicity departed towards Rose Cottages, Zoe waved to Pip, and the inn's landlady, Mrs Biggs, wearing a fur-collared coat, approached May.

"Please tell Mrs Monroe," said the landlady, "that if there's anything I can do, anything at all, if your chef wants to use our kitchen while the tea rooms are closed—"

Felicity wasn't one for eavesdropping, but it was reassuring to overhear that Vera and the Green Ginger had the village's support.

# Chapter Nine

Flanked by high granite walls covered in bright-green fronds of maidenhair fern, which thrived in the dampness supplied by the stream, the village high street climbed gently towards the castle. Passing the churchyard, Felicity dipped her head to look under the lychgate. Police were buzzing around a barn-like building with high, small windows next to the church. It was presumably the church hall, but there was no sign of either Alex or Vera.

After the churchyard, the road became rather steep, and by slowing his pace and gazing up at her forlornly, Pip suggested Felicity might want to carry him.

"I shan't pick you up on this occasion," said Felicity, overtaking the little Yorkie. "But you're in luck, as I believe we've reached our destination."

A painted wooden sign planted in a bed of silver-leaved lavender, droplets of drizzle gathered on the dried flower-heads, announced their arrival at Rose Cottages.

The cottages in question were four independent dwellings arranged around a central yard, its smooth grey cobbles slick with damp. Each of the cottages was thatched and white-washed in the local style, and each had a small front garden, the boundaries defined by hip-height stave fencing. The scent of wood smoke hung in the air.

At work in one of the gardens, pruning a large, unwieldy buddleja whose flowers had gone to seed, was the sour-faced, checked-shirted man who'd caught Vera's attention the evening before, his red Border Collie lying outside the garden's fence.

The Collie stared inquisitively at Pip. The herding dog's manner was rather more polite than that of his master, who gave Felicity a hostile glare as she arrived in the courtyard. The Yorkie kept his distance from the Collie, sniffing at the fences of the other gardens. Was the unfriendly man a resident of Rose Cottages or employed by someone who lived there?

May had said that Mrs Norrington had lived in the cottage at the end. With the four dwellings arranged in a horseshoe pattern, there were two cottages that could be thus described.

One end cottage had a front garden that was a riot of teasels and grasses and other plants that, depending on the situation, could be classed as weeds. Inside, its window sills were stuffed with jungle-like potted plants and knick-knacks belonging to a Victorian curiosity cabinet, from tribal masks to shadow puppets.

The other end cottage's garden was arranged in a rigid pattern. Clipped box hedging bordered herringbone paving with an elegant rosebush bearing bright red hips at the centre. The window sills were entirely free of clutter, the white lace curtains fell in neat pleats, and the brass fittings on the red door shone brightly despite there being no hint of sunshine.

Of the two dwellings, it was clear which was the home of a retired colonel.

Felicity pushed open the gate and made her way up the herringbone path, Pip trotting closely behind her.

Her natural inclination was to avoid disturbing anyone whose spouse had recently met an untimely death. Professionally, however, a quote from Mrs Norrington's widower or anyone else in the deceased's family would be a coup for the newspaper, especially as it seemed Felicity was the first journalist on the scene.

A sign next to the front door read *Briar Cottage*, but before

Felicity could reach for the shining brass knocker, the door opened abruptly.

A stooped woman of a round fifty in a plain black dress squinted at her. "What is it?"

It was an incredibly impolite manner in which to receive a visitor. Luckily, Felicity was well-practised at remaining composed in challenging circumstances. "Good day to you. I'm Lady Felicity Quick, reporter for the—"

"I told the other ones already," said the woman with a sniff. "You'll not find anything for your scandal rags here."

Felicity's heart sank a little. She wasn't the first journalist to reach Rose Cottages. At least the others had been sent away as well.

"Good day to you, indeed," said the black-clad woman as she threw the door shut, the brass knocker jumping in place.

Felicity had been on the point of offering reassurance about her intentions, because while 'scandal rags' certainly existed, the Western Daily News wasn't one of them. But with the window of opportunity for explanations firmly closed, Felicity shrugged off the encounter and turned back down the path. Access to the grieving husband hadn't been guaranteed, and since her days as a society reporter, Felicity had toughened up as a journalist.

She'd reached the garden gate when the front door to the cottage sprang open again.

"Colonel Norrington would like to speak to you, your ladyship."

It was the same black-clad woman with the same stoop and the same squint. She eyed Felicity with the same mistrust and spoke with the same abrupt hostility. The content of her message had, however, changed.

It was enough for Felicity.

"Splendid," she said and collected Pip before making her way back along the garden path. The potential for a scoop was quite thrilling.

With Pip tucked under her arm — listening for objection rather than seeking approval whenever it came to the Yorkie's presence — Felicity followed the hostile housekeeper along a narrow corridor with a dark blue Persian runner and into a cramped yet orderly sitting room that smelt strongly of cigar smoke.

There were two upright wingback chairs and a leather Chesterfield sofa, a couple of small side tables, and in typical cottage fashion, no room for anything else.

In one chair sat a man with no hair on his head, a big white moustache, and small, porcine eyes. He wore a light brown suit with a thin mustard check and held the butt of a cigar between stubby fingers. A walking stick with an ivory handle leaned against his chair, and he had one leg elevated on a small stool.

In front of the fireplace, where hot coals sat in the grate, a wire-haired dog with short legs and a long body lay across a small rug, whimpering in his sleep. Felicity recognised the Dachshund immediately. He'd been in the tea rooms just the day before, with the elegant woman in the wide-brimmed hat.

Felicity shivered. She had seen Mrs Norrington merely hours before the unfortunate woman had met her end.

Pip's tail wagged. Felicity wouldn't put him on the ground to dash about. This was a grieving household.

"Ah, Lady Felicity Quick." Colonel Norrington spoke in a booming voice typical of retired military men. "Mrs Maunder, fetch us a tray of tea."

The woman in black nodded curtly and disappeared from the sitting room doorway.

"Please." Colonel Norrington gestured towards the Chesterfield after a draw on his cigar. "Do sit."

Felicity did as she was instructed, placing Pip on her lap. "May I say how deeply sorry I am about the passing of—"

"Ah, yes. Terrible business. Terrible business." The colonel waved his cigar and shook his jowls. His dismissive reaction to the mention of his wife's death was somewhat jarring, but grief affected people differently.

"Perhaps your housekeeper already informed you, but I work as a reporter for the Western Daily News."

"Of course, of course. Lord Denbury's sister, are you not? I knew your father, you know. We were in South Africa together. Kingsley was absolutely decisive at Mafeking. A very fine officer, he was. Very fine indeed."

In a manner typical of many veterans, her father had never spoken about his involvement in the Boer War. At least, not to Felicity.

"My father was an admirable man," she agreed. *Although he'd be turning in his grave to see me on the staff of his newspaper*, she added silently.

Pip remained obediently on Felicity's lap, despite his pricked ears showing obvious interest in the Dachshund, who continued dreaming fitfully before the fire.

While using her family's standing and connections for advancement could, on occasion, make her uncomfortable, Felicity was determined not to waste her opportunity with Colonel Norrington.

"Would you mind terribly if I took a quote from you for our paper?"

"Not at all, Lady Felicity. Not at all. You may ask any question you care to put to me, and I shall do my utmost to answer. Your family's newspaper is the best our region has. Perhaps even the best the country has. Nothing but meaningless gossip comes out of Fleet Street these days."

Felicity withdrew her notepad and pencil from her pocket. "It may seem like a rather obvious question, but our readers will want to have your own statement on the matter. How has the unexpected passing of your wife affected you, Colonel Norrington?"

The colonel's beady eyes opened wide for a moment, and he peered at Felicity with something like alarm. "I'll tell you what's affected me. The state of this village is what's affected me."

Felicity smiled awkwardly as Mrs Maunder reappeared with a tray of tea. The housekeeper set aside a crystal ashtray and a chocolate tin decorated with a floral pattern, piling them atop one another on a nearby bookshelf to make room on a side table for the tray.

The colonel continued. "Prudence and I came here for peace and quiet, and it's been anything but."

Felicity noted down what Colonel Norrington said, but his lack of open grief for his wife's passing and his complaints about the local community weren't the scoop for which she was hoping.

"We had absolutely no idea there would be so many blooming tourists crawling around the place, encouraged by the tea rooms and the inn, of course. We were told Ippleford was a haven from hustle and bustle."

Felicity nodded as she took notes, thanking Mrs Maunder as she clanked a cup of tea on its saucer down next to her.

"And then there's that blasted play. The chaos it's brought to the village, your ladyship. The absolute chaos." Colonel Norrington waved his cigar as he thundered. "If the police should talk to anyone, it should be those ruddy actors."

Mrs Maunder set the colonel's tea down in the same aggressive manner as she had done Felicity's. The clatter of the teacup against its saucer woke the Dachshund. The wire-haired dog sat up, looked around in a panic, then began howling.

"Rover. Rover! Quiet. Quiet, now. She's not coming back, old chap. It's just you and me now. We'll just have to get used to it, old boy." The colonel seemed more capable of expressing his grief by speaking to his pet.

Felicity stroked a hand over Pip's ears. He'd begun whimpering, perhaps in empathy with poor Rover. It was indeed upsetting to see the dog so disturbed by his mistress' sudden absence.

"Did your wife have any enemies, Colonel Norrington?" If there wasn't to be a quote about the hole in the colonel's heart created by his wife's death, then Felicity would try a different approach.

Again, the colonel's beady eyes widened. "What I'm saying, my dear girl, is that this village is not what it seems. It's not the quiet rural idyll it's cracked up to be. There's something not right about it. I regret the day we came here. I really do."

Felicity used her brisk Pitman shorthand to write every word. "Was Mrs Norrington of the same opinion?"

The colonel frowned. "Oh, yes. Of course. But Prudence was partial to sweets. We all have our weaknesses. She enjoyed cakes, especially the ones made by that Italian or Swiss fellow working at the tea rooms."

Based on the slice of chocolate tart Felicity had tried, Mrs Norrington's weakness was understandable.

"And she was helping with the play," mumbled the colonel between puffs of his cigar.

"Your wife supported the staging of the play at the castle ruins?" It didn't sound as though the Colonel and his wife were aligned in their opinions on the village, after all.

"Only because the Women's Association was involved, you understand. Otherwise, she'd have been against it. We came down here for peace and quiet, as I told you."

Patching together what the colonel was saying into something resembling a scoop would be a challenge. It all seemed highly contradictory.

Felicity took a sip of tea — which had been sweetened, even though Felicity preferred not to drink it that way — and looked at her notes.

"Could you tell me something about your wife's last day? Her activities, who she met with, what might have led to her being at the Green Ginger so late at night?" It didn't feel appropriate to mention that she'd seen Mrs Norrington speaking to the Swiss patisserie chef at the tea rooms. The colonel was already agitated.

Colonel Norrington shook his head hard, his jowls swinging. "I'll tell you what my Prudence didn't do. She didn't take part in any kind of sabotage. That's for certain. The police had the nerve to suggest she'd cut holes into lace napkins! Absolute balderdash. We weren't keen on the place, but any kind of underhand activity on my wife's part is out of the question. Prudence was a thoroughly honest woman."

Felicity nodded and continued to write in her notebook, but her mind wrestled with a puzzle. How could one enjoy the tea rooms' cakes yet disapprove of the establishment?

After a few more sips of sugary tea while listening to complaints about the moral degradation of Ippleford, it became apparent there wasn't much else to glean from the colonel for the article to be written with Alex. Felicity was also not especially keen on spending any longer than necessary intruding on a bereaved household.

Saying farewell to the colonel and again attempting to offer her sympathies, Felicity wondered if the other residents of Rose Cottages might shed light on the contradictory picture Colonel Norrington had painted of his wife.

There was only one way to find out.

# Chapter Ten

Outside, the drizzle had weakened and a little sun even threatened to show through the thinning grey clouds that hung over Ippleford.

Pushing open the colonel's gate, Pip trotting ahead, Felicity contemplated the distinctly unfriendly man with the red Border Collie. He was still working in the front garden of the dwelling upon whose front gate hung the name *Damask Cottage* — each cottage had been named after a type of rose — and his dog still lay obediently outside the fence.

The gardener had moved onto a row of shrub roses in a narrow border, which framed a small lawn. Absorbed in his work, he didn't look in Felicity's direction, his large hands easily manipulating the pruning shears.

Whether or not a resident of Rose Cottages, might he have an opinion on Mrs Prudence Norrington?

"There are some rather beautiful gardens in Ippleford," Felicity said by way of an opener as she gazed admiringly at the neat row of shrub roses.

A lace curtain twitched at the neighbouring cottage. It had a painted sign next to the door announcing its name as *Gallica Cottage.*

The gardener looked up from his work, and Felicity smiled at him. Her utterance had been quite clever, for it worked as a compliment whether the so-far unfriendly man was the owner of the garden or employed to work there.

The man grunted. “We don’t do it for the approval of outsiders,” he said, and returned to trimming the roses with increased vigour.

Felicity kept her composure. “I wouldn’t dare assume otherwise. But it can’t be denied that the village’s gardens are exceptionally well kept.” Her attempt at conversation had already failed, but it didn’t mean the discussion must end without civility.

“Our gardens are beautiful because that’s how we like them.” The man kept his eyes on the rose bushes. “Not because there’s anyone to impress.”

The Collie’s ears twitched as his master spoke. Pip halted his advance across the damp cobbles and stood close to Felicity.

As the challenge of rounding off the encounter politely increased, the door to Damask Cottage opened behind the gardener, and the tall, thin doctor who had attended the incident at the tea rooms during the night appeared on the doorstep. The doctor wore a jacket without a tie, carried a coffee cup, and looked extremely tired. He managed a faintly amused smile.

“Mr Viner does an excellent job of keeping Ippleford’s gardens looking marvellous. While we wouldn’t be without his talents as a groundsman, I don’t believe anyone would employ him as a publicity agent for the village.”

Mr Viner mumbled something without ceasing his pruning.

Again, the curtain twitched at the cottage next door.

The doctor approached his garden gate. “I realise we’ve seen one another, not under the best of circumstances, of course, but I don’t believe we’ve been introduced.”

Felicity smiled, relieved to be back on the firm ground of well-mannered conversation. “That’s quite correct. I’m Lady Felicity Quick, reporter for the Western Daily News.”

“Aha. A journalist. Pleased to meet you, your ladyship. Bartholomew Grant’s the name. You might imagine me a doctor, as that was the part I played when you saw me last night. In truth, I’m retired. So, I'm afraid you shan't get any official statement from me."

"Oh," said Felicity. "How nice to have such a worthwhile career upon which to look back." The news was slightly disappointing, but Felicity wasn't discouraged. From the curtain twitching next door, the doctor wasn't the only one of Mrs Norrington's neighbours at home.

"People still refer to me as Doctor Grant," he continued, "and in a pinch, I can perform that duty — as you saw me doing last night — but I've quite moved on from medicine. My time now is mostly taken up by reading and occasionally pottering around in my garden, although when you have someone as naturally talented as Mr Viner here ready to do the work, I'm afraid I usually take the easy option."

Having finished sculpting the rose bushes, Mr Viner took up a rake and began scraping fallen leaves from the lawn. The action unleashed a rich earthy smell, which made both Pip's and the Collie's noses twitch.

The front door of the cottage where the curtain had been twitching opened to reveal a short woman in a long purple dress and a grey topknot. She was of advanced age and remarkably small in stature, but her energy was bright and her movements lively. She gesticulated as she advanced along her garden path, next to which were neat rows of what looked like vegetables, perhaps the tops of beetroots.

"Did I hear mention of a journalist, Doctor Grant?" asked the diminutive woman.

The retired doctor smiled, amused. "Not much escapes you, does it, Mrs Waverley?"

"Oh, indeed!" The small, lively woman turned to Felicity. "I would simply love to say something useful to a journalist. Really, I would. We depend so much on the papers for our news. But we're so far away from any sort of action here at Rose Cottages. We like the quiet, of course. It's a tonic for my Millie's nerves. But I went down to the Green Ginger just this morning, in case there was any way I might help." The not yet introduced woman opened her garden gate and joined Felicity on the cobbles, barely stopping for a breath. "Only the police were telling everyone to stay away, saying they had work to do and so on. I tried finding the manageress. A most agreeable woman. Mrs Monroe, I believe her name is? Yes, Mrs Monroe. Only there really wasn't anyone to speak to. So I came home. And well, here I am."

The small woman's brow was creased with distress. Whether because of the tragic events at the tea rooms or because she wasn't allowed to meddle in the affairs there, it wasn't clear.

Felicity introduced herself, matching the woman's bright tone. As she spoke, another figure appeared silently in the doorway of Damask Cottage. The woman of about forty had short, wayward brown hair, a tweed skirt and jacket even more shapeless than Felicity's, and a glum yet watchful expression. She remained in the doorway, her eyes bouncing from Mr Viner to Felicity.

"I actually heard you introducing yourself to Doctor Grant just now, your ladyship," continued the small top-knotted woman. "I'm afraid there isn't much that can happen at Rose Cottages without everyone hearing. Luckily, we're all quiet people and mindful of the need for peace." She glanced at the overgrown garden and packed window sills of Alba Cottage. "For the most part, of course." She snapped a wide-eyed gaze back to Felicity. "My goodness. Where are my manners? I'm Mrs Emily Waverley, resident here at Damask Cottage. If you're wondering where Mr Waverley is, well, he's dead, dear. Been dead some twenty years now. I live with my daughter, Millicent."

Mrs Waverley made no gesture towards the woman in the doorway behind her. If this was Millicent, her mother had perhaps not noticed she was there.

"We've no need for Mr Viner," continued Mrs Waverley. "My daughter is quite a wonder when it comes to plants, as you can see." She gestured to the neat green rows in Damask's front garden. "Millie keeps us in vegetables quite through the winter. Why, I believe Mr Viner even seeks her advice on occasion."

*Bang!*

The door to Damask Cottage slammed shut, the woman in the doorway having disappeared inside. Pip's claws skittered on the cobbles as Doctor Grant winced at the sudden noise. Mr Viner didn't look up from his work. The Collie's ears twitched.

Mrs Waverley sighed. "My Millie's nerves aren't what they used to be. Then again, she always was a sensitive girl."

Felicity ruled out an interview with the nervy Millie, at least for the time being. There was a deadline looming, and discussions with Mrs Norrington's neighbours needed to be kept on track.

"I had remarked to Mr Viner that Ippleford's gardens are quite a wonder to behold, even this late in the year," said Felicity. "But even such beauty can be little solace in the face of such tragedy."

Mrs Waverley shook her head slowly. "Of course. Poor, poor Mrs Norrington. She was an awfully sweet woman. And the poor colonel. He is understandably quite beside himself. It's all too, too terrible to think about."

Felicity fished her notepad out of her pocket. Mrs Waverley used language that would appeal to readers of the Western Daily News. "May I take down a quote or two for our paper?"

Mrs Waverley's eyes brightened. "Please do, your ladyship. Please do. What would you like me to say?"

"Our readers should like to know something of Mrs Norrington's character."

There was no hesitation in Mrs Waverley's reply. "Mrs Prudence Norrington was a thoroughly respectful neighbour, a highly moral woman, and a valued contributor to our local chapter of the Women's Association."

Felicity wrote everything down. "Could you summarise your personal reaction to the tragedy?"

"I'm shocked and devastated that we should lose such a woman as Mrs Norrington in such cruel circumstances."

"And what effect do you believe it will have on the village?"

"Oh, disastrous. It's absolutely calamitous for the fabric of our community, especially as the precise details of the incident are not yet known. I mean, there's a murderer in our midst, and we've yet to find out who it is." Mrs Waverley blinked. "Something like that, dear?"

They were exactly the quotes Felicity needed. The reminder that there was a murderer in Ippleford ought perhaps to have made more of an impression, but Felicity pressed on. "Might you know what business Mrs Norrington had at the Green Ginger in the middle of the night?"

The mournful howling of Rover rose from within Briar Cottage. Pip's and the Collie's ears turned towards the heart-breaking noise.

"Well." Mrs Waverley thought for a moment, her forehead creasing. "Not exactly..."

Doctor Grant stepped closer to Felicity and Mrs Waverley. "Publishing idle speculation would surely not be useful to the police's investigations. Wouldn't you say, your ladyship?"

"Oh, I've no desire to muddy any waters." Felicity's tone was a trifle defensive. She considered herself a morally upstanding journalist. "I'm fully confident the police will get to the bottom of things. It is, however, my responsibility towards our readers to share with them whatever I can find out about this tragic affair."

Mrs Waverley glanced confusedly between Felicity and the doctor, as if unable to decide whether to indulge in idle speculation.

"Might you like a quote or two about the cancellation of the play?"

A small cottage window had opened above the chaotic garden. Leaning out of the opening was a young woman in some kind of kimono in an Eastern print. Her frizzy brown hair had been wrestled into a half-successful chignon.

Where had Felicity seen her before?

Mrs Waverley looked at the young woman with open disapproval. Doctor Grant's face soured a little.

Felicity had perhaps not yet exhausted everything there was to glean from Mrs Waverley, but the opportunity to learn more about the play was intriguing. Until the murder, village life seemed to have revolved around the production. And Mrs Norrington had been involved in its staging, had she not?

"Thank you," Felicity called up to the woman in the window. "That would be splendid."

# Chapter Eleven

The interior of the cottage with the nameplate *Alba* was just as cluttered as its front garden. In the hall, a coat rack groaned with jackets, capes, scarves, and an array of hats in various colours. Black-and-white prints, decorated plates, and lacquer paintings depicting scenes from across the world adorned the walls. Even the treads of the narrow stairs were piled with books.

"Ernestine will be down any moment now." The man who'd opened the cottage's front door was tall and classically handsome, with a strong jaw and straight nose, but he peered through thick-lensed glasses and wore ill-fitting trousers with mended holes and a woollen jumper that had seen better days.

"Please, do take a seat," he said, gesturing towards a small sitting room that was, like the hallway, crammed full of items, ranging from Dutch vases and a doll dressed in traditional Welsh clothing to copper pots with plants drooping from them. A sweet, complicated smell hung in the air. Joss sticks, perhaps.

The cottage had the same layout as the colonel's. It was amazing what decor could do to change the atmosphere of a place.

"I'll fetch some tea," said the man with a genial smile, and he disappeared back into the corridor.

Felicity took a seat on a worn velvet bench next to yet another pile of books, which she now saw were the texts of plays.

Pip stiffened under her arm.

Blinking down at them from a tall cabinet, seated among the curios as though he were one himself, was a large ginger and brown cat with wispy ears and long whiskers.

The cat was thankfully rather relaxed about the Yorkie's presence, but Pip's tail wagged enthusiastically. Whether the Yorkie intended to make a feline friend or wanted to embark on a thrilling chase that would see many a curio knocked to the floor, Felicity couldn't quite guess. She would have to ensure Pip remained seated in her lap.

Footsteps on the stairs heralded the reappearance of Ernestine, her hair slightly tamer than when she'd appeared in the window, but only slightly. Her silk kimono billowed in an orange and black paisley, and when she smiled, her eyes lit up.

Felicity stood to greet her.

"Ernestine Heard. How do you do?"

They shook hands, and as Felicity introduced herself, she remembered where she'd already seen the couple. Vera had pointed them out the night before, as everyone was getting ready for the rehearsal.

Ernestine looked affectionately at Pip as Felicity retook her seat. "And this is?"

"Oh." Felicity smiled. Not everyone acknowledged her canine companion's presence positively, but it was usually a good sign when a person did. "This is Pip. I hope your cat has no objection to his presence?"

Taking a seat on a battered wicker chair opposite Felicity, Ernestine glanced up at the cat, who was licking his rather large paws. "Falstaff's the relaxed type. I'm afraid one has to be to live with Phil and I."

The man re-entered the room carrying a large tray of tea, which he placed on a leather pouffe towards the centre of the cramped room. "Terribly sorry. Didn't introduce myself yet, did I? Philip Heard."

He stepped forward to shake Felicity's hand. Felicity introduced herself.

"I'm afraid we've not yet acquainted ourselves properly with the local press." As he spoke, Philip poured the tea, which, from its fragrance, was of the smoked variety. "An oversight on our part. It's important to get word out to the local people however we can about what we're trying to achieve."

"Not that our theatre work should take any of the attention away from last night's tragedy," added Ernestine quickly. "That poor, poor woman. Such a tender soul. The colonel is putting on a brave face, but it'll hit him soon enough. They say she was murdered, don't they?"

"That's the understanding so far, yes." Felicity reached into her pocket for her notepad. "You're the organisers of the play that was to take place at the castle. Is that correct?"

Philip moved a pile of books to take a seat on a stool next to Ernestine. "The former organisers, I suppose you might say. The production's been cancelled now, of course."

"Of course," echoed Ernestine gravely.

Felicity was thankfully adept at accommodating both a notepad and a Yorkshire Terrier on her lap. "May I get a quote from you for the paper about the effect the tragedy has had on the village and on you as residents?"

Ernestine and Philip looked at one another. After some tacit understanding had been reached between them, Ernestine turned towards Felicity. "Naturally, we're extremely upset at the idea of our neighbour, Mrs Norrington, having met her end in such a fashion. We've not been here long, so we didn't know her well."

"How long have you lived in Ippleford?" Felicity took a sip from her tea to be polite. Lapsang souchong was rather an acquired taste.

Philip shook his head. "Just a matter of months."

It was difficult to imagine so much clutter being accumulated in mere months, but there was no reason to distrust the Heards on this point.

"Mrs Norrington was a pleasant neighbour," continued Ernestine.

"Very welcoming and respectful. And she was helping us with the play. Almost all the ladies from the Women's Association were. Mrs Norrington was working on the costumes. I actually suspected she'd have made quite a wonderful actress. Sometimes you can just sense it. I told her as much, but she said she didn't fancy the attention."

"She wasn't critical of the play in any way?" enquired Felicity.

Ernestine frowned. "Why would she be, if she'd decided to help us? No one was forced to do so."

It was another point on which the victim and her husband were perhaps not in agreement. "What kind of woman was Mrs Norrington?"

Again, Ernestine and Philip exchanged glances. Ernestine spoke. "Quiet. Polite. Thoughtful. Discreet. As I said, we didn't know her, so these are just impressions, you understand."

Felicity nodded. At least there was no inconsistency on Mrs Norrington's pleasantness. "And you're actors yourselves?"

Philip answered. "We were on the stage in London."

It occurred to Felicity to ask about someone she knew who'd made quite a career for herself in the London theatres, but she quickly decided against it. It would have been a distraction.

"We were doing quite well," he continued. "Till Ernie got sick."

Philip put a hand on Ernestine's. She gave him a smile tinged with sadness.

"Weak lungs," she said, turning to Felicity. "Not so helpful when you've a theatre full of people straining their ears to hear you. There was nothing for it but to leave the city. And so—" she looked at Philip lovingly "—here we find ourselves."

"Could you tell me something about the play you were staging?" It wasn't an essential piece of information, but it was the colourful context readers of the Western Daily News appreciated.

"You've heard the legend of the Blue Lady, I suppose?" enquired Ernestine.

"I've heard of the Blue Lady Inn," said Felicity, adjusting the Yorkie and her notepad on her lap. "Is there a link?"

"Ah!" Philip sat up straight. "Why, the inn takes its name from the legend. Want to hear it?"

Felicity glanced around the room for a clock among the clutter, but there was no way of telling the time. Her meeting with Alex was approaching fast, and the story likely had no influence on what had happened to Mrs Norrington. "Please. If you're able to be brief. I'm working to a deadline."

"I shall do my best," promised Philip.

Ernestine gave him a reassuring pat on the leg. Falstaff, still perched on the cabinet, stretched his maw into a wide yawn and rested on folded paws. Pip whined quietly.

"The Blue Lady," began the actor, his voice deep and sonorous, "was a princess at Ippleford Castle. She had the misfortune of falling in love with a commoner, a soldier among her father's men-at-arms. Her father wouldn't entertain the idea of their marriage. He gave his daughter's hand to a powerful lord, a cruel man she didn't love. As if that weren't punishment enough, the lord humiliated her by siring children with numerous mistresses. Meanwhile, the princess' true love was sent into battle and died."

"How terribly sad," said Felicity. Such tragedies echoed through the generations, the Great War having ended many love stories.

"Unfortunately, the story doesn't stop there," added Ernestine. "Legend has it the princess ended her own life in a last act of dramatic revenge, flinging herself from the high tower."

"It's said her ghostly image can still be seen in the tower, pining for her one true love," added Philip.

The actor and actress looked deeply into one another's eyes.

"Have you ever seen her?" Felicity had no time for ghosts, but, if written about tastefully, the legend might provide interesting context for coverage of the murder. "The apparition, I mean."

Ernestine laughed warmly. "We're actors, your ladyship. Not spiritualists. But no, in all the time we've spent at the castle, often late into the evening, we've not seen the Blue Lady."

"What we find fascinating is how, despite the tragedy of it all, love is ultimately at the centre of the story." Philip looked again at Ernestine.

"If one looks hard enough, it's at the centre of every story." Ernestine gazed into Philip's thickly lensed eyes. "There's not much that can happen in this world without love."

As a distraction from Ernestine and Philip's open displays of affection, Felicity attempted to apply the rationale to the puzzle of Mrs Norrington's murder. A forceful blow to the back of the head could be an act of passion, but what love story was there at the tea rooms? Perhaps Felicity was insensitive to it, having never been in love herself.

But then, how does one know when one is in love?

Felicity shifted uncomfortably in her seat. "I'm afraid I should be getting along. May I ask, one more thing?"

Philip and Ernestine unlocked their gazes. "Certainly," said Philip.

"Was all going well with the play prior to last night's incident at the tea rooms?"

Ernestine answered. "The production had its detractors, like any work of art, but as I saw it, everything was going swimmingly."

"Better than expected, even," added Philip. "Why do you ask?"

The idea had occurred to Felicity that the tea rooms might not have been the only target of sabotage. However, from the disarray at Alba Cottage, Philip and Ernestine might not have noticed a missing prop or a torn dress.

Felicity stopped writing in her notebook for a moment. "I'm trying to gather a sense of what life was like in the village prior to Mrs Norrington's untimely death. By some accounts, it was undisturbed peace."

Philip huffed. "And by other accounts, depravity had come to town in the form of two actors. Is that right?"

Felicity stroked Pip. "Those weren't the exact words used."

"We knew before coming here we'd be up against traditional ideas," said Ernestine. "But the attitudes in Ippleford can be rather surprising, can't they, Phil?"

"Disapprove of the work we do, by all means. But why disapprove of the tea rooms? Or even the efforts of the inn to attract more customers? A village needs an income, doesn't it? Some people would sooner see village life die out completely than have anything but the traditional way of things continue forever."

Felicity scribbled the last of her notes. If there were underlying tensions in Ippleford, what bearing might this have on the sabotage and murder at the tea rooms? There was very little sense to be made of things, as yet.

"Would you like a biscuit?" Ernestine opened a tin which had a blue-and-white tessellated pattern enamelled on its top.

Pip sniffed inquisitively, but his ears dropped in disappointment. The biscuits were dry and crumbly and contained rather too many sesame seeds.

"That's awfully kind," said Felicity with a gracious smile, "but I really ought to be going. I can't miss my deadline."

Outside in the cool, damp air, Felicity and Pip crossed the shining cobbles of Rose Cottages' courtyard and followed the stream back towards the centre of the village.

Felicity's nerves fizzed with an odd excitement. The variety of contrasting quotes she'd gathered was compelling. At the centre was the most intriguing question of all: if Mrs Norrington was the gentle, honest soul everyone said she was, how did she meet a violent end in the middle of the night at the tea rooms?

Felicity had to find Alex. He'd hopefully uncovered the information that would fill in the gaps.

# Chapter Twelve

With the copy deadline looming, Felicity was pleased to come across Alex on Ippleford's high street, which saved her a jaunt down to the Blue Lady Inn, where they'd agreed to meet.

With her collar turned up against the persistent drizzle, Felicity hung back below a stand of white-barked yellow-leaved birches, Pip sniffing around their roots, and waited for Alex to finish interviewing a young uniformed police officer with another reporter, a thin moustached man from one of the national newspapers. Both journalists wrote furiously in their notebooks as the policeman spoke.

The interview finished rather promptly, and the police officer departed. Alex tucked his notebook into the inside pocket of his jacket and approached Felicity, looking perplexed.

"Why didn't you come over?"

Felicity opened her mouth to speak but hesitated. Why hadn't she? "We agreed my focus would be the softer side of things," she said, wincing a little. "Remember?"

Alex smiled. "A journalist afraid of interrupting will face problems acquiring all the necessary information."

Felicity frowned. Alex was the more experienced reporter, but she'd learned a few things during her time writing for the society pages. "And a journalist who doesn't know how to choose the correct moment might equally face problems."

"Perhaps," said Alex thoughtfully, looking down at Pip sniffing his shoes. He lifted his gaze above the thatched roofs of the cottages lining the village high street. "Been up to the castle yet? Or what's left of it."

The jagged edges of crumbling battlements jutted into the steel grey sky, a single tower still standing proud.

"Not yet," said Felicity. "But I have learned a thing or two about the Blue Lady."

"The inn?"

"Not quite." Felicity raised her eyebrows. "They say she haunts the castle."

Alex mirrored Felicity's expression. "Does she, now?"

The journalist with whom Alex had been interviewing the policeman wasn't far away. He appeared to be gathering quotes from a pair of dazed-looking day-trippers, who perhaps hadn't realised there'd been a murder in Ippleford before setting out to visit the village. The journalist's gaze kept wandering over to Alex and Felicity.

"Shall we go for a stroll?" suggested Alex. "We can get our ideas for the story together without anyone listening in. There's still time before the deadline."

Felicity wholeheartedly supported Alex's suggestion. Walking and clarity of thought went hand in hand, and there was much to work through. "This way?" she suggested.

They started along an alleyway between two rows of cottages, Pip rather predictably in the lead. Beyond rugged granite walls and thick, tree-studded hedges, the alleyway offered views of orderly back gardens and passed several sheds containing horse carts, the odd motor, and even a cider press. Felicity was reminded of when she and Alex worked in Lower Diddleton together, but any enjoyment on her part was selfish.

"No sign of our replacement yet?" enquired Felicity, doing her best to sound hopeful.

"Not yet." Thankfully, Alex didn't sound too dejected. "Interview anyone of interest?"

"I spoke to the deceased's husband."

Alex's eyes widened. He smiled. "That's the ticket. I knew you had it in you."

While Alex's encouragement was welcome, Felicity had to wonder what he'd suspected she didn't have in her.

Glossing over this point, Felicity continued. "Colonel Norrington insists his wife, like himself, disapproved of the tea rooms, even if she was partial to their cakes. He also mentioned their disapproval of the play and of the inn's efforts to attract more business, but he thoroughly rejects any suggestion of Mrs Norrington being responsible for the tea rooms' sabotage."

Alex's eyes narrowed in thought. "Interesting."

The alleyway took a sharp turn along a high stone wall hung with dark green ivy. Pip kept a careful balance between the analysis of interesting smells and leading the pack.

Felicity continued. "I saw Mrs Norrington at the tea rooms yesterday. I didn't recognise her at the time, but I made the connection when I saw her Dachshund with Colonel Norrington. She seemed quite happy to be a patron of the establishment. She had rather a playful encounter with the patisserie chef, in fact."

"Playful?" Alex glanced at Felicity as the alleyway passed under the broad canopy of a gnarled oak tree, fat drops of rain steadily falling from its umber-coloured leaves. "That chef's someone to speak to."

"Absolutely," said Felicity, relieved Alex was fully engaged with the story at hand and not pining for the interview with Judge Hawkins. "I spoke briefly to Mrs Norrington's neighbours, who all describe her as an absolute dear. I also met the organisers of the play. A pair of actors from London. The production's been cancelled, of course, but they told me Mrs Norrington was volunteering in the costume department, which rather undermines what Colonel Norrington had to say about his wife's disapproval of the whole thing."

Felicity and Alex passed Pip as he spent an extended amount of time inspecting a thick patch of tall grass that had sprung up next to a drain.

Alex looked again at Felicity. "And you'd like to put that all in the paper?"

"Oh," said Felicity, flummoxed. "Well, no. I don't think critiquing Mrs Norrington's character would be respectful. Not at this early stage in the investigation. It's not the tone the News is known for, is it?"

"Did you get any quotes we can use?"

"What an odd question. Of course, I did."

Alex smiled. "My apologies, but I had to check. You can't help yourself, can you?"

"Help myself what?"

"Playing detective."

Felicity frowned. "Is it wrong to be curious about what exactly happened and why?"

"I'm just as curious as you are," said Alex. "The difference is, I don't let it get in the way of my reporting."

A burn of indignation rose in Felicity's chest. Coming to Ippleford hadn't been her idea. "I'm not letting anything get in the way of my work. I collected all the quotes we need."

Alex smiled but said nothing.

The alley they'd taken became narrower. A half-crumbled wall lay ahead. It seemed to be a dead end. Having retaken the lead, Pip squeezed under a nearby gate.

"Pip!" Felicity had visions of the little Yorkie tearing through someone's patch of prize-winning fuchsias, but the gate didn't open into a private garden. It led to the churchyard.

Alex held the creaking wooden gate open for Felicity.

"Thank you," she said, perhaps too curtly. Alex could wind her up with incredible ease. Did he do so on purpose?

A gravel path led through rows of lichen-covered graves sprouting from moist, grassy ground. On the other side of the churchyard were the church with its pointed spire and the barn-like church hall, around which policemen bustled purposefully.

Pip disappeared into the unkempt grass.

"What information did you gather for our story?"

Felicity asked this of Alex rather pointedly, but from the calm in his blue gaze, she apparently irked her colleague far less than he bothered her.

"The police are interested in the sabotage angle." Alex put his hands in his pockets as they walked along the path. "To them, it seems likely the murdered woman was responsible."

Felicity lifted her brow. "That's not something to include in our story, though, is it?"

"Not that the murdered woman was the saboteur. That's not proven yet. But we'll mention the police's interest in the sabotage. We can't be the only newspaper not saying anything about it."

Felicity swallowed. Her grandmother would faint at reading all the bad news about the tea rooms, not to mention the impact of the tragedy on Vera.

"The police are also looking for a vital piece of evidence," said Alex. "The handle of the teapot used as the murder weapon is still missing."

Felicity tucked an errant curl under her cloche. "How queer. Why would one keep such a thing, do you suppose?"

Alex shrugged. "It's not up to us to find the answers." He nodded in the direction of the police. "It's up to them."

Pip stopped at a gravestone with a particularly interesting scent. The engraving on the splotchy granite was no longer entirely clear, but the name on it was Viner and the date was somewhere in the Eighteenth Century. The grumpy gardener was a Mr Viner, was he not? That his family had been in Ippleford for centuries went some way to explaining his haughty manner.

"What did you hear about the castle legends?"

Felicity turned towards Alex in mock surprise. "Are you, like me, unable to control your own curiosity? Or is this something you're considering for our article?"

Alex shrugged. "A bit of local colour can draw readers in."

After a brief but biting narrowing of her gaze, Felicity relayed what she'd heard about the Blue Lady, omitting what the actors had said about love being at the core of everything, as it didn't seem remotely relevant. Alex listened with interest as they took a loop of the path that ran behind one of the churchyard's giant, ancient yews.

"So, the death at the tea rooms isn't Ippleford's first tragedy?" he asked.

"If the legend is to be believed," replied Felicity.

Alex stopped on the path and glanced around. Besides Pip and the police by the church hall, who were far away enough to be out of earshot, he and Felicity were alone.

Alex swept a hand over his dark blond hair. "Look, I don't know how much truth there is to it, but I heard mention among my sources of Mrs Monroe for consideration as the main suspect."

Felicity's heart sank. Lady Henrietta had been right. "That's definitely not something we'll be putting in the paper."

"No. Definitely not. There's no official suspect yet, but I know Mrs Monroe's a friend of yours. I thought you'd want to know what's being said, even if it comes to nothing."

Felicity dared not imagine her grandmother's reaction to the news. "But why would Vera do that to her own business?"

Alex frowned. "I'm not saying I agree, but you can see how the police might have arrived at the idea. If you caught the person sabotaging your business red-handed..."

The wide doors of the church hall banged shut. Pip lifted his nose above the wet grass. Vera, her little leather handbag on her wrist and her shoulders stooped, had exited the building. She looked so small compared to the church hall's vast dimensions.

Felicity had come to Ippleford to support Vera. She'd yet to live up to her mission.

It was as if Alex knew what Felicity was thinking. "If you give me the quotes you collected, I'll write our article and call it in. If you trust me with your notes, of course."

Felicity blinked at Alex. "Will you be able to read my shorthand?"

Alex smiled. "It can't be any worse than mine."

With little hesitation, Felicity took her notepad from her pocket, pulled out the pages with the quotes she'd collected at Rose Cottages, and handed them to Alex.

"Good luck," said Alex, as Felicity hurried towards Vera, Pip bounding through the grass after her.

---

Felicity caught up with Vera at the wood-shingled lychgate connecting the churchyard to Ippleford's high street. Vera gave Felicity a weary smile as she approached.

"Oh, Lady Felicity. I haven't told you how terribly sorry I am for everything that's happened. I'm sure this isn't what you expected when you agreed to come to Ippleford."

Felicity was taken aback. "There's no need to apologise to me, Vera. I assure you." She bent to scoop Pip under her arm. His journey through the wet grass had dampened his fur considerably. "The sabotage was quite bad enough. I can't imagine what you must be going through."

Vera sighed. She seemed exhausted, but she kept her smile up. "Please don't worry, my lady. On top of everything, I'd rather not have you wasting your time worrying about me. I'm sure it'll all sort itself out, one way or another."

Had Vera any inkling of the police's thoughts on the murder suspect? It wasn't Felicity's place to broach the subject. As Alex had said, it may still come to nothing.

"If there's anything I can do, Vera. Anything at all. You really must let me know." She attempted to return Vera's smile. The result was something more of a sympathetic grimace.

"There's rather a lot to do at the Green Ginger. I suppose you'll want to interview me for the paper, won't you? If you don't mind speaking to me while I'm working, that's fine by me, my lady."

Felicity had wanted to provide support to Vera. An interview for the Western Daily News was perhaps all she had to offer. "If you wouldn't mind speaking to me in that capacity?"

It wasn't the bold move of which Alex already doubted Felicity capable, and there perhaps wouldn't be time to add Vera's quotes ahead of the upcoming deadline. But was there a chance Felicity's reporting might help Vera? Felicity had to try.

## Chapter Thirteen

The bell above the door of the Green Ginger tinkled as Felicity, Pip in her arms, and Vera entered the premises. Besides the closed sign hanging in the window when the tea rooms would normally have been open, there was no trace of the drama that had unfolded during the night. The tables with their shining cutlery and starched, lace-edged tablecloths looked ready to accommodate patrons. A thick sweet aroma like burnt buttery caramel emanated from the kitchen. It was powerful but also extremely appetising.

At the cake counter, Frances and May, in their black-and-white uniforms and both wearing white gloves, were counting biscuits into cardboard boxes, each decorated with a sweet little etching of a thatched cottage. *With love from Devon* was swirled below the image.

May smiled shyly at Felicity. Frances barely looked up from her work.

"This way, my lady," said Vera, beckoning Felicity through the green swing doors.

The kitchen was spacious and well-organised. Along the walls were a series of ovens and wooden worktops with shelves above and below, the latter covered by green-and-white gingham curtains. At the centre was a worn but solid oak table. A wide slab of smooth, grey-veined marble lay on the table's surface.

Katherine stood at the hob in a pale green knitted dress with an apron tied at her waist. She used a long wooden spoon to stir a tall, bubbling copper pot.

Even with the kitchen door open and a cool breeze wafting in, the rich, toffee-like smell was so thick in the air, one could almost taste it. Pip's little black nose twitched rapidly.

Katherine glanced over her shoulder. Her cheeks glowed under her powder. "I followed your instructions," she said to her sister. "I hope it'll turn out all right."

Vera took off her hat, coat, and bag and tied on an apron. "All will be well, Kathy. I'm sure of it. I can't tell you how thankful I am that you're here."

Stepping away from the stove as Vera took the wooden spoon from her, Katherine untied her apron. "I'm sorry," she said to Felicity. "I suppose you're here to interview us, only I can't stop. Zoe's upstairs by herself. I promised her we'd have a dolls' tea party as soon as her mother got home."

"Of course," said Felicity, full of understanding. The dedication of the women at the Green Ginger was admirable. "Perhaps another time."

As Katherine departed through the swing doors and Vera stirred the copper pot, Felicity glanced around. She rarely spent time in kitchens. It also wasn't appropriate to put Pip on the neatly swept black-and-white tiled floor. Still, she felt the need to ask. "Might there be something I can do to help?"

Vera glanced over her shoulder, still stirring with the wooden spoon. "Of course not, my lady, but I'm afraid I can't stop what I'm doing. We've orders to fill and customers depending on us. You're welcome to take a seat, my lady. You'll have my full attention in just a moment."

Felicity pulled a stool from under the table and perched on it, placing Pip on her lap.

"Aha," said Vera. "Here we go."

She lifted the pot from the stove, brought it to the table, and poured the contents onto the marble slab. The golden-brown mixture oozed out of the pan and settled in a thick puddle atop the stone.

The Yorkie licked his nose as another wave of the heavy buttery scent swept through the kitchen.

"You're making fudge, are you not?" enquired Felicity.

"Precisely so, my lady." Vera smiled and used the back of her hand to mop her forehead. Her cheeks were bright red and her eyes were shining. "We let a bit of the warmth go out of it, then we reshape it before chopping it into slices. When it's fully cooled, we break it into pieces. Crumbly pieces, mind you. None of that sticky stuff. We like fudge that crumbles around here."

Vera never worked in the kitchens of Bradley Court, so her passion for sweet-making hadn't been known to the Quicks.

Felicity smiled. "I prefer crumbly fudge, too."

Vera dusted her hands on her apron. "You're welcome to a piece when it's ready, my lady. Would you care for a cup of tea and an iced bun? Or perhaps a hot buttered crumpet? I imagine you've been too busy to give lunch a second thought."

Felicity had wanted to offer Vera her support, not be waited upon. However, refusing Vera's hospitality risked causing offence. Felicity was also famished. "An iced bun would be lovely, and I shan't say no to a cup of your delicious tea."

"Very well, my lady." Vera smiled proudly.

Felicity tucked into the sweet, sticky bun before the tea was ready, dropping a couple of accidental crumbs for Pip. When Vera brought the brew over, her hand gripping the handle of a fat, red teapot, the spell of cosiness that had enveloped the kitchen broke. That Vera was keen to move on was understandable. It could not, however, be ignored that a murder had occurred just hours ago in the room next door.

It was easy to find a blank page in her notebook, just beyond where Felicity had torn out the notes for Alex. "I realise we saw each other on the street not long after Mrs Norrington was found." Felicity's tone was gentle but serious as Vera took a seat at the table. "I believe the newspaper's readers would like to know from you what happened leading up to the discovery."

Vera's pale eyebrows drew together as she stirred a sugar cube into her tea. "Well, my lady. I went to bed as normal but heard nothing. None of us did. It was Kathy that found her, you see. When she woke me up to tell me, I thought I was dreaming."

An occasion would indeed need to be found to interview Vera's sister. "And how did Katherine come across the dead woman?"

"She went down for a glass of water. That's when she saw Mrs Norrington, all laid out." Vera's hand shook slightly as she picked up her teacup.

"Did you know Mrs Norrington well?"

"She was a customer. We chatted politely, of course. Nothing more."

"What reason did Mrs Norrington have to be at the Green Ginger during the night?"

"None whatever, my lady. None I'm aware of, in any case."

"How might she have gained entry to your premises?"

Vera looked sheepish. She nodded towards the kitchen door. "It was always unlatched, my lady. I wanted everyone living here to come and go as they pleased. No one should feel locked up." Her use of the past tense indicated Vera had seen the error in her ways.

Felicity didn't press the point. "Do you believe Mrs Norrington was sabotaging the tea rooms?"

"I can't think why she would, my lady. She seemed to be a satisfied customer. I'm afraid it rather looks that way though, doesn't it?" Vera sipped her tea and blinked.

If the murder victim had disapproved of the tea rooms as Colonel Norrington said she did, she'd done a good job of hiding the fact.

Felicity nibbled the remains of her iced bun — which was moist and quite delicious — as she considered her next question.

"How did you find your staff? Except for your sister, of course. I imagine you've known her all her life."

Vera looked amused. "Not quite, my lady. Kathy is a couple of years older than me."

Felicity stroked Pip as a flush of embarrassment rose to her cheeks. "Oh, dear. I didn't quite mean it like that."

"It's quite all right, my lady. Kathy dresses with the latest fashions and knows how to use make-up. She worked in one of the big London department stores before she was married, you see."

Felicity sipped her tea. "What brought her to Ippleford?"

"I suppose she won't mind me telling you, my lady. But you'll keep it to yourself, won't you?"

Felicity rested her pencil flat on her notepad. "Of course."

"Her husband put her out on the street. Kathy had nowhere else to go. Even though we were born in Devon, the countryside's not her natural environment. I'm awfully sorry it happened to her, but I've been so grateful for her being here. Especially now."

Curious though it was, it would have been indelicate to ask what led to Katherine's husband making her homeless. A woman's position could become precarious with no wrongdoing on her part, and it seemed hardly relevant to the interview for the paper.

"It sounds as though you have a good relationship with your sister."

"Oh, of course, my lady." Vera chuckled warmly. "My little Zoe adores her, and Kathy has all the patience in the world for her."

Felicity picked up her pencil. "What about Frances and May? Have you known them long?"

Vera took a sip of tea. "I met them when the Green Ginger first opened, when they came to work for me. That'll be about a year ago now. They're extremely competent young ladies, as I'm sure you've already noticed. I was very lucky to find them both."

"Where did you find them, exactly?"

Vera put her teacup down. "I'm afraid you'll think me rather silly, my lady. The police told me as much just this morning."

"It's not my business to judge you, Vera," said Felicity, unimpressed the police saw their business differently, "although I'll admit you have me intrigued."

"How I found them was by going to girls' homes and orphanages and asking for anyone wanting to work hard and learn a profession."

Felicity stroked Pip and tried not to appear surprised. "That sounds incredibly noble." The approach was unorthodox. Had Lady Henrietta been aware?

Vera shrugged. "I don't consider myself noble, my lady. May was at an orphanage in Tiverton, preparing to go into service, and Frances was in Bristol, at a halfway house for young ladies from reformatory."

Felicity remained composed, but the word *reformatory* sent a shiver down her spine. It conjured images of delinquent children and hard regimes. Given everything that had happened, a former criminal employed at the tea rooms couldn't be overlooked, even if Frances must have been rather young when committing whatever acts sent her to reformatory school.

Felicity stroked Pip's ears. "What made you choose this approach?"

"After how generous your grandmother's been to me, I felt I had a duty to help others. I met a great number of girls, my lady. Most of them were unsuitable, you understand. But when I met Frances and May, I knew I could trust them."

Felicity smiled weakly. Trusting the wrong person was easily done. Yet if Alex's report was true, and Vera was the prime suspect for the murder, how had the police ruled out a former reformatory girl living upstairs from where the crime took place?

"Do the police suspect anyone at the tea rooms?" enquired Felicity. She was getting off track in terms of quotes for the newspaper, but she wanted reassurance Vera couldn't possibly be the main suspect.

Vera sniffed. "You can quite imagine the police's suspicions about Frances, but she and May share rather a small room, and it's simply not possible for one to rise without waking the other. They both swear they were in their room together all night."

Rather abruptly, Vera stood and went to the marble slab, where she began moving the thick puddle of still-warm fudge around, creating a fat sausage shape. Felicity sipped her tea and watched as Vera used a large wooden spatula to cut the sausage into generous slices. May and Frances could be heard in the room next door chatting and giggling. The girls clearly had a strong bond.

"Cools down crumblier that way," said Vera as she washed her hands and returned to her seat.

Felicity smiled. It wasn't yet clear how the interview would help Vera, but Felicity's curiosity tugged at her sleeve, urging her onwards. "Is Mr Carli back from London?"

Vera nodded and sipped her tea. "The police are speaking to him, but there's not much he can tell them, of course. He only got back from London this morning. He's very upset about the whole thing, as we all are, although Luca has something of an artist's temperament."

"How did you meet him?"

"At a shelter for young men."

Felicity nodded non-judgementally, although she began to see why the police had reprimanded Vera about her choice of staff.

"He's from Switzerland originally," continued Vera. "When he first came to England, he went straight to London, like so many do. Seeking his fortune. After a bit of bad luck, he ended up sleeping rough." Vera smiled. "It was a blessing to find him. His cakes are to die for. Wouldn't you say so, my lady?"

Vera's choice of words was unfortunate, but she had a point. "The chocolate tart I tried was indeed heavenly."

"We have people coming from as far as Bournemouth and Bristol to try Luca's confections."

Felicity smiled politely and looked at her notepad. *A shame his personality isn't as palatable,* she thought. She tapped her pencil on the open page. "Forgive me for asking this, Vera, but I believe the paper's readers will be wondering. With everyone living upstairs, how do you explain no one hearing anything of the murder? It was, apparently, a violent act."

Vera sighed. "The rehearsal for the play meant Kathy, Frances, and May all got in late, well after Zoe and I went to bed. There were people moving about outside till late into the night. I slept rather fitfully, my lady, I must admit. Perhaps I heard something of the goings-on downstairs and didn't realise what it was." Vera rubbed her temple. She looked tired. "The police had their doubts as well."

Felicity felt a twinge of guilt. She'd used the interview to satisfy her own curiosity, but how had it benefited Vera? "Oh, dear. I've asked too many questions, have I not?"

A faint smile returned to Vera's lips. "You're just doing your job, my lady. And I know you only want to help. It's just... Well. There's not a lot anyone can do, other than solve the crime and help us get back to normal."

Felicity swallowed. She sincerely hoped Alex's source for Vera being the police's chief suspect was mistaken. But what if the murderer was someone else at the tea rooms? How would things go back to normal then?

Vera stood up and slapped her apron. "I need to get on with my fruitcakes. You're, of course, welcome to taste all our sweets, my lady. Although I don't suppose you'll have room in your articles for talk of cakes and such."

Felicity saw her opportunity. "Not exactly, but we shall mention that the Green Ginger Tea Rooms is a purveyor of the very finest cakes and sweets, and that the owner and her staff are getting ready to reopen as soon as possible."

Vera smiled sadly. "That's very kind of you, my lady. We'd like to re-open tomorrow, if we can. I hope the villagers don't find it disrespectful, but I'm afraid we can't go for long without money coming in, and I expect we won't get back to our normal customer numbers for a while."

Felicity stood up, tucking Pip under her arm. Getting matters resolved as quickly as possible was indeed crucial. "Do you suppose I might speak to Frances and May? I realise they're busy. I'll do my best not to disturb their work."

"Be my guest, my lady. Just please be mindful that they've both been through an awful lot." Vera's face was serious. "Not only what's happened here at the tea rooms but also before coming to Ippleford. They've had hard lives. They wanted to move on from all that."

"I shall indeed be mindful." Felicity nodded confidently, but it couldn't yet be ruled out that the murderer had come from within the tea rooms, and the thought gave her goosebumps.

## Chapter Fourteen

Felicity pushed through the kitchen's swing doors and re-entered the tea rooms' seating area with Pip clasped under her elbow. Frances and May were still filling gift boxes at the cake counter. They'd been giggling, but upon Felicity's arrival, the girls fell silent.

"Your ladyship," said May with a nervous little curtsey and the flicker of a welcoming smile.

Frances said nothing. She continued to smirk.

Was it unfair to be suspicious of the red-headed waitress based solely on her background?

"Miss Lee, Miss Pettigrew, do forgive me for interrupting," said Felicity breezily. "Mrs Monroe told me I could put a few questions to you both while you continue to work. Would you have any objection? The readers of the Western Daily News will be eager to hear what effect last night's terrible tragedy has had on you."

May's lips parted but no sound came.

"She was found just over there, my lady." Frances nodded towards a tea table upon which lay a modest bunch of white lilies wrapped in brown paper.

The matter-of-factness of the pronouncement was disquieting.

"Mrs Norrington, you mean?" enquired Felicity rather unnecessarily.

Frances continued dropping biscuits into a box. "Yes, my lady." She folded the box closed with a smooth movement. "That's who I mean."

Pip squiggled in Felicity's arms. She'd been holding onto him for too long. "Would it be a bother if I set my dog on the floor?"

May shook her head enthusiastically. The idea seemed to please her, but compared to when she'd been outside with Zoe, the youngest waitress was more withdrawn in Frances' presence.

"By all means, my lady," said Frances without looking up from her work.

As soon as Felicity set Pip down, he went snuffling off under the tables, on the hunt for fallen titbits rather than any clues to the crime, which by now would have been collected by the police, anyway.

"You've done a wonderful job clearing everything up," said Felicity, admiring the pristine table settings. "Criminal activity aside, I'm aware the police can make quite a mess of things."

"You should see upstairs, my lady," said Frances, her hands moving quickly and automatically as she filled the biscuit boxes. "They went through all our belongings, too. Quite an ordeal, it was."

"We haven't had time to tidy upstairs, your ladyship." May was slower and more careful in putting the biscuits into boxes than Frances. She glanced nervously at both Felicity and Frances as she spoke, which slowed her further. "As soon as the police left, we tidied everything down here so that anyone looking in through the window wouldn't be reminded of the... The... You know."

"I know," said Felicity. She didn't want to make her questioning of the girls into another ordeal for them. As Vera had said, they'd been through a lot, and they were also rather young. Felicity hoped her suspicions were misplaced. "I also know Mrs Monroe appreciates your hard work very much. She speaks highly of you both."

"We know she does, my lady," said Frances. "We'd do anything for her." She looked up briefly from her work. There was a hardness to her gaze. "Mrs Monroe knows that."

Felicity smiled politely. “I’m certain she does.”

Frances’ manner was gruff, but that in itself didn’t mean she was capable of murder. Besides, Felicity needed to keep her mind on her work. Alex would have called in their article by now, but she’d committed to interviewing the witnesses from the tea rooms.

Felicity slipped her notebook from her pocket. “Could you tell me what happened last night?”

Frances set the box in her hands on the cake counter. “That’s just it, isn’t it? No one heard anything. No one saw anything. Did they, May?”

May hesitated, then she shook her head.

“You heard something, Miss Pettigrew?” pressed Felicity.

“Oh, no, your ladyship,” came May’s reply. “Absolutely not.”

Felicity tried a different tack. “Could you say something of the effect the tragedy has had on you?”

“It’s deeply shocking, your ladyship.” May’s voice wobbled. “If Frances and me didn’t share a room, I’d even find it quite frightening.”

Felicity lifted her eyebrows as she nodded. Did May know about Frances’ history?

“Mrs Monroe said she’ll make sure all doors are locked and all windows are latched from now on.” Frances said this more to May than to Felicity. “So we don’t need to be afraid. But we’re not pleased about the effect it’s had on Mrs Monroe’s business.” She looked at Felicity. “Mrs Monroe said she might not open tomorrow out of respect for the dead woman, but I disagreed with her. It’s not Mrs Monroe’s fault the woman’s dead, is it? Why should she suffer?”

Felicity wrote everything the waitresses said in her notebook. Frances was more outspoken than Felicity had realised. Their contrasting personalities weren’t a barrier to the strong bond they seemed to have.

Frances restarted her work with the biscuits, thrusting them a little roughly into the boxes. “I’m also not best pleased that the play’s been cancelled, if we’re being honest about things. We were very much looking forward to it. Weren’t we, May?”

May offered Felicity a pained smile, seemingly more aware than Frances of what society deemed normal behaviour. Expressing disappointment at the play being cancelled in reaction to a brutal murder couldn't be used as a quote. The newspaper's readers would consider it bad taste.

"You had the leading role, didn't you, Miss Lee?"

Frances nodded grimly. "Mr and Mrs Heard say they don't know when the play will go back on, or even if it will. We learned all those lines and sat through all those dress fittings for nothing." As she spoke, she dropped a biscuit. It bounced off the cake counter and onto the ground. "Blast it!" Frances stamped her foot. A flush of red appeared on her cheeks.

Felicity blinked, a little taken aback.

"It's all right, Fran," said May, soothingly. "There are always extra biscuits."

Pip approached the cake counter, his sixth-sense for dropped food finely attuned in any situation. Gingerly, he edged behind the counter and approached the fallen biscuit.

"Pip," said Felicity sternly.

The Yorkie looked up at her pleadingly.

Felicity shook her head. Being allowed to explore the empty tea rooms by paw was enough of a privilege for a little Yorkie. Consumption of a freshly baked shortbread was a step too far, not to mention it hardly being appropriate sustenance for a canine.

May smiled down at Pip. "If you don't mind him eating it, your ladyship, he's welcome to do so. It'll only go in the bin otherwise."

Reluctantly, Felicity relented, and Pip crunched on the biscuit, Frances and May both watching him.

The younger waitress turned to her friend. "See, Fran. It's not going to waste."

Frances was calmer, but her cheeks were still flushed. She had a temper. Could she get angry enough to strike a woman on the back of the head with a teapot?

Felicity tried not to allow any hint of this disturbing thought to display on her face. She didn't feel in any immediate danger from

Frances, but who knew what she might be capable of when provoked?

With May growing more comfortable talking, Felicity was keen to return to questioning the waitresses. Before she could do so, May picked up a biscuit tray and held it towards Felicity.

"Would you like to try one, your ladyship? It doesn't seem right, your sweet little dog getting to taste our shortbread and you not."

Felicity smiled at the girl. "Thank you, Miss Pettigrew, but I just had an iced bun."

"You can't say no, my lady," said Frances forcefully. "Mrs Monroe made them herself. You should try one."

Felicity's smile slipped a little. "Very well." It seemed the easier option than further attempts at protest. Perhaps even the safer option.

The thick, small round of golden biscuit with crinkled edges glistened with a sprinkling of sugar. Could it be salt? If the saboteur had been killed, there should have been no danger of that. It was a relief when the biscuit melted on Felicity's tongue, deliciously buttery, intensely sweet, and utterly wasted on Pip.

"It's delightful," she said.

The girls both beamed.

"Mrs Monroe's a wonderful baker," said Frances, excitement in her eyes. "But have you tried Mr Carli's chocolates?"

"His chocolates?" Felicity wasn't in the mood for further sweets, but that seemed by the bye.

Frances turned to the shelves behind the cake counter. There were multiple boxes of biscuits and packets of fudge stacked in neat rows. On one of the higher shelves was a small array of unique-looking boxes. From that higher shelf, Frances took down a tin decorated with an intricate, foreign-looking floral design.

Two memories raced through Felicity's mind.

The first was of Mrs Norrington in her wide-brimmed hat, standing approximately where Felicity was now situated. She had requested something from the same shelf from which Frances had produced the chocolate box. Luca had been behind the counter, and he'd smiled at her and shaken his head.

The second memory related to the chocolate tin itself. Felicity had seen precisely such a floral box before. There'd been an identical tin at Colonel Norrington's cottage.

Had Mrs Norrington been attempting to buy some of Luca's chocolates? Or had she wanted something else?

As Frances popped the lid of the chocolate box open, Felicity gestured towards a row of small plain-looking tins next to the gap where the chocolate box had been. Each tin had a set of hand-drawn initials on the side. *FL. MP. LC. KE.*

"May I ask what those boxes are?"

Frances frowned, displeased to have been interrupted in her presentation of Luca's chocolates.

"They're our tips boxes, your ladyship," said May, helpfully.

"Do you wish to tip us, my lady?" challenged Frances.

Felicity had to think quickly. "Aren't tips normally left at the end of a customer's visit? I don't believe we're finished here yet."

Frances grunted. She tipped the open chocolate box towards Felicity. "This is the sample box we let customers try from, but be warned. An ordinary chocolate bar won't taste the same after this."

With refusal not an option, Felicity cloaked her uneasiness with a polite smile and took a chocolate from the tin. It was a simple, round brown ball dusted with cocoa powder. It didn't look like much, but its deep, velvety taste was a different story altogether.

"My goodness," said Felicity when she was finished.

May nodded, beaming with pride. Pip sat expectantly and even raised a paw.

"Mr Carli is extremely talented," said Frances, with a hint of snootiness. "A genius, in fact. He's wasted here."

"I'm sure his talents are appreciated locally," said Felicity. Mrs Norrington had highly likely been among Luca's fans.

"Oh, they certainly are," said Frances. "But Ippleford's just a little village."

Felicity was about to come to Ippleford's defence, and to the defence of Devonshire villages in general, when raised voices outside caught everyone's attention.

---

Without a second thought, Felicity rushed to the tea rooms' front window. Frances joined her, as did Pip, although he was too short to see outside, even on his hind legs.

On the high street, which was still slick with drizzle, Vera was walking away from Mr Viner, the grumpy gardener Felicity had seen earlier at Rose Cottages.

As Vera disappeared around the side of the tea rooms, presumably to use the kitchen door, she swatted her hand at Mr Viner in a dismissive gesture. Mr Viner looked even less happy than usual, his hands falling with a slap to his sides.

"That man's a gardener, is he not?" enquired Felicity. "Does Mrs Monroe employ his services?"

A flush of red returned to Frances' cheeks. "Yes, but he's a... He's a blooming swine."

Felicity appreciated that Frances made the effort to not use more colourful language. "Why do you say that?"

"He's very disagreeable." Frances continued to watch the high street. "He's got too many opinions. Mrs Monroe is sick of him sticking his oar in."

Mr Viner said something to Vera as she retreated. It wasn't possible to hear everything. "Why don't—" and "—take care of—" was all Felicity could catch.

The kitchen door slammed.

"The absolute swine," muttered Frances under her breath.

Mr Viner shook his head and turned his attention towards a large pot of spent flowers he'd been digging up outside the tea rooms. His Border Collie lay nearby, unfazed by the argument or the wet ground.

Pip whined in a heartstring-tugging manner typical of small yet canny dogs. With a sigh, Felicity tucked the Yorkie under her arm.

Frances returned to May and her work with the biscuit boxes.

"Is there anything else you need from us for your newspaper article?" asked Frances, with typical gruffness.

Felicity was about to respond with a question about the play — for surely the girls must have engaged with Mrs Norrington outside of the tea rooms, if they were all working on the production together — when they were again interrupted.

"Perhaps Lady Felicity would like to talk to me?" Katherine had appeared in the doorway at the back of the tea rooms that led to the living quarters. She had on her grass-green topcoat and matching hat. She approached the cake counter. "I've given Zoe a book to read, and I've got a task to do for Vera. Perhaps we can talk on the way? If you're finished speaking to May and Frances, that is."

Felicity considered the girls counting the shortbread biscuits into boxes. There was more she could ask them, but Katherine had discovered Mrs Norrington's body. It was the kind of witness testimony that would sell many extra newspapers.

"I believe I've taken up enough of Frances and May's time," said Felicity in a grateful tone. "And if I stay in the tea rooms much longer, I might find myself without need of food for the coming week."

The young waitresses giggled.

"You're very welcome, my lady." Frances' warm, genuine smile gave Felicity a pang of guilt for suspecting the girl. For while Frances was older than May, she couldn't be described as much more than that. A girl.

"It shan't be a bother if I accompany you?" said Felicity to Katherine. "I'd indeed appreciate a quote or two from you for the paper."

"I'd be glad of the company," said Katherine.

# Chapter Fifteen

Katherine was to take a delivery of biscuits to Ippleford's post office, where they'd been selling more than usual because of the tea rooms' closure. Felicity watched as Frances and May placed the required number of boxes into two jute bags, which Katherine slipped into the crook of her arm.

"Can I help carrying the biscuits?" asked Felicity as she stepped onto the high street after Katherine, placing Pip on the ground. It was no longer raining, but the air was damp and cool. Gentle gusts of wind shook the occasional patter of rain loose from the trees dotted along the thoroughfare.

"Oh, no." Katherine had painted her lips with something of a cupid's bow. At a glance, it was indeed easy to mistake her for younger than Vera. Much younger. "The biscuits weigh nothing at all. And you'll want to take notes, surely?"

Pip trotted ahead of Felicity and Katherine, as if he somehow knew they were heading for the post office, which lay a little way up the hill in the castle's direction.

Taking Katherine's comment as an invitation, Felicity removed her notebook from her pocket. Precisely how long the errand to the post office would take wasn't clear. "I hope you don't mind me diving straight into matters. You found Mrs Norrington's body, did you not?"

"That's right." A horse and cart clattered by, but Katherine's eyes remained fixed on the street ahead of her. "I got out of bed for a glass of water. I even went into the kitchen and made the drink before I noticed her." Katherine glanced at Felicity. "The body, I mean. It's a wonder I didn't drop my glass, but I somehow held onto it. I didn't even scream. It was the queerest thing. My first thought was, I must be dreaming. Only the bottom half of her was visible, the rest under the table. I already knew it wasn't good, but when I lifted the table cloth, I saw enough." Katherine glanced again at Felicity, her jaw tight. "Whether the woman was dragged under there or that's where she fell, I couldn't tell you. You'd need to ask the police about that."

Felicity nodded. She was certain Alex would have all the details from his interviews. "What time was it?"

"Couldn't say for sure. Somewhere towards one o'clock. Pitch dark outside, of course."

With the post office in sight, Felicity slowed her pace. "After finding the victim, what did you do?"

"I woke my sister. It was only when Vera confirmed I wasn't dreaming that I realised the seriousness of it. And how completely odd it was. As far as anyone is aware, the woman had no business in the tea rooms in the middle of the night. Anyway, that's when the whole circus started. Everyone up and out of bed, the police racing into the village, the neighbours all wondering what was going on."

"How long have you been in Ippleford, Mrs Evans?"

"Let's see." Katherine glanced around, as if the answer lay in the neat cottage gardens they were passing. "A couple of months, I suppose. It's not my intention to stay here for very long, of course. But my sister is just about the only family I have." Katherine smiled a little bitterly. "You know, I used to tease her about how gullible she was. How anyone with a sob story could have room and board with her within half-an-hour of meeting her. I suppose I'm one of her strays now."

"They say blood is thicker than water," offered Felicity.

Katherine's expression softened. "I suppose so."

"What brought you to the Green Ginger, if I may ask?" Would Katherine offer more information than Vera had?

Katherine looked squarely at Felicity. "My husband had enough of me. He told me to pack my bags and leave." She shrugged. "I had nowhere else to go. So, here I am."

It wasn't extra information, but it would have to do. "I'm very sorry to hear that." As much as independence appealed to Felicity, being alone in the world as a woman could be a rather tough spot to be in.

"It could be worse." Katherine's bitter smile returned. "My husband was never mean to me. Never laid a finger on me, in fact, which was part of the problem."

It took Felicity a couple of extra beats to realise what Katherine had said. She now had too much information.

Before Felicity could muster a response, Katherine went on. "Say, I don't suppose you'd mind me asking you a question?"

With Pip having halted for a thorough, nose-led inspection of a gatepost, Felicity stopped and turned to face Katherine. "Please, go ahead."

"I saw you with a rather handsome-looking fellow out and about in the village." Katherine wrinkled her nose mischievously. "Are you some kind of husband-and-wife reporting duo?"

Embarrassment bloomed across Felicity's cheeks. "No. No." She laughed from awkwardness. "You've got that quite wrong. Mr Cooper and I are colleagues. Nothing more."

"Oh." Katherine's cupid bow drew into a pout of disappointment. "But you work closely together, do you not?"

Felicity cleared her throat, her composure returning. "We're reporting on the murder together."

"That's funny." Katherine put a fingertip to her chin. "I thought I saw your Mr Cooper the day before the murder occurred. Was that my mistake?"

Felicity couldn't lie. "No, you're quite right. We were also to work on the Ippleford piece for the leisure supplement together."

Katherine raised her eyebrows. "It takes two journalists to write up an inn, tea rooms, and a set of castle ruins, does it?"

Her embarrassment intensifying, Felicity regretted accompanying Katherine on her trip to the post office. Had the interrogation about Alex been Katherine's motive for inviting her along?

Relief came in the form of Luca walking at a brisk pace in the opposite direction. He had on his tan overcoat, under which bright white trousers were visible, presumably part of his chef's attire. He wore a bright red neckerchief. His dark brown eyes stood out against his pale skin.

"Oh, why," said Felicity airily. "I do believe that's Mr Carli."

Katherine turned and huffed. "I suppose the police must have finished with him."

As Luca drew closer, Felicity attempted a salutation. "Good day, Mr Carli."

The patisserie chef looked at Felicity without smiling, mumbled something unintelligible, and continued walking in the direction of the tea rooms with no proper acknowledgment of the greeting.

Felicity frowned in confusion. The contrast with Luca's charm when they'd first met was drastic. Had the police given him a hard time when interviewing him? She'd like to speak to him herself.

"Well, I'm afraid that's just typical," said Katherine.

Felicity blinked. "Typical?"

"I'm sorry to say it, but he's the sort of man who won't give you the time of day unless you're a particular type of woman."

"I'm not sure I follow," said Felicity innocently. Had Mrs Norrington perhaps been the patisserie chef's type of woman?

It was Katherine's turn to be flustered. "I can understand my sister's sympathy for the likes of Frances and May, but I fail to see how she tolerates that ridiculous man and his fanciful ways."

"He makes exceedingly delicious chocolates." It was perhaps unfair to needle Katherine, but Felicity was curious to find out more, if she could. "I happened to try one just this morning. Might that be reason enough for Vera to keep Mr Carli in her employ?"

Katherine harrumphed and resumed walking towards the post

office. "I've got to get back to Zoe. She shouldn't be left alone for too long. She's only seven, poor dear, and she's been through quite enough even before all this murder business. Vera, too."

Felicity continued to accompany Katherine in the direction of the post office. "The war claimed so many lives and irreparably damaged so many more," she said, referring obliquely to the father Zoe had lost.

Katherine looked at Felicity with confusion, then nodded. "Of course. Yes. But I'm here to look after them now, and I'll jolly well do my best to make sure nothing else happens to them."

They arrived at the post office. The building was newer than most in the village, being constructed from brick instead of cob and with a slate roof rather than thatch. The door, like the window frames, was painted bright pillar-box red.

Pip sniffed at an A-framed board announcing that the post office sold souvenirs for tourists as well as fresh bread, eggs, and newspapers. A poster in the window announced the play. *The Blue Lady of Ippleford Castle* had been the production's name. The poster now bore a strip of paper bearing the word *CANCELLED* in red, hand-painted lettering.

"Just on time." A large, grey-haired man with spectacles in his top pocket stepped out from the establishment's front door to accept the jute bags from Katherine. "We've had a charabanc come by. They bought up almost everything we have. The tea rooms remaining closed is quite understandable, of course, but Mrs Monroe's missing rather a lot of customers, I must say."

Katherine smiled graciously. "We're just pleased you've found success selling the Green Ginger's products, Mr Stanton."

Mr Stanton nodded proudly. "Mrs Stanton's done a wonderful job of the presentation." He peered at Felicity. "We've not been introduced, have we?"

Katherine made the requisite introduction.

The post master's eyes lit up. "A reporter for the Western Daily News, you say?"

"If you'll excuse me," said Katherine, straightening the sleeves of her bright green coat as a fine drizzle resumed. "I've got to get back to my niece," she added and promptly departed towards the tea rooms.

"If you'd like a quote from Mrs Stanton and myself, your ladyship," said the post master, "we'd be happy to oblige. As you can imagine, we sell rather a large number of copies of your fine paper here at the post office, as there's not a dedicated newsagent in the village."

Felicity smiled amiably. She would have liked to have returned to the Green Ginger and put several questions to Luca, but to turn down Mr Stanton's invitation would likely have a negative impact on the paper's reputation in Ippleford, especially if the post office was the only establishment selling newspapers.

As though sensing the inevitable — or perhaps the post office also sold dog biscuits — Pip had already trotted inside.

"Thank you, Mr Stanton. If you'd be able to spare me the time, that would be lovely."

---

As feared, the Stantons told Felicity nothing she hadn't already heard. With her notepad perched on the post office's counter and Pip tucked under one arm — because weaving between the ankles of a steady stream of customers grew quickly tiring for the little dog — Felicity wrote what a polite woman Mrs Norrington had been and how out of character for the peaceful village of Ippleford the whole affair of murder was.

The Stantons also mentioned the Green Ginger's success. A proof point was the extra footfall the post office and inn were attracting with the tea rooms closed. While it was gratifying to have collected a positive quote about Vera's business to put in the paper, had it been worth the precious time the interview at the post office had taken? A replacement reporter could arrive in the village at any moment, and Felicity still wanted to speak to Luca.

Thanking the Stantons, who were preparing to close the post office when she and Pip finally emerged back onto the high street,

Felicity hurried to the Green Ginger, yellow and orange leaves falling like confetti in the wind.

Felicity tapped on the tea rooms' front door. Vera let Felicity and Pip inside, the Yorkie squeezing through the door nose-first to conduct an investigation into fallen food. The warm, spiced smell of fruit cake hung in the air.

"I'm ever so sorry, my lady," said Vera, gently smacking flour from her apron, her cheeks red from her work in the kitchen. "Luca's gone to lie down. He has a headache, and I can't disturb him. If we're to re-open tomorrow, he needs his rest."

"Have you an indication of when I might speak to him?"

Pip made his way to the cake counter, nose twitching towards where Frances and May were now busy boxing up the fresh batch of fudge.

Vera's brow creased. "Difficult to say, my lady. He's usually—"

A rather urgent knocking at the tea rooms' front door caught everyone's attention.

Vera squinted through the small leaded panes of the tea rooms' front door. "Now, just who could that be?"

"I'll get it, Mrs Monroe." Frances bounded towards the door, slipping off her white gloves.

"That's kind of you, Frances." Vera sighed. "It's been an awfully long day. None of us got much rest last night, of course, and I should wonder if we'll sleep tonight. Poor Mrs Norrington." She glanced at the lilies on the tea table where the murder victim had been found. They'd not been put in a vase and were already wilting. "Should I prepare you a basket for your dinner, my lady? I'd invite you to dine with us here, but after everything that's happened, I doubt any of us will be decent company."

"Please, Vera. It's not your responsibility to keep me entertained." Indeed, Felicity had come to Ippleford to help Vera. She'd yet to live up to the commitment.

Frances approached from the door. "It was Mr and Mrs Biggs from the inn. Wanting to know if there's anything they can do."

"Oh." Vera's bottom lip trembled, as if the gesture might move her to tears. "That's so extremely kind of them. I hope you didn't send them away with a flea in their ear, Frances."

May glanced up from her work at the cake counter. She seemed uneasy.

"Course I didn't, Mrs Monroe." Frances pulled her gloves back on and returned to boxing the fudge. "I said how very kind, but no thank you very much. We have everything in hand."

Vera nodded. "That's right. There's no reason anyone else should be inconvenienced by this whole affair."

An idea sprang into Felicity's mind. "Actually, Vera, I might see if there's a table at the inn for dinner this evening. My colleague, Mr Cooper, should be there. And, well..."

She went to the cake counter and collected Pip. He wriggled with protest as Felicity tucked him under her arm, his hopes of a dropped piece of fudge dashed.

"If you don't mind, Vera, I'll head off." Felicity approached the front door. "I'll come back later to speak to Mr Carli. Hopefully, his headache will have subsided by then."

"Very well, my lady," said Vera, with a confused little wave.

The bell tinkled above the tea rooms' door as Felicity exited the Green Ginger. Her plan was decided. She would catch up with Mr and Mrs Biggs — who were lumbering towards the inn — and collect another positive quote about the Green Ginger to put in the paper, as there was clearly no animosity between the inn and the tea rooms. It wasn't much, but Felicity hoped it would help.

Only it wasn't to be.

On the tea rooms' doorstep stood the two policemen Alex had been interviewing earlier, the uniformed officer with the dark grey moustache and the severe-looking young detective.

Both policemen stared at Felicity with a degree of intensity she didn't appreciate.

She gripped Pip a little harder. "C-can I help you?"

"I'm Sergeant Hewitt. This here's Detective Inspector Daniels." The uniformed officer spoke slowly, as though Felicity's mental faculties might not be up to scratch. "And unless I'm mistaken, you're Lady Felicity Quick."

"I am," said Felicity, doing her best to regain her composure. "How may I help you?"

"We'd like to speak to you, your ladyship," said Sergeant Hewitt with a grim raise of his eyebrows. "Now."

# Chapter Sixteen

The wind picked up as Felicity followed Sergeant Hewitt and Detective Inspector Daniels towards the churchyard. Turning up the collar of her tweed jacket and hugging Pip to her chest, Felicity's mood was rather low. She wasn't being much help to Vera, and she ought really to have reported back to Alex by now. The policemen's curt manner gave the impression she'd done something wrong. Had she?

As its exterior suggested, the church hall was a cavernous building, roughly put together with bare stone walls inside. A series of small windows were positioned too high to offer much light or a decent view, and a handful of electric lights strung from thick, cobwebbed roof beams struggled to compete with the dimness of the interior. A chilly draft whistled through the building.

Pip shivered in Felicity's arms.

"Over here, please, your ladyship." Sergeant Hewitt gestured stiffly to a desk with chairs on either side of it in the corner of the barn-like space.

Felicity took a seat and placed Pip on her lap. To her dismay, neither Sergeant Hewitt nor Detective Inspector Daniels joined her. At some distance away, they spoke in hushed tones with one another, then approached several policemen. Some were seated at desks, poring over documents. Others had been awaiting instruction from the senior officers before departing for police business elsewhere in the village.

While stroking Pip and doing her best to remain calm while waiting — for there was much to get on with — a colourful pile of cloth caught Felicity's attention. The gold and red banners were recognisable from the items Philip and Ernestine Heard had been transporting to the castle for the rehearsal.

It seemed like a lifetime ago now, but Felicity had only arrived in Ippleford on the previous evening.

Bundled up with the banners was also clothing. A dark blue dress with a laced front and broad cuffs was distinguishable in the pile. Was this the dress Frances would have worn as the Blue Lady? Might Mrs Norrington have worked on it? The police had presumably bundled up the play's decor and costumes in their takeover of the church hall. No one who cared about the play would treat the items like that.

At long last, the detective and the sergeant joined Felicity, removing their hats and sitting at the opposite side of the table.

Detective Inspector Daniels took a notepad from the inside of his single-breasted jacket. "Apologies for the delay, Lady Felicity."

Felicity gave a tight smile. "That's quite all right, Detective Inspector." Being polite and helpful was always an excellent policy when dealing with the authorities, but not knowing why one was being questioned was rather disquieting, even if one had done nothing wrong.

"We'll come straight to the point, your ladyship," said the sergeant, leaning forward. "You were in the village at the time of Mrs Norrington's death, were you not?"

"That's correct." Felicity stroked Pip.

"We're speaking to everyone who was in the village last night," continued the sergeant. "As I'm sure you can appreciate, it's a rather unusual crime, so we're leaving no stone unturned. If you don't mind, your ladyship, we should like your statement as a witness."

"I have absolutely no objection to that," said Felicity, relieved.

"However, I'm afraid I didn't hear or see anything that could be of use to you," she added, attempting to cut the conversation short.

The detective gave a little smile. "Do please allow us to be the judges of that, Lady Felicity." He found a blank page in his notebook. "I understand you arrived in Ippleford yesterday afternoon. Is that correct, your ladyship?"

Felicity nodded.

The detective made a note. "Could you take us through the hours leading up to Mrs Norrington's death? Where you were, who you met, what you saw or heard. Anything you can remember. Even if it doesn't stand out to you as noteworthy, it might be of use to us."

The local sergeant had also produced a notebook. He eyed Felicity sharply.

"Well." Felicity's thoughts skipped ahead. She was keen to leave the church hall as soon as possible. How could she condense her testimony yet satisfy the policemen? "I arrived in Ippleford yesterday afternoon. I spent a short while at the tea rooms before being shown to the cottage where I spent the night."

"What business did you have in Ippleford?" asked the sergeant.

Felicity's insides tightened. "I was to write an article about the village as a destination for day-trippers." It wasn't correct to withhold information from the police. "I'd also been asked to look into the sabotage at the Green Ginger."

The detective gave a knowing nod.

Sergeant Hewitt's eyes widened. "Didn't realise you were a private detective, your ladyship," he said with a distinctly unimpressed air.

Felicity's protest was immediate. "Oh, I'm not. Nothing of the sort. Mrs Monroe is a dear friend of my grandmother's. It was as a favour to my grandmother that I agreed to look into things. To be honest, I didn't feel completely comfortable about it. I'm a reporter, and I know how to investigate a story, but I'm not any kind of detective. Only Mrs Monroe was quite desperate, you see. She didn't know to whom to turn."

"Indeed," said Detective Inspector Daniels with a sharp glance at the sergeant. Having already interviewed Vera at length, he was likely aware of the local constabulary's inaction on the matter.

The sergeant sat up even straighter in his chair. "And may I ask just how far you got with your investigations into the goings-on at the Green Ginger, your ladyship?"

"Precisely nowhere, if I'm entirely honest, Sergeant. I arrived at the tea rooms, had tea and cake and spoke to Mrs Monroe and her staff. Mrs Norrington came into the tea rooms while I was there, although I didn't recognise her at the time." Felicity stroked a hand over Pip's ears, remembering the Dachshund's pained howls.

"We're aware of Mrs Norrington's movements on the day of her death," said the sergeant a little impatiently.

Felicity was more than happy to hurry onwards. "I was then taken to the cottage where I stayed the night. I happened upon my colleague, Mr Alexander Cooper, on the high street, but I spent the rest of the evening in my cottage."

Detective Inspector Daniels smiled. "I know him. Sharp as a tack, that one."

Sergeant Hewitt twitched his moustache. "When you say 'happened upon', your ladyship, do you mean you didn't know another journalist from the same newspaper you work for — your brother's newspaper, no less — would come to Ippleford?"

Felicity frowned. It was true she'd been surprised by Alex's arrival, but how was it related to the murder investigation? Valuable minutes were ticking by. "I'd not been informed of Mr Cooper's plans beforehand, Sergeant. It's not unusual for last-minute decisions to be made at a daily newspaper. We produce morning, afternoon, and evening editions, as I'm sure you're aware."

"Could you elaborate on your time spent at the cottage?" asked the detective.

"I dined there alone with provisions supplied by the tea rooms. Then I read a book by the fire. I must admit, I had some difficulty falling asleep as the village remained alive with activity until late into the night."

"What do you mean by 'activity'?" enquired Sergeant Hewitt.

"People walking, sometimes running. Talking, laughing. I suppose it was all related to the rehearsal of the play at the castle. I couldn't say what time I fell asleep."

Detective Inspector Daniels flicked back through his notebook. "I understand you arrived at the scene of the crime not long after the police did. What caused you to wake up?"

The memory of Alex standing outside the cottage and the relief on his face when she opened the door made Felicity shift in her seat and adjust Pip in her lap. "Mr Cooper woke me up. He'd heard a commotion and was checking on me. We decided to see what was happening, and we quickly noticed the police vehicles and the ambulance."

Sergeant Hewitt lowered his brow. "And since then, you and Mr Cooper have been reporting on the murder, have you not?"

"That's correct," said Felicity, although she was rather neglecting her fair share of the work.

"You cover the reactions of the people affected by the crime while Mr Cooper chases us around. Something along those lines?" Detective Inspector Daniels smiled ambiguously.

Felicity briefly returned the smile. How seriously did these policemen take her?

The detective continued to smile. "Our Chief Inspector mentioned you have some talent when it comes to criminal investigations."

"Oh." Felicity was taken aback. "Chief Inspector Luscombe, you mean?"

"You've met him on a couple of occasions, if I understand correctly."

"That's right." Felicity spoke with caution. She still couldn't make out what was meant by the detective's smile.

"Have no fear, your ladyship," continued the detective. "Our Chief Inspector speaks highly of you."

Felicity swallowed. "He does?"

Sergeant Hewitt turned to his colleague, looking as surprised as Felicity felt.

Detective Inspector Daniels nodded. "He said you can be a little cavalier in terms of method, but he believes you have something of a knack for understanding people."

Felicity blinked, doing her best to conceal the hesitant pride glowing faintly in her chest. "Is that so?" The news was especially surprising given that Chief Inspector Luscombe had always cultivated a vague air of disapproval in his dealings with her.

The detective's face became serious. "I therefore hope you don't mind my asking for your opinion on the situation we're facing here, your ladyship."

The local sergeant looked on with astonishment as Detective Inspector Daniels closed his notepad, indicating that the detective's question wasn't a part of the official investigation.

Had an opportunity to help Vera presented itself?

Felicity stroked Pip. "If Mrs Norrington was responsible for the sabotage, and the motive for the murder was to punish her for this, then the murderer is likely someone with close ties to the tea rooms." As Felicity spoke, uneasiness slithered through her.

It was one's duty to give the police all the necessary information. Did that duty extend to giving one's honest opinion?

"Someone living there, you mean?" pressed the detective.

Felicity hesitated. "I couldn't say that with full confidence."

"Do you have anyone in particular in mind?" enquired Sergeant Hewitt, the disbelief on his face replaced with interest.

"Not exactly," said Felicity. "But I've been made aware of background information on members of the household. I believe there's more to be uncovered there."

Detective Inspector Daniels flashed an eager glance at the sergeant.

Was it not unfair to judge a person by their past actions, especially if they were a child at the time of any wrong-doing? Had Felicity said too much?

Her mouth had gone dry. She licked her lips. "How long do you think it will be before you have someone for the crime?"

"Oh, not long now, your ladyship," said Sergeant Hewitt confidently. "Not long at all."

"Thank you, Lady Felicity." The detective tucked his notepad into his jacket pocket. "You've been most helpful."

"Yes, your ladyship." The sergeant rose from his seat, his tone with Felicity quite changed. "Thank you for your time. It's most appreciated."

Felicity stood, tucking Pip under her arm. She needed to speak to Alex.

She turned to leave but stopped. "There's actually something I simply cannot fathom."

Detective Inspector Daniels lifted his brow. "What might that be?"

"Mrs Norrington's motive for sabotaging the tea rooms," said Felicity.

The detective and sergeant looked at Felicity in mild confusion.

"Have you been able to uncover anything in that regard?" she enquired.

"It's not always possible to say for certain why people do things," said the detective. "What matters to us is whether or not they did them."

Sergeant Hewitt smiled under his steel-grey moustache. "We'll leave the 'why' of it up to the likes of you and Mr Cooper, your ladyship."

# Chapter Seventeen

Outside the church hall, under a darkening sky of thick, rolling clouds, Felicity breathed deep lungs of chilly air scented with the herby earthiness of the graveyard. She'd been nothing but honest with Detective Inspector Daniels and Sergeant Hewitt. Why, then, did she feel so uncomfortable about their discussion?

The church's bells struck the hour. It was much later than she'd hoped.

Alex. Felicity had to speak to him. Together, they could make sense of things. But where to find him? She would try the Blue Lady Inn first.

Setting Pip on the ground, Felicity hurried towards the high street. The lychgate connecting the churchyard to the street being a medieval structure, passing through it meant ducking one's head.

With her head bowed, Felicity almost knocked into someone coming the other way. "Oh, dear. How clumsy of me. I'm awfully sorry."

The person she'd nearly bumped into took a step back. It was Luca.

He brought a hand to his Homburg hat and scratched his temple, his gaze jumping between Felicity and the churchyard behind her. He looked even paler than earlier and still had on his chef's whites under his tan overcoat.

Pip edged forward as if to sniff the man's shoes. Changing his mind, the Yorkie retreated for some sniffing under the lychgate, his bright little eyes keeping watch over the patisserie chef.

"Mr Carli." Felicity stood up straight and tugged on her tweed jacket. Here was an opportunity she hadn't expected. "I'd understood from Vera that you had a headache. I was sorry to hear it. Are you feeling better now?"

The patisserie chef gave a little shrug. "I think so. Yes." The charm Luca had so obviously attempted to use on Felicity the first time they met had entirely disappeared. He seemed even agitated by her presence.

"I'm happy to hear that." Felicity wasted no time in reaching for her notebook. "In fact, I was hoping I might speak to you for the Western Daily News."

"I ignored you."

Felicity paused, her pencil hovering above a blank page. A horse and cart clattered by on the high street next to where they were standing. "Ignored me?"

"Earlier. Further up the road. You greeted me. I didn't reply to you. It wasn't on purpose. It wasn't polite, and I'm sorry for that."

"Not to worry." Whether using his charms or not, Luca clearly preferred to take charge of a conversation. Felicity would have to be as direct as possible. "You weren't in Ippleford the night of Mrs Norrington's death, were you, Mr Carli?"

"I was not." Again, his eyes darted to the churchyard.

"Do you have witnesses to confirm your whereabouts?"

He squinted at Felicity. "What is this? A police interrogation? I thought you were a journalist." He shook his head angrily. "Of course, I have witnesses. The hostel I stayed in, it was very busy."

Felicity cleared her throat. Being direct wasn't her usual style. "When you returned to the tea rooms and heard the news of what happened, what was your reaction?"

Luca sighed heavily. "Very bad. Very bad indeed. It's bad for me. Bad for everyone. Very bad."

"You knew the dead woman, did you not?"

The patisserie chef stared wide-eyed at Felicity. "Mrs Prudence Norrington was a customer of the tea rooms. We all knew her."

"The day I arrived in Ippleford, I believe I saw you speaking to Mrs Norrington at the cake counter. Do you remember the interaction you had with her? Can you recall what she said?"

Luca frowned deeply. The frown developed into a queer sort of smile. "She spoke to me about my work. About my talent. She wanted to see me do well." His gaze hardened. "Did you try my chocolates?"

"The waitresses had me try one, but I don't see what that has to do with the matter at hand, Mr Carli."

The patisserie chef's eyes burned like coals. "So you understand me when I say that I cannot allow my talent to go to waste here?"

The statement contained not an ounce of politeness or modesty. In the context of Mrs Norrington's murder, it was a particularly unsettling remark.

"Is that how you would like to be quoted in the newspaper in reaction to the murder?"

Luca waved his hand, as though Felicity was talking nonsense. "Already, this village is too small, and now a murder? The reputation. It does nothing for the reputation."

If Lower Diddleton's experience of murder was anything to go by, violent crime had the potential to raise a village's profile.

Felicity felt no urge to comfort the patisserie chef. "Are you saying the local community has been quite shaken by events?" she proposed, curious to know if Luca could think about anyone but himself.

His eyes went again to the churchyard. A pair of policemen were coming towards the lychgate.

"You know what?" Luca stepped backwards. "I change my mind. I look after myself. Everyone must look after himself."

"Change your mind about what, Mr Carli?"

But the patisserie chef was already hastening towards the tea rooms. A passing van had to toot its horn and swerve to avoid him, but Luca remained oblivious.

Felicity could have given chase, but to what end? Although her suspicions about Luca remained strong, he'd given her no concrete evidence to build on. He did a splendid job at stonewalling any attempt to extract information from him. Had Mrs Norrington really been at the Green Ginger to pay her respects to Luca's talents?

Pip emerged from the cover of the lychgate and stood with a paw raised, sniffing the air.

"I was told the police had taken you in for questioning."

Felicity turned.

Alex stood with his hands in his pockets, his dark blue eyes shining. Pip darted forward for an enthusiastic sniffing of his shoes.

Felicity smiled at Alex, pleased to see him, but her smile quickly died. Her stomach tensed at the memory of the police interview. "Detective Inspector Daniels and Sergeant Hewitt indeed interviewed me, although I fear I might have told them too much."

Alex's eyebrows drew together. "I doubt it. I'm sure they're grateful for any information you have."

The reassurance was mildly comforting.

He continued. "Quite the baffling case, this one, although the police certainly have something cooking. Were you able to offer any help to Mrs Monroe?"

"No," admitted Felicity with a twinge of regret, "but I've interviewed everyone at the tea rooms, just about."

Alex grinned. "That's a scoop and a half. The other reporters have been given the cold shoulder."

Felicity smiled back, weakly. It wasn't much help to Vera, was it? "Did you call in our story?" she asked. "I'm terribly grateful to you."

"Don't mention it. Your notes were clear." Alex peered down at Pip as he continued to talk. "And when I called the story in, I received a spot of good news."

Felicity raised her brow expectantly. "Oh?"

Alex looked up. "The journalist relieving us arrives tomorrow."

The announcement hit her like a brick. How had the replacement slipped Felicity's mind? She'd engineered it herself.

"I wasn't given a time," continued Alex, "but we're free to leave as soon as he arrives."

"Super." Felicity did her best to sound enthusiastic. The Ippleford mystery had become thoroughly absorbing, but after everything Alex had done — and continued to do — for her, Felicity had no right to be selfish. "And the interview with Judge Hawkins is still on?"

Alex looked quite pleased as he nodded.

"Splendid," said Felicity convincingly.

Would matters in Ippleford be rounded off in a satisfactory manner before they left? Felicity had done so little to help Vera. And in speaking so frankly to the police, she may even have brought more suffering to Vera's door.

Was there time to set things right?

Felicity had quite desperately wanted to discuss matters with him, but she decided against burdening Alex with her worries. It hadn't been his idea to come to Ippleford. She refocused her mind on what mattered both to her and Alex in equal measure: journalism.

"Do you think we have enough to call in another story?" Felicity asked. "We'll curry favour with the copy editors if we deliver ahead of the next edition's deadline."

Alex tucked his hands in his pockets and rocked back on his heels. "That's not a bad idea at all. Never hurts to have the copy editors on one's side."

---

Ippleford's high street wasn't yet back to regular levels of activity, although there were a few more people moving about than there had been that morning. Immune to village events, the castle ruins remained on their hill, the stream continued to babble at the side of the road, and the autumn wind harried the leaves still clinging to the trees.

Felicity and Alex arrived at the telephone box to find it occupied by another journalist, an older man working for a newspaper in Bristol. They used the time to put their notes into some kind of order suitable for an article.

Flicking through the two notebooks, Felicity called in the story, which someone at the newspaper's headquarters would no doubt put under a headline like *Tea Rooms Reacts To On-Site Slaying*, but then headlines were rarely the reporter's decision. Alex stood outside the booth talking to the other journalist while Pip snuffled around the base of the giant oak.

By the time Felicity's call to the paper had finished, the other journalist had left, and the day's light was growing dim.

She relayed to Alex something the copy editor had mentioned to her. "Initial reports are that circulation figures for today are through the roof."

"I'm not surprised," said Alex, kicking at a stone as though a bit bored. "Jasper ought to be jolly pleased with us, although there's not much else we can report on for now."

Felicity's stomach tightened. "I suppose we're now simply waiting for the police to announce they've arrested someone." And it was highly unlikely Vera would be happy about who it would be.

Alex nodded. "The inquest will be a mere formality, as we already know it to be an unlawful killing. Perhaps the whole case will be rounded off before the replacement journalist even gets here?"

Felicity pressed her lips together. It was a desirable outcome, was it not? To leave Ippleford with everything settled and still interview Judge Hawkins. But if the case unravelled, would it settle things for Vera? Or would it mean even more difficulties?

Alex redirected his gaze up the hill. "Been to the castle yet?"

Pip lifted his nose from the oak's base and wagged his tail.

Felicity blinked. A distraction. Yes, she needed a distraction.

# Chapter Eighteen

Felicity's legs burned with the surprising amount of effort needed to make it up the hill, which became rather steep as it rose towards the castle. That the weather had cooled further was convenient, the sun descending behind angry-looking clouds. Otherwise, Felicity's cheeks might have become quite pink.

Passing cottages and their gardens and the occasional sloping field containing sheep or a solitary horse, Pip trotted happily ahead, and Alex's long stride made light work of the climb.

Coming down the hill towards them were Philip and Ernestine Heard, their arms full of unlit wooden torches. Felicity introduced Alex to the actors and again offered commiserations at the cancellation of the evening's performance, although everyone agreed it was entirely appropriate under the circumstances.

"Be careful not to run into any ghosts." Ernestine's eyes twinkled with a hint of mischief.

Alex frowned sceptically. Pip sniffed an errant line of bunting attached to a torch in Philip's arms.

"I was under the impression you were actors, not spiritualists." Felicity matched Ernestine's playful tone.

"Quite correct." Philip adjusted his glasses. "The only Blue Lady we've ever seen was the young woman we cast for the role in our play.

It's been an awful disappointment for our amateur actors, of course. Let's hope for better luck next year," he said, looking at his wife.

Ernestine laughed. "Unless we've been run out of the village by then."

Following a round of farewells, Felicity, Alex, and Pip continued up the hill.

"A curious couple," remarked Alex.

"Pleasant enough," said Felicity, too breathless to say more, although actors were, on the whole, not like most people.

The ground levelled out at a set of well-used wooden stiles. Beyond, a muddy, stony path led through wet grass up to what was left of the castle. As they approached the ruins, Alex stopped and looked up at the edifice's first line of defence. A curtain wall built in impenetrable granite was identifiable despite sections of it having crumbled and dense dark-green ivy clinging to the remains.

"Impressive," said Alex. "Or it would have been. I don't suppose you know what led to the castle's downfall?"

Felicity pushed her hands deep into the pockets of her tweed jacket. Even after the bracing hill climb, the cold air still had a bite to it. "I know only a little of the history, as shared with me by my grandmother. Between internal strife and external pressures, I'm afraid it doesn't take much to unseat a powerful family."

Alex raised an eyebrow. "The Quicks have done well to hang on for this long."

Felicity arched an eyebrow in return. "I suppose we're lucky to have had a rather dull history."

Pip looked up from the tuft of grass he'd been munching on. A low growl rose from his tiny chest. Coming around the curtain wall were Mr Viner and his red Border Collie. How such a handsome, placid dog could tolerate a character like Mr Viner's was mystifying.

The Collie stopped at a distance from Pip, head cocked, as though offended by Pip's growl. The Yorkie's reaction seemed more directed at the Collie's owner.

Alex nodded in greeting. "Good afternoon."

The gardener nodded back almost imperceptibly.

"Good afternoon, Mr Viner." Felicity always did her best to remain polite, even when faced with rudeness.

"Be careful up there." The gardener's tone was menacing.

"Careful in what sense?" enquired Felicity.

"That you don't end up with a stone on your head," came Mr Viner's cheerless reply.

"Oh, we shall be vigilant." Felicity smiled brightly but couldn't help wondering. Had the gardener's words been a warning or a threat?

Alex let out a long breath as Mr Viner and his dog exited the castle grounds via the stiles. "Not the typically friendly Devonian I've grown used to in my time here."

"I doubt he cares for the welfare of two outsiders like us," replied Felicity. *Perhaps to the point of wishing us harm*, she considered, but another thought seized her. "You enjoy living in Devon, then?" Felicity glanced at Alex as they continued into the castle grounds. "You've no desire to return to London?"

As they passed through the remains of the curtain wall, a clattering of jackdaws flew out from crevices in the stonework and went swooping and cawing around the hilltop.

Alex watched the birds for a moment. "Not in the immediate future, no. I'm rather comfortable here."

There was an inexplicable fluttering in Felicity's stomach. "Jasper will be pleased," she said, and pressed on into what remained of the castle's courtyard.

The shells of stone buildings several storeys high, with arched doors and mullioned windows, surrounded what would once have been a smoothly cobbled floor but was now scraggy earth with tufts of grass. A solitary remaining tower reached up into the dark grey sky, its crenellations ragged with disrepair. In the far corner grew a large elm, decades or perhaps even centuries old. It threatened to push down a section of wall, albeit at a snail's pace, the stones leaning dangerously outwards. The tree's dried up leaves hissed in the breeze.

Pip trotted over to inspect the tree. A single flailing line of coloured bunting caught on a branch was the only indication of a performance ever having been planned at the site.

Alex pushed back his jacket and stood with his hands on his hips, impervious to the cold wind. "Do you suppose we'll see her?"

Felicity frowned. "Who?"

"Who do you think? The Blue Lady, of course."

Felicity's mind went to the crumpled blue dress she'd seen in the church hall. It was to have been Frances' part in the play. Her stomach tightened. "I don't believe in ghosts," she said.

Alex's brow creased, the scar on his forehead showing. "Say, are you quite all right? I didn't intend to frighten you with talk of spirits."

The wind picked up, the jackdaws still calling in the distance.

Felicity could hold back no longer. "I'm worried about something I said."

"Something you said when?" The concern in Alex's dark blue eyes was earnest.

"When I spoke to the police."

Alex looked relieved. "That's nothing to worry about. You can't have told them too much. The police interviewed me as well, you know. They're interviewing everyone."

"They asked for my opinion."

Alex raised his eyebrows. "Did they, indeed?"

Felicity continued. "Chief Inspector Luscombe had apparently told Detective Inspector Daniels I know a thing or two about unravelling murders."

Alex pulled back his chin. "I say. That's quite the compliment, isn't it?"

Felicity gave a little shrug, although she appreciated Alex's attempt to lift her spirits.

"What did you tell them?" asked Alex.

Felicity pushed her hands deeper into her pockets. "I gave them my honest opinion."

"Which was?"

The knot tightened in Felicity's stomach. "That someone at the tea rooms is responsible for the death of Mrs Norrington."

Alex sighed, as if let down. "That's not anything the police didn't already know."

Felicity frowned, slightly affronted. "What makes you say that?"

"Well." Alex paced the courtyard. "In the beginning, they were looking closely at Mrs Monroe. As the business owner, she had the strongest motive to do away with her saboteur. But from looking into the backgrounds of the other tea rooms' residents, the police have found a few pieces of compelling information."

Felicity's relief was mixed with dread. She needn't blame herself for putting Frances or anyone else from the tea rooms on the police's suspects list, but someone would surely hang for the crime. Someone Vera cared about.

"I'm sure things will be wrapped up soon enough," continued Alex. "And although the police have every reason to trust your opinion on the matter, I doubt you'll have said anything to change the course of things."

Alex was doing his best to reassure her, but Felicity couldn't help but wonder. What if she'd arrived in Ipplcford a day earlier? What if she'd been able to investigate the sabotage properly and identify Mrs Norrington before she was murdered?

Felicity approached the tall tower, stepping over masonry that seemed freshly fallen, likely due to the combined efforts of ivy and strong winds.

"I say, be careful, won't you?" Alex followed her. "What do you expect to find in there?"

On the other side of the tower, beyond a winding stone staircase, was another empty doorway.

"This," said Felicity. Through the doorway, an expansive view of the village opened out before them, with its long, gently bending high street, the church with its pointed spire, and a peppering of cottages arranged higgledy-piggledy along the main artery of the high street. Beyond, the countryside was a patchwork of green and brown fields spread over rolling hills, a low bank of rain clouds squalling across them.

Looking down on the village from atop the steep, rocky bank supporting the side of the castle gave Felicity a queer, unbalanced feeling. From a distance, Ippleford belonged on a biscuit box. From within, it was a rather different story.

Felicity drew damp, cool air deep into her lungs. Ippleford would soon be behind them. The interview with Judge Hawkins would go ahead. It was what Alex deserved, and it would be good for Felicity's career.

"It is rather beautiful," said Alex, leaning against the doorway, "even on a day like this. That rain's coming this way, though."

In turning towards Alex to agree it was high time they returned to the village to seek cover, or at least umbrellas, Felicity took a step to the side. But where she expected her trusty Oxfords to meet with solid ground, something shifted under her feet. A stone went hurtling down the bank, bouncing off rocks along the way.

Felicity had stumbled. She was falling.

## Chapter Nineteen

Her hands flailing, the steep bank below her, Felicity did her best to right herself.

"Felicity!" Alex stretched out a hand, but he was too late.

Felicity had grabbed a length of ivy protruding from the castle's crumbling walls. The vine was thick and tough, and she was able to find her footing and right herself, her heart pounding.

"Are you all right?" Alex's eyes searched Felicity's.

"I-I'm fine." Felicity looked down at the bank. It was a long drop littered with stones that had crumbled from the castle over the years. "Gosh. How silly of me."

"Nothing silly about it. Ruins can be dangerous. Some are better managed than others." Alex looked around at the castle as though angry with it. "This one isn't managed at all, I'd say."

Pip trotted through the tower's doorway. *Did I miss anything?* his pricked ears and bright eyes seemed to say. Felicity smoothed her tweed skirt, even though it hadn't come into contact with anything. She breathed deeply, her heart calming.

"Thank you," she said.

Alex frowned. "For what? You saved yourself."

It was true. Considering the multiple occasions Alex had come to

Felicity's aid, a tradition had been broken. Still, it was an enormous comfort that he'd been nearby and ready to act. The thought prompted a blush to creep into Felicity's cheeks.

Alex's thick eyebrows drew together. "Are you sure you're all right?"

"I believe so. Other than the surprise of nearly falling to one's death."

Alex laughed, though not unkindly. "You might have lost your hat and landed in a bramble patch with a couple of bruises, but you're made of tougher stuff than you think."

Felicity cast a gaze down the rocky bank. It looked deadly enough. Was Alex just trying to make her feel better?

His nose to the ground, Pip was approaching the same spot where Felicity had stumbled. She swept him off the ground and into her arms. "No, Pip. Not another round of heart-stopping drama, thank you very much."

Pip wriggled in mild protest, but quickly relaxed in Felicity's arms. The walk up to the castle had been a big ask on his little legs.

"That rain will be here soon," said Alex, staring out across the fields and hills. "We'd best head back to the village."

Fat raindrops splatted on the grass before they reached the stiles, and by the time they'd started down the hill, the rain was bouncing off the street. Felicity was careful not to slip on the wet ground as they hurried back into the village. The rain intensifying further, her cloche hat grew soggy — perhaps to the point of being ruined — and the shoulders of her tweed jacket became heavy and cold. She gripped Pip as tightly to her as possible.

On the deserted village high street, Felicity and Alex stopped outside Felicity's cottage and ducked under the tiny porch, both of them panting.

Felicity laughed as the rain battered the porch roof. "Rather silly of us not to have taken coats or umbrellas."

"I suppose so." Alex smiled. "Will you dine with me at the inn?"

It was an extremely tempting offer. Another blush rose towards Felicity's cheeks. She and Alex were standing awfully close to one another. "That's kind of you, but I need to get dry." That was part of it, at least.

Alex nodded, as though he'd expected to be turned down.

"What about breakfast?" suggested Felicity as Alex went to leave. "Mr and Mrs Biggs shan't forgive me if I don't eat at least one meal with them."

Alex agreed, and after refusing Felicity's offer of an umbrella and bidding her a pleasant evening, he jogged towards the inn, the rain thankfully easing. It was somehow sad to watch him leave but good to know he wasn't far away. So why hadn't Felicity wanted to dine with Alex? The source of her awkwardness was quite baffling.

Inside the cottage, the fire had already been lit. There was also a new basket of provisions in the kitchen, including a pat of bright yellow butter, tea cakes so fresh they were still warm, a slice of game pie, and a small canister of fragrant Earl Grey tea. Food hadn't been on Felicity's mind, but she now realised she was, in fact, ravenous.

As she sat before the warmth of the fire with a toasted tea cake, her jacket and hat hanging to dry on the chair opposite, and Pip enjoying some of the game pie's filling from a saucer on the floor, Felicity watched the flames dance in the grate and reflected on her short time in Ippleford.

Her goal to solve the sabotage promptly and to everyone's satisfaction had been naïve. She saw that now. The murder had, of course, been beyond her control. The reporting she and Alex had so far done had been well-received, but nothing about the situation was satisfactory.

Vera would be utterly devastated when the police arrested someone from her household for the murder. There was nothing Felicity could do to ease that pain.

With a long sigh, she took her empty plate to the kitchen. As soon as the replacement journalist arrived, Felicity would leave Ippleford with Alex for their next assignment. Would she still be in the village when the arrest took place? It was a cowardly thought, but she hoped not.

She went to bed with the detective book she'd brought with her and Pip curled at her ankles on the patchwork quilt. The patter of the rain at the windows slowed, then stopped. When Felicity finally fell asleep, she did so with the book still in her hand and the old oil lamp burning.

When she awoke with a start a few hours later, the book fell out of her hand and onto the floor.

---

The noise was, at first, confusing.

When Pip began barking, it became apparent that despite it still being rather dark outside, the banging was at the cottage door.

*Bang, bang, bang!* A pause. *Bang, bang, bang!*

Pip's barks were interspersed with gruff little growls.

Whoever was at the door clearly needed Felicity's attention. Frowning, she slid out from the warmth of her bed and pulled on her grey silk robe, tying it tightly at the middle. If this was Alex, strong words would be needed. Pebbles at the window were one thing, but such an awakening simply wouldn't do.

*Bang, bang, bang!*

Squeezing her hair to ensure her curls weren't egregiously errant, Felicity went into the sitting room, Pip growling at her heels. The clock said half-past six.

*Bang, bang, bang!*

The door's latch jumped, adding a metallic rattle to the thumping on the wood. Felicity hoped it wasn't Alex. If it was, then he was in rather a desperate state.

Standing on tiptoes, she looked through the tiny, diamond-shaped pane of glass set high in the cottage door.

Vera stood on the doorstep, the first red rays of dawn breaking in the sky beyond. She was hatless and crying, her straw-coloured hair in disarray.

Felicity's stomach sank as she scooped Pip under her arm and quickly opened the door.

"Vera—" she began, but she was cut off.

"Oh, my lady. I'm so sorry. Can I come in?" The tea rooms' owner clasped a handkerchief in both hands.

"But of course."

Felicity barely had time to stand aside as Vera bustled urgently into the cottage's sitting room and sat down, unheeding of the jacket and hat which Felicity had been drying in front of the fire and which Vera crushed as she sat. She put her head in her hands and sobbed, her shoulders shaking.

Alarm rose in Felicity. She had dreaded Vera's anguish, yet here it was, in her tiny sitting room. Pip shivered as Felicity placed him on the floor, his earlier zeal for barking at the intruder completely gone.

"Sh-should I put on water for tea?" suggested Felicity weakly. Alex had reassured her that the police had already come to the conclusion by themselves, but Felicity still felt guilty about what she'd told them. Guilty for the hurt it would cause Vera.

Vera continued to cry without looking up.

"I'll make tea." Felicity started towards the kitchen.

"Forgive me, my lady." Vera lifted her tear-streaked face. "I didn't know where else to go, who else to turn to. I don't want my Zoe to see me like this."

Felicity went to Vera and crouched beside her, putting a hand on hers. "Are you able to tell me what's happened?" She asked this despite feeling she already knew.

Vera shook her head and buried her face in her hands again, wave upon wave of despair convulsing through her body.

Felicity rose and went to the bedroom to fetch a fresh handkerchief from her valise. Lady Henrietta would be deeply upset to know Vera was this distraught. The least Felicity could do was be there in Vera's hour of need.

Crouching back down beside her, Felicity offered Vera the handkerchief.

Vera didn't take it. Her hands fell limply into her lap. She blinked her swollen eyes, her big red cheeks glistening with tears. "Oh, my lady. The worst possible thing has happened."

"What is it, Vera?" asked Felicity gently.

"It's Frances, my lady."

Felicity took a deep, steadying breath. Had there not been some way Felicity might have helped prevent this whole mess of a situation? It didn't matter now. It was over. "Did the police come for her?"

"The police?" Vera tilted her head, confused. "No, my lady. She's dead. Frances is dead."

# Chapter Twenty

Grey daylight arrived at the cottage's windows. In the tiny sitting room, beside the unlit fireplace and still in her silk robe, Felicity sat opposite Vera, perching on the edge of a high-backed chair with Pip in her lap.

Still wearing her overcoat and between bouts of uncontrollable crying, Vera berated herself for not taking better care of Frances. "The poor, poor girl. She had no family to speak of besides us. Besides me."

Felicity listened without interrupting. Her own shock at the news and her questions about the waitress' death could wait. She wanted to be a comfort to her grandmother's friend, although there was nothing anyone could do to bring Frances back.

Despite Vera's protests, Felicity eventually made a pot of tea. She used the time it took to boil the water to get quickly dressed, pulling on her tweeds, which had dried nicely, and reshaping her blue felt cloche as best she could after Vera had sat upon it. The day had evidently and rather inauspiciously begun.

After a few sips of strong, milky tea and some gentle coaxing, Vera's sobbing subsided enough for her to explain that Frances' body had been discovered beside the castle ruins by Mr Viner. Because of his work as a gardener, he rose early, often before dawn, and walked his dog around the castle grounds at least once a day.

"Do you know what happened to her?" Felicity spoke as gently as possible, stroking Pip's silken back. The Yorkie watched Vera with interest, his tufted ears pricked.

Vera blew her nose on the handkerchief Felicity had supplied. She shook her head. "We don't yet know for certain, my lady. It seems likely she fell."

Felicity's chest tightened at the memory of her own stumble at the ruins. Had Alex indeed played down the danger of that steep, rocky bank?

"It would have been slippery up there after all that rain," continued Vera. "Frances would have known that. She isn't a silly girl. Wasn't a silly girl." She dropped her face into the handkerchief and sobbed. "Oh, goodness only knows what she was doing up there after dark. First Mrs Norrington. Now my poor Frances. Could things get any worse, my lady?"

"I doubt that very much," said Felicity reassuringly. As her own shock subsided, Felicity's curiosity grew, but Vera was in no state to be pressed on any point.

With her face buried in the handkerchief, Vera returned to crying uncontrollably. It was painful to witness and left Felicity feeling powerless. She dreaded to think what her grandmother's reaction would be to the news of the waitress' death and Vera's despair. Felicity supposed she would be the one to inform Lady Henrietta. It was a rather depressing prospect, especially in light of why she had come to Ippleford in the first place.

There was a polite tapping on the cottage's front door, nothing like the impassioned pounding that had announced Vera's arrival. On the doorstep was a young uniformed police officer. He'd been sent to collect Vera, the police being keen for her assistance back at the tea rooms. Pip came to the door and sniffed the cool morning air. A horse and cart went by, the cart's driver and the agricultural workers riding in the back, peering with interest at the policeman in attendance at the cottage.

Vera approached the doorway. She turned to Felicity, her eyes wide with fear. "But I don't want Zoe to see me like this."

Felicity put a hand on Vera's shoulder. "Vera, she shan't." She spoke confidently, though where her confidence came from, Felicity didn't know. She wasn't any sort of expert in such matters. "You were right to come to me to let out your pain. Now, when you return to your home, you'll find the courage within yourself to be a pillar of strength for your daughter. She needs the comfort of her mother nearby, and you're more than capable of providing her that comfort. I'm certain of it."

Vera nodded. "Thank you, my lady. I can't tell you how grateful I am that you're here."

Felicity smiled sadly. She didn't feel she was being helpful, but she was glad Vera thought so.

Vera went to join the policeman waiting outside on the high street, leaves swirling about their ankles in the breeze.

Felicity advanced onto the doorstep, hugging herself against the early morning chill. "Do you wish me to accompany you, Vera?"

Pip trotted outside, as though quite certain of the tea rooms' owner's answer.

A glimmer of hope in Vera's shimmering blue eyes. "Oh, my lady. Would you?" Her breath appeared in white plumes as she spoke. "I shouldn't like to place more burden on you than I already have."

"It's no burden, Vera. It's the least I can do."

Closing the cottage door behind her as she stepped outside into the cold, Felicity simmered with curiosity about what had happened to Frances. She imagined herself relaying what she would discover to Alex over breakfast at the inn, but that wasn't her primary motivation for accompanying Vera. If she could, Felicity still wanted to help.

---

"Mummy!"

Little Zoe, still in her night shirt, dashed between the tea tables and flung her arms around Vera's waist. She had a well-loved rag doll in her hand, and her eyes were ringed with red.

There were several policemen present at the tea rooms, including

Detective Inspector Daniels, who was talking to an agitated-looking Luca at the cake counter. Katherine, who had been holding Zoe's hand until Vera's entrance, approached her sister. May was nowhere to be seen.

"There, there, my darling." Vera stroked her daughter's cheek. Her composure had returned, just as Felicity had said. "There's nothing for you to worry about. All shall be well, my darling. All shall be well."

In a well-tailored blue wool dress and her face without powder, Katherine watched her sister and niece's reunion. The anxiety in her crumpled brow aged her.

Before he made a nuisance of himself sniffing around the policemen, Felicity scooped Pip into her arms. "How are you bearing up, Mrs Evans?" she enquired.

"I'm all right." Katherine forced a grim smile. "But poor Zoe. She knows something's not right, although she doesn't understand what's happened. Not yet." She lowered her voice, the creases in her brow deepening. "The police suspect it to be suicide."

Felicity swallowed. "Suicide?" A ghastly and familiar puzzle piece fell into place. Frances must have known the police's investigation was closing in on her, and death by one's own hand was perhaps preferable to the hangman's noose.

"She was in that play, you know," continued Katherine. "And rather obsessed with the whole thing. Both Frances and May were. They were terribly disappointed when it got cancelled, but I wonder if that's where she got the idea."

"The idea?"

"To end her own life as the Blue Lady did."

Felicity turned the suggestion over in her mind. "Would that have been in keeping with what you knew of Miss Lee's character?" Felicity had had her impressions of and suspicions about Frances, but she hadn't known her at all well.

Katherine shrugged. "People have hidden depths."

The observation rang absolutely true.

"Still, I suppose it's for the best, really," continued Katherine.

"Saves Vera the heartache of the trial. She's been through so much. We all have."

"What will Miss Lee's passing do to your sister, do you think?" Felicity's grandmother's response would be linked to that of her cherished former lady's maid.

With a sigh, Katherine folded her arms. "Vera was incredibly keen on Frances. And after I practically tripped over that poor woman's body just the other night, well. It's all a bit much, isn't it? Vera's been through tough times before. Perhaps not as tough as this, but she's always pulled through somehow." Katherine cast a gaze over the well-stocked cake counter and the empty tables and chairs of the tea rooms, all poised for the re-opening, which would likely be cancelled. "Whether her business will survive is a different question."

Felicity's mind whirred. If, for the police, Frances' death confirmed her as guilty of murdering Mrs Norrington, then the case was closed. Yes, it had to be reported on, but what could Felicity do to help Vera and her business recover?

"Mrs Monroe." Detective Inspector Daniels' tone was — for a policeman — gentle, but his face was grave. "We appreciate your need for time with your daughter, but we urgently require your help in getting Miss Pettigrew to open her bedroom door. Given everything that's occurred, we'd prefer the use of force to be a last resort."

Vera hugged her daughter close. "May's locked herself in her room?"

"My men have been trying to coax Miss Pettigrew out," said the inspector. "I'm afraid she sounds rather distressed. She shared the room with the deceased, did she not?"

Vera wobbled a little, blinking back tears. She looked at her daughter and wiped her golden hair from her forehead. "Zoe, dearest, will you wait with Aunt Kathy a little longer? There's something I need to do. I promise I'll return directly."

Zoe's clear blue eyes widened. She looked from her mother to her aunt, her well-loved rag doll swinging from the crook of her little elbow.

"Come," said Katherine gently, offering the little girl her hand. "What would you say to a warm mug of cocoa?"

Katherine and Zoe disappeared through the green swing doors of the kitchen as Vera went upstairs with Detective Inspector Daniels and his men. This left Felicity, with Pip still tucked under her arm, at something of a loose end. It wasn't exactly the role Felicity had envisioned for herself.

Despite it being still too early for breakfast, Felicity knew Alex would appreciate hearing about Frances' unexpected passing as soon as possible. Until the replacement journalist arrived, it would be their duty to write it up for the paper. But Felicity wasn't yet ready to leave the Green Ginger.

A single uniformed police officer was stationed inside the front door. The only other person present was Luca. He was behind the cake counter, bending over.

Felicity approached, stroking Pip. "Simply ghastly news about poor Miss Lee, isn't it?"

The patisserie chef straightened without turning around. He had on his chef's whites, as though expecting to work. When he turned to face Felicity, he had his arms folded over his smock. His dark eyes burned with resentment "I will have to find another job," he said. "Again, moving on. Again, another job."

Either Luca was blissfully unaware of how selfish he was, or he simply had no shame in it. But that wasn't the most curious aspect of his reaction. "What makes you so certain this is the end of the Green Ginger, Mr Carli?" enquired Felicity.

A smile twisted his lips. He seemed darkly amused by the question. "Before coming to such a small village, I had my doubts. With my talent, how could I not have doubts? In the end, I found my own way of doing things. But this—" he jutted his chin, gesturing to the tea rooms, or perhaps the whole of Ippleford "—this is too much. I cannot stay. I am not certain what will happen to the tea rooms, but it matters to me not what Mrs Monroe does next. For me, it is over."

The patisserie chef's 'own way of doing things' warranted further investigation, but Felicity couldn't help but take offence on Vera's behalf. When she'd found him destitute in London, Vera had helped him. Luca apparently had no intention of repaying the favour. Perhaps, with his marvellous talent, he didn't even consider Vera as having saved him.

Regardless of Luca's appalling attitude, it would be yet another blow to Vera if her patisserie chef walked out, not that there was much chance of the police allowing anyone from the tea rooms to leave the village for the time being.

"Were you to move on from Ippleford, Mr Carli, I'm certain your talent would be sorely missed." It was difficult to sound earnest, but Felicity somehow managed it. The sensation was as uncomfortable as dragging one's nails across a blackboard. "And not just here in the village. I understand people regularly come from Exeter and even further afield to enjoy your creations. It's possible you underestimate your influence."

A flicker of satisfaction passed over Luca's features. "I have opened their eyes to what a sweet can truly be." It was as if he wanted to gesture with his hands but stopped himself. Instead, he tightened the fold of his arms and huffed. "But I should have left when the first one died."

Felicity could keep up the pretence no longer. "'The first one'? I'm sorry, Mr Carli, but your grasp of the English language is surely competent enough for you to realise quite how disrespectful that sounds."

Luca edged along the cake counter, seeking an exit. "Is it a crime to want something more?" He sounded like a chastised child. "Something better?" As he emerged from behind the counter and started towards the doorway at the back of the tea rooms that led to the living accommodation, something glinted under Luca's tightly folded arms.

Was the selfish swine hiding something?

A wail went up from the kitchen. Zoe had started to cry, and Katherine's hushing was having no effect.

After a deep calming breath — for Luca's horrid attitude had quite infuriated her — and with Pip still in her arms, Felicity pushed through the kitchen's swing doors, ready to bring Vera's daughter whatever succour she could.

At last, Felicity could help. Yet her mind was elsewhere.

# Chapter Twenty-One

Seated at the tea rooms' kitchen table, Felicity and Katherine stared dotingly at Zoe. Felicity had set Pip on the little girl's lap and encouraged her to stroke him, which the Yorkie tolerated admirably. Felicity had a powerful urge to speak to Alex, not to mention an appointment to keep with him, but as Pip's presence calmed and distracted Zoe, Felicity's withdrawal would need to be delicate.

Flattening her palm to stroke his back, Zoe spoke to the Yorkie in a gentle, whispery voice, as though there was no one else around. "Hello, Mr Pip. How are you today? It's so very nice to see you."

The scene was heart-warming. Still, Felicity's mind raced with the innumerable topics she and Alex had to discuss. She also needed to speak to her grandmother, the thought of which made her chest tighten. Frances' death had changed so much.

"Thank you." Katherine smiled at Felicity as she stood to clear the cocoa mugs from the table. "Zoe simply adores animals. I'm sure she'll be all right now. Won't you, Zoe, my love?"

The little girl nodded enthusiastically, although she couldn't hide her disappointment when Felicity gently collected Pip from her lap.

"I'm sure there'll be another opportunity for you to meet again," said Felicity. "I believe Mr Pip rather likes you, you know. He's usually rather choosy when it comes to laps."

The little girl smiled and blushed, and Felicity gave Pip a good scratch under the chin. He'd been an exceedingly good boy.

"I suppose you've got to get on with your reporting," said Katherine from the sink, where she'd begun washing up. "We shouldn't like to hold you up. We're here if you want to speak to us, of course."

Felicity nodded, grateful. "I need to discuss things with my colleague first. He's down at the inn. This latest development rather changes things." Felicity chose her words carefully, not wanting to insist upon the subject of death or even Frances' absence in front of Zoe.

"Yes," said Katherine thoughtfully, as she turned the cocoa mugs up to dry. "It rather changes everything, doesn't it?"

---

Besides the solitary uniformed officer at the front door, the tea rooms were deserted. Outside, it was raining. The clattering of the drops at the windows combined with the sombre grey morning light gave the empty tables a mournful quality. The Green Ginger certainly wouldn't open today. Given how upset Vera was, the state May was in, and Luca's ideas about leaving, how long would it be before the tea rooms got back to normal?

Felicity nodded politely at the policeman as she approached the door to the high street. On her way to the inn, she would stop at the cottage to collect an umbrella.

"Lady Felicity."

Detective Inspector Daniels appeared in the stairway at the back of the tea rooms, stooping under the doorway's low lintel.

"Do you have a moment, please?"

The policeman's timing was, again, impeccable. "Of course, Detective Inspector."

They sat down together at one of the empty tables, Felicity

placing a fidgety Pip on her lap. He was as keen to get outside as she was. The detective asked the expected questions about what Felicity had seen and heard the day before.

Felicity confirmed she'd seen Frances, and that although she hadn't known the waitress well, there seemed nothing the matter with her. "When Vera came and found me at the cottage—" an action the police weren't too pleased about, but which they'd allowed to happen given Vera's obvious distress "—with news of Frances' death, I was just as shocked as anyone, Detective Inspector."

"I see." The young detective looked thoughtful as he made notes, his lips pressed together under his thin moustache. It was highly unusual to have to investigate a single dramatic death in a quiet village like Ippleford. Having to resolve two such incidents occurring within barely a day of each other must have increased the pressure tremendously.

"Is it true Miss Lee ended her own life?" Despite her burning desire to get to the inn to meet Alex, Felicity was powerless to resist the opportunity to put her own questions to the detective.

The policeman narrowed his eyes. "Is this for your newspaper, your ladyship? I'd been led to believe you work on the softer side of the newspaper's coverage."

Felicity smiled reluctantly. She was guilty of using the term herself, but she was coming to resent her work being called soft. Approaching a freshly bereaved relative to request their comment for the newspaper was subtle work.

"Please consider me off duty for the moment, Detective Inspector. Mrs Monroe is a dear friend of the Quicks. I'm asking out of personal concern for her and her family."

The detective let out a sigh and tucked his notepad away in his pocket. "We have our ideas about things, of course, but it's too early for conclusions. Sergeant Hewitt and his men are still at the castle searching the scene of the incident. We'll know more when they're finished." He turned to the rain-splattered windows. "Although this weather won't help matters."

Felicity stroked Pip. "Have you interviewed Mr Carli?"

Detective Inspector Daniels twisted towards her, but his face revealed nothing. "Not myself. Not yet, but I'll be speaking to everyone at the Green Ginger in due course."

"Is there much known about his background?"

The detective smiled. "I thought you said you were off duty, your ladyship." The rebuff came as no surprise.

Felicity couldn't be sure what, if anything, she'd seen hidden under the patisserie chef's arms. Having somehow earned their respect, she didn't want to get a reputation among Devon's detectives as a dilettante and a meddler, so she didn't continue asking about Luca, despite her interest in learning more about him. "Will you be conducting another thorough search of the premises, Detective Inspector, including the accommodation upstairs?"

Detective Inspector Daniels blinked. "Do you not trust us to do our work?"

"Oh, no. I didn't mean that at all. Not at all." Felicity hurriedly changed the subject. "The man who found poor Miss Lee early this morning was a certain Mr Viner, was it not?"

The detective gave a curt nod.

"He was up at the castle yesterday evening. Mr Cooper and I saw him. I suppose you've spoken to him already?"

The detective made no motion to retrieve his notepad from his pocket. "We're aware of Mr Viner's movements, your ladyship, and we'll be releasing the relevant information to the press at the appropriate time." The detective stood up from the table. "In fact, we're holding a conference for the journalists at the inn within the hour. I'm on my way there now. Can I assume you'll be joining us, your ladyship?"

Noiselessly, May had come downstairs and entered the tea rooms. She had a thick red woollen jumper pulled over her night gown, and her brown hair was uncombed. She stopped with her hands on the cake counter, where she and Frances had been packing biscuits and fudge the day before. The haunted expression on her face implied she was still comprehending what had happened.

Felicity matched the detective's gesture and stood up from the table, Pip in her arms. "If I'm not there for the announcement, then my colleague, Mr Cooper, shall be."

The bell above the door tinkled as the detective exited onto the high street, a cold waft of air and the hiss of the rain washing into the tea rooms as the door open and closed. Felicity should perhaps have followed Detective Inspector Daniels to the inn. But there was something she had to do first.

---

May turned with a start as Felicity approached the Green Ginger's cake counter, Pip still tucked under her elbow. With her eyes ringed with red, the young waitress looked pale and shaken, which was to be expected. She'd not long found out her colleague and dear friend had passed away.

"My apologies, Miss Pettigrew," said Felicity with genuine regret. "I didn't mean to startle you. The news of Miss Lee's demise must have been a terrible shock. May I ask how are you coping?"

May twisted the hem of her red jumper, her eyes flooding instantly with tears. "Not so well, your ladyship."

Felicity offered the waitress a handkerchief, which she refused, preferring to use the frayed sleeve of her jumper to wipe away her tears. Stroking Pip, Felicity said nothing further, giving the girl time to compose herself.

May sniffed, wiping her cheeks. "She was still in bed when I fell asleep. I didn't hear her leave, your ladyship. If I'd have known she was going out in the middle of the night, I wouldn't have let her go on her own. I wouldn't have let this happen."

May and Frances had been one another's alibis in the murder of Mrs Norrington, each swearing they would certainly have been aware had one of them left the room. The facts looked rather different now.

"Miss Lee will be sorely missed, will she not?" said Felicity gently.

May nodded, her eyes threatening to once again overflow with tears.

With someone so young and so clearly upset, it wasn't right to whip out a reporter's notebook, but it didn't prevent Felicity from asking her questions. "I understand you were both extremely close." She continued to speak in the same soothing manner.

"Oh, yes, your ladyship. We only met when we both came to Ippleford to work here, but it was as if we'd known each other much longer." May was quiet for a moment. Having remembered the good times she and Frances had shared, the waitress had to adjust to such times having ground to a violent halt. "I shall miss her such an awful lot, your ladyship. Really an awful lot. And it's so cruel what they're saying about her."

Felicity tipped her head, stroking Pip. "Who is saying what about her?"

"The police. Asking me about why Frances did away with herself. I told them she didn't. She wouldn't."

Felicity couldn't help raise an eyebrow. Was there a chance Frances' death wasn't suicide?

May continued, defiant. "I know they don't believe me, but I knew Frances. They didn't."

"I'm certain you knew Miss Lee better than anyone," said Felicity carefully, "but may I ask, what makes you so sure?"

"Frances had plans for herself, your ladyship. She wanted something more out of life. Something more than just waitressing."

In the short time Felicity had known her, Frances had indeed seemed ambitious. "Do you happen to know what plans she had?"

May frowned. "Not exactly, your ladyship, but she was very interested in improving herself. Frances got the lead role in the play because she worked hard to remember the lines. I haven't got the head for that sort of thing. And she was taking lessons. Arithmetic. History. All sorts. She wanted to be ready for whatever opportunity came along. That's what she used to tell me." May wiped away another tear. "She wouldn't do away with herself. Why would she? She was excited about her future. I don't understand why they can't see that."

"The lessons Miss Lee was taking," said Felicity, keen to unpack this new information. "Were they here in Ippleford?"

May nodded.

"Do you know who with?"

"She used to go up to Rose Cottages every week. Alba, I think. Or Gallica. Oh, I forget which one. They've all got such funny names."

Felicity suppressed the urge to pull out her notepad. It risked interrupting May's openness, and the questions she was asking weren't strictly newspaper business. "This might sound quite awful to you," she said, "and I'm terribly sorry for bringing it up, but do you believe Miss Lee's passing might be related to the death of Mrs Norrington?"

May's expression darkened. She crossed her arms over her chest. "I know what people are thinking, your ladyship. I know what the police want to believe. Yes, Frances and I were furious about the sabotage when we found out, but we never heard about it until that poor woman was found dead in our tea rooms. Mrs Monroe didn't tell us because she didn't want to upset us. She's been so awfully kind. But that any of us from the tea rooms did away with Mrs Norrington... It just doesn't add up, your ladyship. It's so damaging for the business, and we all care so much about Mrs Monroe."

"You're quite right," said Felicity. Luca was the exception, of course, but he wasn't in Ippleford on the night of Mrs Norrington's death. "It doesn't add up."

May held Felicity's gaze, then looked away. "There was something odd Frances said to me after Katherine found Mrs Norrington."

Felicity waited to see if May would speak further. "What was that?" she coaxed.

May returned her gaze to Felicity's. "She said the murder presented an opportunity. I asked her what, but she wouldn't tell me. She could be secretive like that. I told the police, of course, but they didn't seem to think it meant anything."

"You knew Frances better than anyone in Ippleford, though, didn't you?"

May nodded enthusiastically.

Sometimes, one had to pull on the loose threads in order for things to unravel. "What do you suppose she meant by Mrs Norrington's death being an opportunity?"

"We were such good friends in so many ways." May turned away, looking up at the shelves beyond the cake counter. "But there are things I didn't know about Frances. Things she didn't want me to know, perhaps. I honestly couldn't fathom what she meant." May's gaze shot back to Felicity, full of a new kind of energy. "You've solved mysteries before, haven't you, your ladyship?"

Felicity was caught off-guard. "Well, I wouldn't say that, exactly."

May paid no heed. "Will you solve this one for us? Find out the truth about how Frances died?"

Felicity sighed sadly. *If only I could*, she thought.

"You've been through such an awful lot, Miss Pettigrew. You should really get some rest if you can."

May wiped away another tear. "I keep thinking, what if I'd woken up? What if I'd stopped her?"

"Will you join us for a cup of tea, May?" Katherine appeared in the kitchen doorway. "Zoe's going to toast some tea cakes for us. Aren't you Zoe?"

The blonde-headed little girl appeared beside her aunt and nodded shyly.

May gave a little smile. "Thank you, Mrs Evans. That sounds lovely."

With the clock ticking down to the police's announcement, Felicity took this as her cue to leave the tea rooms and hurry through the rain towards the inn. There was an increasing amount she needed to share with Alex, and not all of it could appear in the Western Daily News. Not yet.

# Chapter Twenty-Two

On her way to the inn, Felicity stopped at the cottage to collect an umbrella. Re-emerging into the hammering rain under the umbrella's shelter, Pip, who was standing next to Felicity's ankles, growled. Coming up the high street, from the direction of the inn, was Mr Viner.

His hat was pulled low over his brow, its brim dripping with rain, and his hands were tucked deep into the pockets of a thick corduroy jacket. His long legs and lean physique carried him swiftly along. As usual, walking beside the gardener was his bright-eyed Border Collie, for whom the rain had no influence on his ability to enjoy a walk.

They were passing on the other side of the high street, hugging the stream, which hurtled along with the extra water. The Collie looked over at Felicity and Pip, but Mr Viner kept his eyes fixed on the street ahead.

Felicity couldn't resist. Scooping Pip under her arm, she crossed the road.

"Mr Viner, good morning to you," Felicity called out brightly above the clatter of the rain. She wouldn't allow herself to be snubbed. Not this time.

To begin with, Mr Viner hardly glanced in Felicity's direction, but when she positioned herself and her generously sized umbrella in the direction of his travel, he came to a stop, having no option but to acknowledge her.

Felicity gently squeezed Pip as a signal to him to cease growling. The Yorkie's hostility was clearly aimed at Mr Viner rather than the Collie, who'd come to a patient halt at his master's side.

"My apologies for interrupting your morning stroll with your dog, but you discovered the unfortunate Miss Frances Lee at the castle earlier this morning, did you not?"

"I'm not talking to the papers." The gardener's voice was gruff, and his eyes flashed with barely concealed misgivings. At another moment, on another day, and in different circumstances, Mr Viner would have been intimidating. He was, like most men, a good deal taller than Felicity, and he displayed an open dislike for her.

For some reason, Felicity wasn't in the mood to fear much. "I assumed that." The distance between her work for the Western Daily News and her interest in the Ippleford mysteries was growing. "It's not as a journalist that I want to speak to you."

"Why do you want to speak to me, then?" The lines on the gardener's face deepened with disbelief, rain dripping from his hat before his eyes.

"I want to understand what's happening. Mrs Monroe is a dear friend of my family's. If I can help her and the tea rooms, then I shall do that. And I believe that for the best possible chance, I need a full understanding of all the facts." It was a bold pronouncement, but it was the truth of Felicity's position.

The gardener stared at Felicity as the rain beat on her umbrella. It was a most uncomfortable silence, but Felicity stood her ground. Was it reckless? Had she just accosted the murderer? Felicity had, in the past, been accused of a disregard for her own safety, and Frances had described Mr Viner as a swine, but Felicity had her wits about her, and despite the rain, the village high street wasn't entirely deserted. She side-stepped slightly as a van bearing the name of a greengrocer splashed past.

While Mr Viner was an unpleasant man in many ways, he put effort into controlling his negative reactions, even if the effort itself was so obvious as to negate the intended effect. “I can’t help you. I’d like to, but I can’t.” While his jaw was tight, his manner had softened, albeit almost imperceptibly so.

It was more than Felicity had hoped.

The gardener went to step around her, but Felicity easily continued obstructing his progress thanks to the ample dimensions of her umbrella. “You mean there are things you would like to say, Mr Viner, but cannot?”

“There’s nothing I can say that’ll change anything,” the gardener growled.

With a concerted effort, he stepped firmly around Felicity and her umbrella, and set off in the castle’s direction, the red Collie trotting obediently after his master.

Felicity was on the brink of chastising herself for not being bolder and more direct with her questioning, but she hushed the negative voice within her. There was a time when she wouldn’t have dared accost a man like Mr Viner in the street. And even when feeling brave, she often allowed the fear of her brother’s disapproval to hold her back.

She’d come a long way. And she knew what she had to do next.

---

Arriving at the Blue Lady Inn, Pip shivering in her arms, Felicity shook the rain from her umbrella, dodged the rivulets running off the thick, low thatch, and stepped inside. She was just in time. Thunder rumbled in the distance, and the rain bounced off the outdoor tables in a downpour that reduced visibility to a matter of feet. Even her broad umbrella would have provided little protection.

Felicity marched towards the public bar with the intention of asking for Alex, but her fearlessness shrank somewhat when she saw the bar packed with people.

Except for Mrs Biggs and the odd barmaid, who squeezed through the crowd carrying trays of food and drinks and collecting empties, the gathering was overwhelmingly male, being made up mainly of journalists. Despite it hardly being later than breakfast time, pints of beer were being pulled, and despite another death having occurred, laughter rose to the black-painted rafters of the bar's smoke-stained ceiling.

With a fortifying deep breath and Pip clutched to her chest, Felicity began easing through the throng.

"Here to give Coop his orders for the day. Are you, your ladyship?"

"Look sharp, Coop. Your guvnor's sister's here."

"Need help walking your little doggy, do you, your ladyship?"

The remarks triggered waves of laughter through the bar, but Felicity kept her chin high as she pressed through the crowd.

Reporters were accustomed to dealing with people from all walks of life, which Felicity had learned left them with less respect for social hierarchy than the average British subject. Men also tended to be less polite when in large groups. The only reason the journalists of the Western Daily News never made such jokes at Felicity's expense — at least not so as she could hear them — was because her brother paid their wages. She was under no illusion about that.

Felicity didn't take the comments personally. With her career, she'd known from the start what she was up against as a woman and had accordingly become rather thick-skinned. It was, however, painful to hear Alex being teased.

The jeering helped her locate him. He was standing beside a fireplace in which a small fire glowed, looking through his notebook and sipping from a coffee cup. He had on a dark brown suit and a burgundy tie.

As their eyes met, Felicity felt a sudden lightness.

Alex shook his head. "Quite incredible, isn't it?"

Setting a grateful Pip down in front of the warmth of the fire, Felicity stepped closer to Alex in order to hear him above the hubbub of the bar. The smell of his coffee mingled with the fresh and reassuring scent of meadows he always had about him. It was an extremely welcome odour compared to the stench of pipe smoke and spilt beer that was the typical aroma of drinking houses.

"Incredible how dreadfully rude our peers can be, you mean?" surmised Felicity.

"No." Alex's dark blue eyes were deadly serious. "The death of the waitress."

"Did the police already hold their conference?"

"Not yet," said Alex, looking out over the crowded bar. "Any minute now. But the news is spreading like wildfire." He returned his gaze to Felicity. "Somehow, I just didn't expect it all to wrap itself up so neatly. Looks like we'll be done here much sooner than expected. The inquest from the tea rooms' murder has been adjourned. It was supposed to take place this afternoon. They'll probably combine the two, the way it's looking now."

"How is it looking now?" Considering what Felicity had learned at the Green Ginger, she was equal parts curious and concerned.

Alex took another sip of coffee. "Word is the police aren't looking for anyone else in connection with either death. From their point of view, the case is as good as closed."

Felicity took a steadying breath. "Is that your take on the matter as well?"

"My take?" Alex narrowed his eyes. "Wait. I know that look."

Felicity blinked rapidly. "What look?"

"You've other ideas, haven't you?"

Before Felicity could confirm that she didn't just have other ideas but also other information to share, Mrs Biggs swung by, collecting empty cups and glasses. She had on a roomy floral dress that was somewhat low cut, with a string of pearls at her neck and an apron tied at her waist.

"The weather is absolutely appalling, isn't it?" Mrs Biggs looked at Felicity and Alex as she spoke, but she didn't wait for their reply. "Fitting, I suppose. The heavens crying at the waste of such a young life. Sad. Very sad. As if there hadn't been enough loss of young life these past years. My poor Robert, for one." The landlady raised her eyes upwards in a dramatic, sorrowful manner. "May his soul rest in peace. But there's no use complaining about things, is there? We've all got to keep going, haven't we?"

Felicity smiled awkwardly at Mrs Biggs, but the landlady's attention had already moved on, and she flitted off in search of more empty vessels.

"I know it's not the conclusion you were hoping for." Alex fixed Felicity with his calm, blue gaze.

Felicity cocked her head. "I don't follow."

Alex swept an errant lock of hair from his forehead. "Mrs Monroe looks upon her staff as family, and your grandmother has a special place in her heart for the woman. I know that from speaking to Lady Henrietta myself before coming here."

He was right, of course, although these weren't Felicity's chief preoccupations at that precise point in time.

"But you know as well as I do," he continued tactfully, "that these things rarely round themselves off in a way that ensures everyone is happy. It's the way of the world, unfortunately."

Pip gave a satisfied little groan as he stretched luxuriantly in front of the fire, the clamour of the bar no obstacle to canine rest.

Felicity considered Alex's comments. Was it foolhardy to not accept the police's interpretation of events? Was it Felicity's drive to improve Vera's lot and, with it, her grandmother's by seeking a culprit from outside the tea rooms?

Alex hadn't said it — he wouldn't, because he wasn't self-centred or presumptuous like that — but Felicity also had to consider Alex in all of this. She was the reason he'd been kept away from interviewing Judge Hawkins.

Was it not in everyone's interest to wrap things up as quickly as possible, to rip the bandage off, and move on?

Mr Biggs, a tea towel over his shoulder and his forehead glistening, appeared through the crowd proffering a tray of baked goods. "Sausage roll, anyone? They're fresh out of the oven. Seeing as we couldn't put on a normal breakfast this morning with the police commandeering the dining room for their announcement. Not that we have any objection, of course. All important business."

Alex declined, but Felicity's stomach growled. She hadn't yet eaten a thing.

The innkeeper pounced on her hesitation. "Our sausage rolls are just as good as anything from the Green Ginger, your ladyship. Mrs Biggs makes the sausage meat herself."

"I don't doubt it." Felicity smiled in a way she hoped erased any hint of snootiness that may have accidentally been communicated. "And I shall indeed indulge in one, thank you very much."

Using a starched napkin supplied by Mr Biggs, she lifted a warm, savoury pastry from the tray. Pip was suddenly awake, craning his neck upwards, his black nose twitching. Alex politely averted his gaze as Felicity bit into the flaky pastry. Mr Biggs moved swiftly onto the next group of journalists.

Eating with one's hands from a napkin wasn't among the etiquette lessons Felicity had received growing up, but the discomfort was worth it. The salty, tender filling contrasted perfectly with the buttery, crispy outside. The sausage roll was absolutely delicious and exactly what Felicity needed.

Ever the gentleman, Alex passed no comment on Felicity's hungry attack on the sausage roll, nor on Pip's eager consumption of the flakes of pastry that drifted down towards the hearthside rug.

"How should we round things off?" asked Alex when Felicity had finished eating. "I don't suppose it'll be long before the journalist replacing us is here, but we might have everything we need by then, anyway. Would you care to pick up a few reactions from the villagers to the new developments? And I'll attend the police's conference? If they make it official that they're not looking for anyone else, I'll telephone it in directly."

Using the napkin supplied with the sausage roll, Felicity did her best to remove any crumbs from her person in a ladylike fashion. She hadn't yet told Alex about her suspicions over Luca, May's insistence Frances would never commit suicide, and Mr Viner's queer reaction to her questions. Casting doubt on the simplicity of the case's solution wouldn't bode well for wrapping things up neatly before moving onto the interview with Judge Hawkins, but it wasn't right to keep her colleague in the dark.

"Alex…" she began.

"Lady Felicity!" The landlord's voice boomed across the crowded bar. "Lady Felicity! Telephone call for Lady Felicity!"

## Chapter Twenty-Three

Having picked up a drowsy Pip and navigated as quickly as she could through the crowd towards the bar with its shining brass taps and rows of tankards, Felicity was led by a smiling, red-cheeked barmaid to a small back room. The room had no windows and was lined with shelves containing ledgers. On a desk with a scuffed green-leather inlay piled high with paperwork, sat a candlestick telephone, its receiver off the hook, waiting.

Felicity knew who she'd find on the other end of the line. She should have probably already contacted Jasper, given the developments. But while her brother had every right to demand Felicity's attention, she would need to keep discussions with him brief. There was so much she had to tell Alex.

The little room's only chair creaked as Felicity sat down. Placing Pip on her lap, she lifted the receiver and mouthpiece. A light frown passed over her features as she wondered how she'd been traced to the Blue Lady Inn. Then again, Jasper had contacts just about everywhere. He was not only the editor-in-chief of the Westcountry's leading daily newspaper but a well-connected peer of the realm. Only it wasn't Jasper on the other end of the line.

"Terribly sorry to disturb you, my lady." It was Kitson, the Quick family's butler. "Lord Quick had to hurry to Plymouth for a meeting.

He left behind a note that he asked to be read aloud to you on a rather urgent basis."

"Thank you, Kitson. I'm listening." At least the call would be short.

"Lord Quick's note reads as follows: *Case in Ippleford will soon be wrapped up. Circulation figures through the roof. You and Coop are doing absolutely splendid work. Sending no replacement reporter. Interview with the judge to take place at Exeter Crown Court tomorrow. Wants to be photographed in his wig and all that. Silly old—*" The butler cleared his throat. "And that's where his lordship's message ends."

Felicity stroked Pip as she considered the news. That there wasn't a replacement journalist coming was something of a relief. It gave her more time, but not much more. To be ready to interview Judge Hawkins the following day meant Felicity would need to be back at Bradley Court that very evening.

It also wasn't reassuring that Jasper had received the news of a speedy resolution for the case. That Frances committed suicide because of her guilt at being a murderess seemed a foregone conclusion. A conclusion by which Felicity wasn't yet convinced. Would there be time enough to tug on more threads and unravel the deeper goings-on at the Green Ginger?

There was muffled discussion on the other end of the line. Kitson returned to the mouthpiece. "My lady, your grandmother would like a word."

There wasn't time for Felicity to protest, although it was only right that Felicity provide Lady Henrietta with an update.

Except that wasn't what her grandmother had in mind. "Felicity, dear. Jasper told me what happened. Oh! Poor, poor Vera. As if that woman hasn't suffered enough. I'm coming to Ippleford to lend her my moral support."

"To Ippleford?" The news sucked the air from Felicity's chest. Having her grandmother in the village would be an enormous distraction from unravelling anything. It was also unlikely a visit from the Dowager Countess of Denbury was the assistance Vera and her family needed.

"It's simply the very least I can do," continued the dowager. "Finnegan's preparing the Rolls as we speak."

"Grandmama, I understand your desire to do whatever you can—"

Lady Henrietta spoke over her granddaughter. "You've done your best, Felicity dear. I know you have. There's nothing anyone can do to change the outcome. It's been a tremendously gruesome run of events, but at least it's over now. Still, two untimely deaths in two days is rather a lot, and I should like to be poor Vera's rock in these unprecedented times."

"Grandmama," said Felicity, increasing the volume of her voice in case a poor line between Ippleford and Lower Diddleton had caused Lady Henrietta to ignore her earlier plea. "Forgive my directness, but please don't come to Ippleford. It's too soon. The police are still at the scene of the incident. Vera and her family are only just coming to terms with the news. I'm certain your support will be appreciated if you wait."

Felicity paused. Bizarrely, her grandmother had nothing to say in response. "Grandmama?"

A nasal-toned fast-talking operator came on the line. "Apologies, there's a fault. Trying to reconnect you, but no luck so far. Will you hold? Can't say how long it'll take, I'm afraid."

Felicity repressed a frustrated sigh. "Thank you, but not on this occasion." She had to get back to Alex. There was no time to lose.

---

Re-emerging from the back office and into the public bar of the Blue Lady Inn, Felicity was not only unable to find Alex. Besides the red-cheeked barmaid, who stood polishing glasses with a checked tea towel, the bar was deserted.

"Where is everyone?" Felicity asked as Pip wriggled in her arms, quite desperate to get onto the floor, which was littered with debris from the crumbly sausage rolls.

"In the dining room for that police thing, your ladyship." The barmaid spoke with a broad mid-Devon accent. "It's through there." She tipped her head, indicating a door at the back of the bar, which indeed bore a gold-lettered wooden sign that read *Dining Room.*

It was an option to pass quietly through the door, take a seat, and listen to the police's announcement, like all the other journalists. But Alex would be there, taking notes for the paper, and nothing the police would say to the press would be news to Felicity. There were other angles that needed to be explored.

"Thank you," she said politely to the barmaid. "I have other business to which I must attend and limited time in which to do it."

Collecting her umbrella from the stand by the door, and brushing an errant piece of pastry crust from her tweed jacket, Felicity carried a reluctant Pip back out onto the village high street and into the rain.

# Chapter Twenty-Four

The ideal situation would have been to have had the time to discuss matters with Alex and come to a sensible agreement together about a plan of what to do next. The ideal situation would also not have involved the threat of Lady Henrietta arriving in Ippleford at any moment. Felicity was thankfully accustomed to operating in situations that were less than ideal. She had a firm idea of what needed to be done next.

The rain had eased somewhat, so the umbrella remained folded. Pip had been eager to set all four paws on the ground, but he was now dawdling, sniffing the brook that ran alongside the high street, which was still bubbling along at quite a pace.

Felicity wasted no time in scooping the little terrier up once again, with no concern about dampening her jacket. "I am sorry, old chap. But we're on rather a tight deadline." If there was another side to the story, it had to be pieced together quickly, otherwise the narrative of Frances' guilt-driven suicide would become immutable.

As the church bells struck the hour, the castle's jackdaws spread cackling across the dark grey sky. Motor vehicles moved slowly through the village, containing mainly men on police business. The post office was open and shoppers popped in and out, but with the tea rooms closed and a distinct absence of day-trippers, the village had a quieter, more melancholy feel than there had been even the morning following Mrs Norrington's violent end.

It occurred to Felicity to knock on the door of the Green Ginger and warn Vera of the risk that Lady Henrietta could arrive in Ippleford in the not very distant future. She decided against it. There was a chance — a hope — that her grandmother would remain at Bradley Court, as Felicity had advised. And Felicity had to stay focused. Her remaining time in Ippleford must be used wisely.

A little out of puff for having ascended the hill rather rapidly, Felicity arrived in the courtyard of Rose Cottages and paused. May had provided a piece of potentially vital information: Frances had been a frequent visitor to the cottages, with the purpose of expanding her education and bettering herself. But at which of the cottages had she been a frequent visitor? Alba, Briar, Damask, or Gallica? In their dimensions and construction, each of the cottages was identical. Yet, as suggested by the styles of their gardens and the furnishings visible at the windows, these were four very different households.

Pip lifted his little black nose. The damp air was fresh and earthy with just a hint of wood smoke.

"Yoo-hoo, Lady Felicity!"

Behind the tall, dense foliage of Alba Cottage's front garden, Ernestine Heard stood on her doorstep in a typical kimono-style dress with billowing sleeves, her hair loose and whipping in the breeze.

"Please, your ladyship, if you have a moment." The actress beckoned to Felicity. "I'm awfully pleased to see you. There's actually something I'm quite desperate to share."

It was as good a place to start as any, and perhaps even better than most. The Heards certainly knew Frances from her starring role in their cancelled play, although they hadn't mentioned her taking lessons.

As Felicity headed up the path to Alba Cottage, the rain worsened, falling in ever fatter drops. Falstaff peeked out from beside Ernestine's legs, his long, elegant whiskers twitching, but he retreated quickly from the intensifying rain.

"Do come in," said Ernestine, stepping aside for Felicity to enter the cottage. "I've just made a pot of tea."

While Felicity longed for a cup of hot tea with which to wash down the sausage roll she'd enjoyed at the inn, she had no desire to ever again taste the particular blend of heavily smoked tea favoured in the Heard household. In addition, if the Heards didn't have the information Felicity was looking for, she would need to remove herself from the situation promptly.

"No, thank you, Mrs Heard," she said politely but firmly. "I'm afraid I can't. There's a deadline hanging over me." Felicity had stepped out of the rain but stopped in the doorway, preventing Ernestine from closing the cottage's front door. "But I'm nevertheless eager to hear what it is you want to tell me."

Pip strained in Felicity's arms, keen to follow Falstaff, who had disappeared down the cottage's narrow and cluttered hallway. Felicity held the Yorkie firmly.

Ernestine's face fell a little. She tugged her kimono wrap more tightly around her as the wind breezed in. "Very well. Let me fetch Philip."

The actress flitted into the sitting room and reappeared promptly with her husband, who was in shirtsleeves and braces that had been repaired at least once. He peered at Felicity through his thick-lensed spectacles, then looked at his wife rather doubtfully.

"Tell Lady Felicity what you told the police earlier," urged Ernestine, blinking up at her husband.

"Well, I, err..." Philip's gazed hopped between Felicity and Ernestine. "The police didn't seem very interested in the idea, and I shouldn't like to share it about if it's not of any consequence."

A tingle of interest went through Felicity. Shifting awkwardly with Pip still in her arms, she leant her folded umbrella against the cottage's door and withdrew her notepad from her pocket. "Please," she insisted. "I'm interested to hear it."

Philip sighed. "Well, the police came by early this morning. They were going through the whole village, apparently. Very thorough work. Commendable, of course. Anyway. They told us what happened to poor Miss Lee. Utterly tragic, of course. Such a waste of a young life. And when they told us how they'd found her..." He looked to his wife.

"Tell her," Ernestine hissed.

"Well." Philip scratched his head. "There's a scene in the play where the princess goes up to the tower and..." The actor's face darkened with seriousness. "Well, she throws herself to her death, you see."

Felicity raised her eyebrows. She'd heard this already, had she not? "You're saying Miss Lee's death mimics a scene from the play?"

Ernestine clapped her hands together, a little too excitedly. "Exactly that. Exactly that, Lady Felicity."

"And is that a coincidence, do you think? Or deliberate?" It wasn't yet clear what this brought to bear on the situation.

"Oh, but how could it be any kind of coincidence?" Ernestine drew a hand to her chest. "Miss Lee had a role in the play, you know. The leading role, in fact. And that was part of her role." Ernestine had turned pale, a hand squeezing the fabric tie of her kimono wrap. "To die falling from the tower."

Felicity raised her eyebrows further as she continued to take notes. If true, it was an utterly gruesome detail.

Philip put a hand on his wife's shoulder. "Darling, please, do go and sit down. It's not good for you to get so worked up. I'll stay and speak to Lady Felicity."

Ernestine squeezed her husband's hand, and with an apologetic nod towards Felicity, she disappeared down the cottage's narrow corridor.

Philip watched his wife and waited till the door of the sitting room closed behind her. He adjusted his spectacles and spoke quietly. "It's all very upsetting, because we're now rather uncertain about our own role in all this."

It was an odd turn of phrase. "I'm afraid I don't follow," said Felicity, her pencil poised. Either one was involved in a murder or one wasn't, surely?

"Well..." Philip pulled his shoulders upward, his hands firmly in his pockets. "Did we inspire Miss Lee to do this in some way?"

Felicity nodded sympathetically. The Heards accepted Frances' suicide as the explanation for her death. "I can imagine how you might think that."

"It's how I see it, at least." The actor lowered his voice to almost a whisper. "Ernie had another idea, of course. She tends towards the catastrophic."

"And what's Mrs Heard's view of the situation?"

"A rather selfish idea, really. But she wondered if someone wasn't trying to harm the play by doing away with our lead actress."

Felicity frowned. "Your play had already been cancelled at the time of Miss Lee's death, had it not?"

Philip nodded. "I mentioned that to Ernie, of course, but there's something she doesn't quite like about the explanation of suicide for the girl's death."

A ghastly fizz of excitement shot through Felicity. There were people outside the tea rooms who had suspicions about Frances' demise.

Like any good journalist, Felicity remained cynical. "What about an accident?"

The actor pressed his hands further into his pockets. "Miss Lee would often go up there to rehearse by herself. She wasn't the most naturally talented of actresses, but she was very dedicated. It's possible she could have tripped and fell, except..." He made a clicking sound with his tongue. "We'd been warned of the dangers posed by the ruins on multiple occasions, and everyone was always very careful. Frances included."

Felicity almost blushed at the memory of her own misstep at the site. Had she been so careless?

"But then, as you say," continued Philip, "the play had already been cancelled. So why would Miss Lee have been up there rehearsing?"

"Did you know her well?" asked Felicity, continuing to make

notes despite Pip struggling at her side. She couldn't put him down and have him go racing after the cat.

"Not really. We knew her in the context of the play only."

"You never saw her outside of rehearsals?"

"Only for costume fittings and the like."

"Did she ever come to visit you at Rose Cottages?"

"Here? Our little place is far too small for organising a play. We did all our preparations either at the church hall or up at the ruins. No, Miss Lee never came to our cottage."

So, the Heards weren't the ones giving Frances her lessons for self-betterment.

The actor went on. "But you know, there was a kind of restless energy to her. One can't help but imagine what would have become of such a girl had she been born into a situation with more opportunity. She was diligent about rehearsing, as I told you. When we announced the play's cancellation, she took it in her stride. Honestly, I'd expected her to be more disappointed."

Felicity took advantage of Philip's willingness to talk about Frances. "Was there anyone with whom Miss Lee didn't get on?"

"Not that I'm aware of. She could be a trifle direct, but she was a sweet girl underneath it all. Why do you ask?" Philip's brow crumpled. "Do you suppose someone hurt her?" he whispered. "Ernie is convinced there's something dark lurking beneath all this. It's doing absolutely nothing for her health, as you can imagine."

"Please tell your wife not to worry," said Felicity reassuringly and with a hint of evasion. "I'm just trying to create a picture of what Miss Lee's life was like."

A gust of wind sent rain clattering onto the floor of the cottage's narrow hall. Felicity had remained in the Heards' doorway rather longer than planned. Not every interviewee spoke as openly as Philip did. "I've just a couple of further questions, if you don't mind?" she said. "They might seem a little incongruous, but I hope you'll bear with me."

"That's quite all right. As we told you before, we're happy to work with the press." The actor smiled self-consciously and scratched the back of his head. "As long as our goodwill is not forgotten the next time we're able to put on a play."

Felicity smiled tightly. She hardly ever wrote for the entertainment section of the Western Daily News, so couldn't make any promises. "What do you know about Mr Luca Carli, the patisserie chef at the Green Ginger?"

Philip looked confused. "Why, nothing at all. I don't believe I've ever spoken to the man. Ernie and I have never frequented the tea rooms because of Ernie's dietary requirements. And Mr Carli wasn't involved in the play at all."

Felicity nodded. She'd drawn a blank. "And the gardener, Mr Lewis Viner. Do you know him well?"

Philip's eyes widened, as though the thought of Mr Viner gave him pause. "We know him from the castle. He's something of the unofficial groundsman up there. He wasn't too keen on the play at first. I believe he's from one of the families that's always lived around here. Very traditional, as some people can be. But once he realised there was no getting rid of us, he adapted his approach. Told us about areas to stay away from, where the structure was unsteady. All in his rather gruff and unappealing manner, of course. He's a rather useful chap to have around, if not a pleasant one."

Would Frances have called Mr Viner a swine based on his unpleasant manner alone? Given her own lack of tact, it would have been rather hypocritical.

Felicity closed her notebook. Time was pressing. She needed to move on. "Thank you for all you've shared, Mr Heard. I do hope Mrs Heard feels better soon."

Philip adjusted his spectacles and stood up straighter. "Well, the police say they'll have everything wrapped up soon enough. We can hopefully go back to normal after that. Although looking at the weather, there'll be no more outdoor productions till next year."

Heading down Alba Cottage's overgrown garden path, Felicity opened her umbrella and leaned into the wind as it drove the rain towards her and Pip. If the police could indeed wrap everything up and return the village to order, was Felicity selfish for wanting to examine what lay beneath the surface of things? She didn't give the idea too much thought. Another question preoccupied her.

If Frances hadn't received lessons at Alba, at which of the remaining three cottages had the waitress been a regular visitor?

# Chapter Twenty-Five

Felicity stopped at the centre of Rose Cottages' cobbled courtyard, the rain tapping on her umbrella. Ernestine's doubts about Frances taking her own life had galvanised Felicity's own. What if there was a link between Mrs Norrington and Frances outside of the tea rooms, something unrelated to the sabotage? Unfortunately, the curtains at Briar Cottage were drawn. Colonel Norrington appeared not to be home.

"The colonel's gone to his nephew on the Isle of Wight."

Doctor Grant was on the front step of Damask Cottage, a thatched porch sheltering him from the rain. He had a pipe with him, and he sent plumes of smoke dissipating into the rainy air. Under his jacket, he wore a rather garish knitted jumper in shades of orange and green. "Doctor's orders, I'm afraid," he added with a half-smile.

Felicity approached the gate to the doctor's cottage, where the clipped, flowerless rose bushes danced in the wind. "How disappointing. I was indeed hoping to speak to Colonel Norrington again. Does he continue to be in good health?"

The doctor puffed on his pipe. "The strain was getting rather too much for the old boy, I'm afraid. He's done his best to put on a brave face, of course, but you can't get to an age like that, have your other half taken from you so violently, and expect everything to be the same afterwards. Thankfully, he left before this business with the waitress. Very sorry state of affairs indeed."

"Were you called to attend to Miss Lee?" Felicity hugged Pip tighter to her side. Standing around in the rain, one became cold quite rapidly.

"I was." The doctor grimaced. "Although I'd prefer not to give any comment to the papers. It's up to the police to make the announcements."

"Of course." Felicity made no move to reach for her notepad. "I have a personal interest in the story, you understand. The owner of the tea rooms is a cherished family friend."

Doctor Grant sucked on his pipe. "As I already told you, your ladyship, I came to Ippleford for a quiet life. Murders and suicides do not fit into that picture at all. But of course, there are worse situations to be in than mine. I'm still alive, at least," added the doctor with a dark twist of humour.

"So the waitress' death was definitely suicide?"

The doctor narrowed his eyes. "You're a sharp one, Lady Felicity."

Doctor Grant seemed resilient enough to be pushed further. "Was it?"

There was a pause as Doctor Grant puffed on his pipe and peered at Felicity. "As a doctor — and a retired one, please don't forget — I cannot deduce the circumstances leading up to a person's death beyond the medical facts of the situation. Miss Lee suffered a fall from the castle's tower that severely injured her neck. I believe she died immediately upon reaching the ground. What caused her to fall from the castle's tower is, however, not my area of expertise. That's for the police to ascertain."

Felicity tightened her grip on the handle of her umbrella as the wind gusted. "Is it possible to say what Miss Lee's chances might have been of surviving the fall?"

The doctor eyed Felicity. "I would say she would have been extremely lucky to walk away from such a fall. Had she not died, she would have suffered some dire injury that would have left her incapacitated for the rest of her life."

"Either it was a deeply unfortunate accident, or there was some deadly intent behind the incident."

Doctor Grant nodded, somewhat reticently.

An idea sprang into Felicity's mind. "And Mrs Norrington. Was there any chance she might have survived her injuries?"

The doctor frowned. "Lady Felicity, what a mind you have for gruesome details."

Felicity smiled without mirth. Would Alex or any other male journalist have received the same response from the doctor to the question? "I've no intention to quote you in our paper, Doctor Grant, but I remain a journalist. Our view of the world is not limited to only what's pleasant. I'm sure the same can be said for your line of work."

The doctor squinted at Felicity through a puff of smoke. "A blow to the head isn't always guaranteed to be fatal, but there was nothing accidental about the wound sustained by Mrs Norrington. There was a clear intent to harm, and no regard for the risk — or perhaps reliance on the risk — of the blow being fatal."

Felicity's mind whirred. In a vague way, wasn't there something similar in how the two women had died? There was nothing of the carefully administered poison or the thoughtfully procured pistol. If someone else had been involved in Frances' demise, then these were intimate deaths, with the assailant up close, and not necessarily pre-planned. Whoever did it used whatever was at hand.

"Doctor Grant," said Felicity, "are you aware of Miss Lee being a regular visitor to Rose Cottages before her death?"

The doctor nodded. "I would see the girl visiting Gallica on occasion."

Felicity looked around the courtyard to orient herself with the cottage names. Gallica was the cottage next to the Heards'. "To visit Mrs Waverley?" Felicity had only met her once, but the diminutive, forthright woman with the top-knot made an unforgettable impression.

"To visit Miss Waverley," corrected the doctor.

Felicity looked over at Gallica Cottage. She'd not met Mrs

Waverley's daughter, but Felicity had seen her, hadn't she? She recalled the slam of a door.

"You'll not find Mrs Waverley at home," continued the doctor. "She has business with the Women's Association. I believe they're busy with some sort of memorial for Mrs Norrington. But you'll likely find Miss Waverley out in her vegetable patch at the back, picking slugs off her cabbages or digging up a beetroot or something of the sort."

Felicity turned, looking for a route to the rear of the dwelling.

Doctor Grant gestured with his pipe. "That cutting down the side of Alba will take you to the back of the cottages. You'll find Miss Waverley there. I don't doubt it."

---

Hurrying down the cutting, Felicity manipulated her umbrella so it snagged neither on the hawthorn hedge on one side nor the white-washed cottage wall on the other.

How had she not spoken to Miss Waverley till now? It was an oversight on her part. No doubt the police, in their thoroughness, had collected all available information. Perhaps they were one or even several steps ahead of Felicity in that respect, and her suspicions would all fritter away to nothing before the day was out.

And that would be quite all right by her. Felicity wanted nothing more than to go with Alex to interview Judge Hawkins with her conscience crystal clear, safe in the knowledge she'd done all she could to put matters right in Ippleford. But she wasn't there yet.

At the end of the cutting, surrounded by low split-wood fencing, was a methodically organised vegetable garden. Rows of enormous savoy cabbages with dark green glaucous leaves covering the ground adjoined a rambling area of thriving pumpkins, their big-leaved vines snaking around the bright orange squashes. Lines of canes supporting raspberries protected by netting occupied one corner, while ordered spires of Brussels sprouts sat opposite.

Among the fruit and vegetables, in a long waxed jacket and a wide-brimmed hat dripping with rain, a figure bent over the soil, examining where she'd just turned over the red earth with a wide-pronged fork. Reaching down with hands covered in large, rough gardening gloves, the woman pulled mud-smeared potatoes from the heap of earth and tossed them one by one into a wooden stave basket, each landing with a gentle thud.

Pip's little black nose sniffed the air eagerly. It wasn't unknown for him to enjoy a dig in the usually pristine grounds of Bradley Court. Felicity approached a gap in the fencing but didn't step through. "Miss Waverley?"

The woman's shoulders shot up and her garden fork fell from her hand, landing on the turned earth. She spun round with wide, frightened eyes.

"Forgive me," said Felicity quickly. "I'm awfully sorry to have startled you. It wasn't at all my intention. You are Miss Waverley, are you not?"

The woman had a long gaunt face and brown hair cut short but not neatly enough to be considered a fashionable bob. Her frightened eyes jumped between Felicity and the back door to Gallica Cottage, which stood ajar at the foot of the garden path. She was considering flight. "M-mother's not home."

"It's not Mrs Waverley I was hoping to speak to." Felicity stroked Pip to calm his craning neck and eager sniffing. She used the sort of soothing voice one employed on skittish horses. "I'm Lady Felicity Quick, a reporter for the Western Daily News. You knew Miss Frances Lee, did you not? I'd like to know more about her. I was wondering if—"

"I shan't talk to the papers," snapped Miss Waverley in a manner reminiscent of Mr Viner's. She took a step back from her potato patch.

The chances of Miss Waverley disappearing inside her cottage were growing by the moment. Why was she so scared of Felicity? "That's perfectly fine, Miss Waverley," she said gently. "I shan't write down anything you tell me, and I shan't put your name in our newspaper. I want to understand a little more about Miss Lee so I can get a clear picture of her. We don't want her misrepresented."

Felicity couldn't be too direct at this stage in the discussion, but she hoped that if Miss Waverley cared at all about Frances, then this hint at what was at stake would prompt her into action.

Slowly, Miss Waverley picked up her garden fork from where it had fallen onto the pile of earth and grasped it with both hands, pulling the long wooden handle tight to her chest. Again, she eyed the cottage door, considering her escape route, but Felicity had her attention. The woman watched both Pip and Felicity. Felicity hoped the little dog in her arms underlined she was no threat.

"Miss Lee used to visit you here at Rose Cottages, didn't she?"

Miss Waverley's mouth turned down further. Reluctantly, she nodded.

"Could you tell me why she came to see you?"

The gaunt woman blinked at Felicity from under the dripping brim of her hat. There was a haunted look in her eyes. "To better herself."

"She was taking lessons from you?"

Miss Waverley hesitated, then nodded.

"What lessons?"

"I taught her reading and arithmetic." The woman's hands tightened around the handle of the garden fork. "History. Some piano."

"Are you a tutor by profession?"

Miss Waverley looked down. "I was a teacher, once."

Felicity remembered Mrs Waverley mentioning her daughter's poor health. Physically, she seemed extremely capable. Gardening in the rain wasn't the activity of someone with poor resistance. What had stopped Miss Waverley from her work as a teacher? Felicity couldn't risk delving into Miss Waverley's private life. It might put her off sharing what she knew about Frances. "Do you offer lessons to many in the village?"

"Few around these parts have the money for private tuition."

Felicity raised her eyebrows. "Miss Lee had more money than most?"

"Money enough for her lessons."

"Do you know where her money for the lessons came from?"

Miss Waverley shook her head. "None of my business."

It was a curious but incomplete detail about the dead waitress. If Frances indeed had extra funds, as Miss Waverley seemed to imply, then from where did she get the money? Was she very careful with her tips from the tea rooms? Or was there something else? "Did Miss Lee ever explain why she was taking lessons from you?"

Miss Waverley gave a small shrug, her broad shoulders tight. "She wanted to do something more than just waitress for the rest of her life. She was clever enough."

Felicity nodded. Frances hadn't stood out to her as particularly intelligent, but as her tutor, Miss Waverley would know more about that. "Did the police come to ask you about Miss Lee yet?"

Miss Waverley nodded.

The rain pattered steadily on the cabbage leaves and on Felicity's umbrella. "May I ask what you told them about Miss Lee?"

Miss Waverley said nothing. She glanced again towards the cottage door. Felicity was losing her.

"Do you have any idea about what might have happened at—"

"They're not right about Frances." Miss Waverley blurted. "They've got it all wrong." Was Miss Waverley crying? It was difficult to see in the rain.

"You don't believe Frances committed suicide, Miss Waverley?"

Felicity was met with silence. Miss Waverley's hands gripped the garden fork, her eyes darkening.

"Did Frances ever say anything to you about Mr Luca Carli, the patisserie chef at the tea rooms?"

"No," said Miss Waverley firmly.

"What about the gardener, Mr Viner?"

Miss Waverley's eyes widened, this time not with fear, but with anger. "Why the deuce would she have anything to say about him?"

Felicity was losing control of the situation. She fumbled for a change of subject, still rather desperate to make the most of the opportunity to speak to Miss Waverley. "Did you know Mrs Norrington at all well?"

"No," snarled Miss Waverley. "Barely spoke to the woman."

Perhaps against her better judgement, Felicity persisted, feeling she was a safe distance from the reach of Miss Waverley's fork. "Can you imagine a reason your neighbour would have been sabotaging the Green Ginger?"

"The sabotage was a trifling thing. A silly thing." Miss Waverley lifted the garden fork up high. "It should never have happened." She threw down her fork. It landed upright in the red earth, and she marched up her garden path, slamming the cottage door behind her.

Felicity let out a slow exhale and relaxed her grip on both her umbrella and on Pip. She'd been considering how best to use her umbrella to parry an attack from the fork. The fire in Miss Waverley's eyes had told her the woman could be unpredictable.

Despite this, their exchange had been oddly satisfying. Felicity had new information, and her ideas about it were already forming, but before she jumped to conclusions, she needed a second opinion, and with Lady Henrietta due to arrive in Ippleford at any moment, she needed it fast.

# Chapter Twenty-Six

With Pip still under her arm, for the little dog had no wish to walk through the rain and wet leaves, Felicity left Rose Cottages and hastened down Ippleford high street, the rain hammering on her umbrella. She was heading for the Blue Lady Inn, where she hoped to find Alex.

By sharing her suspicions with him, Felicity intended not only to piece together the fragments of information uncovered since Frances' death. She hoped to make sense of everything that had happened in Ippleford since Felicity and Alex had arrived in the village.

While he never said as much directly, Felicity knew Alex disapproved of the way she allowed her curiosity to get the better of her. Despite this, he had a knack for helping Felicity figure things out, which was what she needed.

It was a relief to see no sign of Lady Henrietta or the Quick family Rolls outside the Green Ginger, but as the rain bounced off the high street and the brook beside the road gargled with the effort of carrying the extra water, there came a disappointing *pop* from above her head.

Felicity's umbrella had given way. The contraption was closing around her shoulders. Pip wriggled and growled in her arms, confused by the darkness enveloping them, and dismayed by the rivulets of water that were now sluicing both the Yorkie and Felicity.

Wrestling with the collapsed umbrella and finally breaking free of it, a sharp whistle pierced through the clatter of the rain and the frantic babbling of the stream. Katherine was leaning out of the tea rooms' front door, gesturing urgently to Felicity to join her.

With her umbrella as good as useless, and the rain coming down so heavily she would soon be soaked to the skin, Felicity made a dash for the Green Ginger. She would shelter there at least until the heavy shower had passed, and perhaps even borrow an umbrella, for it wouldn't do to arrive at the inn looking like she'd been for a swim in the Exe.

"Goodness," said Katherine, closing the door behind Felicity and Pip, as they dripped onto the tea rooms' floor. "What terrible weather. Let me fetch you a towel. I'll come back directly." She had on the same blue wool dress as earlier and had now also applied make-up.

"That's incredibly kind of you, Mrs Evans."

"Not at all." As Katherine trotted up the narrow stairs to the tea rooms' living quarters, Felicity placed Pip on the floor, and he shook himself from nose to tail. Besides Zoe, who sat alone at a table, busy with drawing pencils and paper, the tea rooms were empty.

Katherine was good for her word and reappeared promptly, handing Felicity a pink towel with embroidered edging.

"Thank you," said Felicity, patting herself down before doing the same for Pip. "Where's Vera, may I ask?"

Katherine sighed. "She had some business with the Women's Association. They want to put up a memorial to Mrs Norrington. I told her not to go, as it would only upset her further. A memorial for Frances is out of the question now since the announcement."

"The announcement?" Felicity could be rather good at playing dumb.

Katherine flicked her eyes in Zoe's direction. She lowered her voice. "Well, the police have made it as good as official now. You know, that Frances did for herself, and that it's all connected to what happened to Mrs Norrington." Katherine indicated with a glance the spot where she'd come across the body. "They're not looking for anyone else. That's what they told the journalists at the inn. The case is, essentially, closed. The reporters have all been up here, of course, but we won't speak to them. We'll only speak to you."

Felicity smiled weakly. It was a compliment, of course, but reporting for her brother's newspaper had shifted from being her highest priority.

A gust of wind blew the rain against the tea rooms' windows. It sounded as though the building were being pelted with stones. Pip wandered across the tea rooms' floor, his nose to the ground, searching for fallen morsels. As he reached the table where Zoe was sitting, the little girl bent down and stroked the Yorkie in her typically awkward fashion. Pip, honourable gentleman that he was, gave up his search for cake crumbs and submitted only slightly unwillingly to the little girl's affections.

"Zoe's doing extremely well," said Katherine, her voice still lowered. "All things considered. What's happened is absolutely dreadful, but in a way I'm glad I was here. I'd like to think I've been able to help Vera and Zoe."

"I've no doubt you have." Felicity lowered her voice. "May I ask, is that how you see matters as well?"

Katherine raised her eyebrows quizzically. "See which matters?"

"Mrs Norrington as the saboteur." For Zoe's sake, Felicity kept her voice barely above a whisper. "And Frances as the vengeful murderess who did away with herself in a fit of guilt."

Katherine laughed. It was rather jarring. "I'm sorry," she said, "but when you put it like that, well. It sounds like a story from the pictures. But yes, I suppose that's the way things will be settled. Vera's not happy about it, of course, but she insisted on taking the risk of hiring staff with troubled backgrounds." Katherine narrowed her eyes. "Why do you ask? Do you see it differently?"

As desperate as Felicity was to talk to someone about her ideas, that person had to be someone she trusted. It had to be Alex. "I've no doubt the police know exactly what they're doing. But for the work I do, I seek people's opinions to add colour and emotion to our articles.

I believe our readers would get tremendously bored if we only wrote up the statements made to us by the police."

Katherine smiled. "Would you like a quote or two from me now?"

"Not yet," said Felicity, thinking on her feet. She needed to get to the inn. "I'd prefer to speak to Vera first on the angle I'm taking."

"You might be waiting a while." Katherine sighed and folded her arms over her chest. "After Vera's been with the Women's Association, she wants to talk to the police about what happens to Frances' remains. She's got May with her. They're awfully concerned because it's likely Frances has no discernible next of kin, and considering the manner in which she died, well. Things can get tricky."

Again, the rain lashed the windows. Felicity wished no ill on her grandmother, but if she'd set off for Ippleford, the weather was perhaps slowing the Rolls' progress. Felicity couldn't say exactly how the situation would become even more complicated after Lady Henrietta's arrival. She just knew it would.

"Shall I put the kettle on while we wait for them? I can even make you a sandwich, if you're hungry. I'm not the mother hen type like my sister, but I know how to put cheese between two slices of bread."

"Thank you," said Felicity graciously, "but I'll be on my way to the inn just as soon as this rain stops. I've a meeting with a colleague." It would be an impromptu rather than a planned meeting with Alex, but Katherine didn't need to know that. "Say, where's Mr Carli?"

Katherine folded her arms and glowered. "I don't know where he is, and quite frankly, neither do I care."

Felicity repressed a raise of her eyebrows. Was this an opportunity to learn more? "He mentioned to me he may seek employment elsewhere," she said. "Could that explain his departure?"

Katherine scoffed. "Oh, that doesn't surprise me. My sister's been played for a fool, but show me a woman able to resist a handsome chap down on his luck with a story to tell."

Felicity was taken aback. "Were Vera and Mr Carli..."

"Oh, no," said Katherine with a wave of her hand. "Nothing of the sort. Not that my sister is squeaky clean, and I've no doubt he tried it. Vera is simply too smart to mix business with pleasure. Luca got all the attention he needed from elsewhere, anyway."

Felicity drew her chin back. "From Frances?"

"Frances? Goodness, no. She was full of admiration for him. Heaven knows why, but as I told you, Luca has a type. And that type is a woman of certain means."

"Frances had money though, didn't she?" offered Felicity, attempting to piece together what Katherine was saying with what she'd heard at Rose Cottages.

"Hardly. Despite lacking in grace, Frances was good at making customers feel special and careful with her tips, but I'm talking about real money. And I'm sorry to say it, but I know this from experience." Katherine looked away, her jaw tight.

"Mr Carli turned you down, you mean?"

A grim smile spread over Katherine's face. "I suppose I deserved it. I suppose I needed to be taken down a peg or two."

Felicity was becoming a little lost. "Why would you deserve rejection?"

Katherine sighed. "I have a piece of advice for you, Lady Felicity. If you ever find a good man, don't let him go. He might not be the most exciting thing around, but if he's decent to you, and you get on well, don't let him go."

Felicity blinked. The conversation was heading off-track. "You mentioned that Mr Carli was courting interest from different women around the village. Do you know which women?"

"Oh, I would say just about anyone from whom he might get a bob or two on a regular basis. Anyone who might mention him in her will."

"He took money from customers? Beyond his tips, I mean?" Felicity remembered the flash of metal under Luca's arm.

"I've no proof, but you've seen how he is. He can turn the charm on, and he can turn it off. Some women are more susceptible than others."

"Mrs Norrington?"

Katherine shrugged. “Couldn’t say for sure, but I wouldn’t be surprised.”

“Do the police know this?”

“Oh, I told them everything. I’ve no loyalty to the man, and I’m quite certain he was up to something. Still is, probably. Deuced if I know what.”

Felicity’s heart rate quickened. Her suspicions about Luca were solidifying. But Katherine had been jilted by him, had she not? Did that cloud her judgement?

“Do you think he...?”

Again, Katherine laughed. “Luca wasn’t in Mrs Norrington’s will, if that’s what you’re getting at. The police checked. Plus, the slippery fellow was away in London that night, remember? Something to do with his passport, although goodness knows what he was really doing up there.”

Felicity didn’t quite know what to think. She’d unearthed crucial information, but it wasn’t evident how it fitted together.

A small yelp of distress caught her attention. Zoe had hoisted Pip onto her lap, rolling him onto his back like a baby. If Felicity attempted something similar, she’d receive a nip on the hand as punishment.

Alex. Felicity had to get to Alex.

“Mrs Evans, do you have an umbrella I might borrow?”

# Chapter Twenty-Seven

The umbrella Felicity borrowed from the tea rooms was only half the size of the one that had broken. As she hurried down the high street, rain hit Felicity's skirt — which still wasn't fully dry from the soaking she'd got when her own umbrella had broken — and she struggled to hold Pip high enough to keep him from getting wet.

On a normal day, venturing outside in such heavy rain would be out of the question. Since arriving in Ippleford, however, there'd been no such thing as a normal day, and so long as there was no sign of Lady Henrietta, Felicity had a clear goal in mind.

She and Pip were both shivering by the time she folded away the borrowed umbrella under the big thatched porch of the Blue Lady Inn. The bar wasn't deserted like it had been earlier, although most of the journalists had dispersed, presumably to write up and call in their stories about the police's announcement. Those that remained in the bar were conducting interviews with policemen or local people, or furiously flicking through and scribbling in notebooks.

"Oh, it's nasty out there, isn't it?"

Mrs Biggs had arrived on the porch behind Felicity. She had on her fur-collared coat and was shaking an umbrella out into the rain.

"Still, I suppose it's appropriate weather," continued the

landlady. "Very maudlin. I was just with the Women's Association. Laying flowers, we were." Mrs Biggs shrugged out of her coat, under which she still had on her apron over her floral dress. "But in rain like this, they'll all be turned to mush in no time." She sighed. "I tried warning them, but they'd not listen to me." Mrs Biggs was exactly the garrulous type of woman one expected to find running an inn.

"Did the Women's Association lay flowers at the castle?" enquired Felicity.

Mrs Biggs' nose wrinkled. "We came to a compromise and put the flowers at the church doors, your ladyship. It would have been inside the church had the vicar been about, but he's not too keen on spending time in Ippleford lately." The landlady lowered her voice. "It's not entirely appropriate to put flowers at the scene of a suicide prompted by guilt for murder."

Felicity gripped Pip tightly. It ought to have been no surprise that Frances' guilt had become an accepted fact in the village, only it didn't feel right to Felicity. Not yet. "Even a murderer can have a family who cares about him," she suggested.

The landlady chuckled. "I suppose that's one way of looking at it, your ladyship. Good that we can put this matter behind us, but I believe it'll take a while longer for things to get back to normal around here." Mrs Biggs looked at Felicity rather seriously. "I must say, things haven't really been normal since those actors came to town. Stirred up some odd ideas, they did. Not fitting for a village like Ippleford, if you ask me."

Felicity blinked. "I can't help noticing you have a poster for the play in your window."

Mrs Biggs looked over her shoulder at the offending item. "Well, Mr Biggs and I didn't see the harm in it at the time. But considering everything that's happened..." The landlady trailed off, raising her eyebrows as though Felicity could fill in the gaps by herself. "And I heard there are echoes of the play to be found in how that poor waitress died."

Felicity didn't react. If news was spreading about the parallels between Frances' death and the play at the castle, it wouldn't make life easy for the Heards. Surely the police hadn't included that level of salacious detail in their announcement?

"I'm looking for my colleague, Mr Cooper," said Felicity, rather bluntly changing the subject. "I don't suppose you know where he might be?"

"Ah, the dashing young man with the scar on his forehead. I know exactly who you mean, your ladyship. One of the polite ones. Not many of these journalists are as well behaved as your Mr Cooper. In any case, you shan't find him here."

"Oh," said Felicity. It was a blow. If Lady Henrietta was indeed on her way to Ippleford, there wasn't time to go hunting around the village for Alex.

Further inside the inn, Mr Biggs appeared behind the bar, beckoning for his wife to join him. Mrs Biggs made a gesture of acknowledgement.

"I saw him just now up at the church," said the landlady.

"You did?" Felicity couldn't hide her relief.

"He's there with his photography equipment, of all things. In this weather."

Felicity was well-versed in the risks of taking pictures in the rain. What could Alex be up to?

"I'm sorry, your ladyship, but duty calls." The landlady nodded towards her impatient-looking husband. "We'll be serving luncheon soon. Will you and Mr Cooper be joining us? We've smoked mackerel and cured ham on the menu."

Pip's little nose was exploring the warm air wafting out of the bar area, which was already scented with the preparations for lunch.

The idea of enjoying a hearty meal while drying off beside the inn's fire was frightfully enticing. "I appreciate the invitation, Mrs Biggs, but I doubt there'll be much time for lunch today. I have an awful lot still to do."

"Very well, your ladyship," said the landlady, as Felicity reopened the borrowed umbrella and walked with purpose back out into the rain. "Just mind you don't catch a cold."

---

Felicity sighed with relief when she found Alex in the churchyard, just as Mrs Biggs had said. He stood talking to a uniformed officer beside the doors of the barn-like church hall, his hands in the pockets of his grey overcoat and his fedora hat dripping with rain. At the doors of the church opposite, just as the landlady had said, were bunches of flowers wrapped in brown paper and pummelled by the rain.

The crunch of Felicity's Oxfords on the gravel path made Alex turn. He immediately excused himself from conversing with the policeman. "I wondered where you'd got to," he said, adjusting his dripping hat. "I presumed you'd gone knocking on cottage doors gathering reactions."

Felicity's smile was weak. "Something like that."

"Everything all right?"

Did Felicity look as perturbed as she felt? Either that or Alex had some kind of sixth sense.

"Can we talk?" She raised her voice above the sound of the rain hitting her umbrella.

Alex gestured towards a giant, knobbly yew tree on a small mound, its vast limbs snaking in all directions. The shelter it provided wasn't entirely free of raindrops, but it was enough for Felicity to fold away the borrowed umbrella and place Pip on the ground. They still had a view of both the church and the church hall. A camera tripod stood at the ready, Alex's photography equipment case unlatched but unopened at its base. A sweet, turfy scent rose from the dirt under their feet.

As was his custom, the little Yorkie went to Alex and gave his shoes an enthusiastic sniffing. Alex smiled down at Pip as he took off his hat and gave it a tremendous shake.

"Do you expect good images in this weather?" enquired Felicity, trying to swipe what dampness she could from her tweeds.

Alex smiled wryly. "Do you not recognise a ruse when you see one? If the police thought I was hanging around simply to ask questions and get exclusive quotes when the detectives appear —

which is exactly what I am doing, of course — they'd chase me away. As it is, they're rather keen on photos of themselves in action." His face turned serious. He nodded towards the church hall. "Mrs Monroe and Miss Pettigrew are in there, you know."

Felicity remembered what Katherine had told her about Vera concerning herself with a proper burial for Frances. "It's officially a suicide, isn't it?"

Alex rocked on his heels. "Technically, nothing's official until there's been an inquest. But the announcement this morning was that the police aren't looking for any other suspects. They didn't spell it out, exactly, but the understanding is that Miss Lee murdered Mrs Norrington and then died by her own hand. For them, the case is as good as closed, and our work here is as good as done. No reason we shan't make it to the interview with Judge Hawkins tomorrow."

Felicity took a deep breath. "Alex..." She hesitated. What if things were left the way they were? Life would go back to normal, eventually. Not just in Ippleford, but for Felicity and Alex, too.

Alex watched as the policeman at the church hall's door disappeared inside. "Mm-hmm?"

It was perhaps selfish, but if she kept her suspicions to herself, Felicity wouldn't ever feel as though things had gone back to normal. There was also the risk that Lady Henrietta might arrive at any moment and turn the whole situation upside down with attempts to improve matters.

Felicity swallowed. "What if the case wasn't as simple as that?"

Alex glanced at Felicity, his eyes narrowed. "Meaning what, exactly?"

The rain fell in heavy drops through the yew's canopy.

"What if Frances didn't harm Mrs Norrington? What if she didn't harm herself?"

Alex stared at Felicity for a moment. "Go on."

"I just... I heard some things that caused me to re-evaluate matters." Felicity did her best to sound spirited and open-minded rather than distrustful.

"Aside from the fact your friend Mrs Monroe would rather Miss Lee had nothing to do with any of this, you mean?"

Felicity brushed the comment off. "Do you happen to know if the police found anything interesting in Mr Carli's background?"

Alex narrowed his eyes. "The cake fellow?"

Felicity nodded.

"Why do you ask?"

"He may have been involved with Mrs Norrington. Perhaps there was even something between him and Frances. I believe I saw him smuggling something out of the tea rooms, and now he seems to have disappeared."

Pip left Alex's feet and went to sniff around the yew's knobbly trunk.

"All right." Alex folded his arms. "What else?"

"Well." Felicity had been prepared for Alex's scepticism. "There's the matter of Frances' supposed suicide. No one who knows her at all well considers it possible. She was an ambitious young woman with plans for her future. It makes little sense. Then there's that awfully stern gardener. He knows something, and he's not letting on." The more she spoke, the lighter Felicity felt. "I also met Miss Waverley up at Rose Cottages. Frances was paying her for lessons, but something's not quite right there, either."

Alex watched Felicity for a moment before speaking. "You've been doing more than getting quotes for the paper, haven't you?"

Felicity's eyes widened. It was somehow easy to forget that Alex was, above all else, a colleague. "I have quotes for the paper." She reached for her notebook, though she knew it contained little of use to the News. "I spoke to—"

"Why don't we tell the police?" Alex's dark blue gaze was steady.

"About what? Everything that I just told you?"

Alex nodded.

"But it makes no sense."

"It's not our job to make sense of it. We can leave that to the police."

"You're not angry at me for sleuthing?"

Alex frowned deeply. "After everything we've been through together, why would I choose now, of all occasions, to lose my temper with you?"

"Are you not worried you'll miss the interview with Judge Hawkins?"

"Who says we will?"

That Alex was still confident they'd make the interview meant he didn't take Felicity's suspicions incredibly seriously, but it was better than her ideas being dismissed. She felt an odd flutter of excitement. Perhaps there was nothing to her suspicions and she was being overly sensitive about the whole case. Felicity didn't have to be right. She just had to be certain.

"I want to tell Vera first," she said decisively. "Before we tell the police." As much as Felicity disliked Luca, Vera regarded him as family, as she had done Frances.

"Then we're in luck." Alex nodded towards the church hall, where Vera had just stepped through the barn-like doors. Glancing at the sky, she opened her umbrella. May soon joined her, looping her arm through Vera's. They moved slowly towards the lychgate, their shoulders slumped. May looked ashen.

With a firm nod in Alex's direction and leaving Pip still sniffing around the yew, Felicity opened the borrowed umbrella and again stepped into the rain.

# Chapter Twenty-Eight

The tired, haunted stares of the two women halted Felicity's approach across the gravel outside the church hall. Vera looked haggard, her cornflower eyes dull and her straw-coloured hair frizzed by the rain, despite the protection of her hat and an umbrella. In a large grey overcoat and clinging to Vera's arm, May looked thinner and sallower than usual.

"My lady," said Vera. It was a lacklustre greeting, which was entirely understandable. Who in Vera's position wouldn't feel worn down?

"How are you both managing?" Time was pressing, and the answer to Felicity's question was perhaps rather obvious, but she couldn't be too direct about things. Vera and May were fragile.

"As well as expected, my lady," said Vera. She offered a fleeting smile.

May sniffed. She was doing her best not to cry. The air was awash with the sound of rain tapping on umbrellas and hitting the gravel.

Felicity bit her lip. "It's not my intention to prolong your discomfort, but I was wondering if I might have a word with you, Vera?"

"Oh, my lady." Tears welled in Vera's eyes. "There's no bringing our poor Frances back. What further harm could a conversation do?" She handed her umbrella to May, pressing the waitress' hand firmly around the handle. "Get along to the Green Ginger, my dear. You'll catch your death if you spend too long in this awful weather."

May did as she was told, glancing nervously back at Vera and Felicity before ducking under the lychgate. The uniformed officer who had escorted Vera and May out of the church hall now stood beside the doors, stoic in the downpour. Alex watched them from the edge of the rain shadow cast by the yew, Pip sitting at his side, unusually obedient.

Vera hugged her little leather handbag as rain dripped off the brim of her hat, its single dowdy silk rose already sodden. Felicity did her best to position the small umbrella so that it sheltered both her and Vera. The rain hit the back of Felicity's tweeds.

"Your sister informed me of your concern about what will happen to Frances."

Vera nodded sadly. "In the eyes of the law, we aren't family, my lady. The police are understanding, but they can't help us. I went to the Women's Association earlier, and they refused to lay flowers at the castle for her. I understand it, but it feels so cruel. Frances had so few supporters in life, and now even fewer in death." Vera took a handkerchief from her bag and wiped her eyes. "I suppose we must get on with things. The Green Ginger must open again. I've Zoe to provide for, and I don't want Katherine, May, or Luca back out on the street."

Vera's strength was admirable. How much more bad news could she take?

There was no point beating about the bush. Felicity took a deep breath. "It feels quite terrible to have to do this, but I've made some discoveries about which I feel it's my duty to inform the police. Before I go to them, I should like to tell you first."

Vera glanced wearily over her shoulder at the policeman standing beside the church hall door, his uniform made darker by the rain. "The police must surely know everything by now, my lady. They've asked us enough questions."

Felicity lowered her voice. "Do you believe they know everything about your patisserie chef?"

Vera's eyes widened. She looked again at the policeman and also at Alex, who, along with Pip, watched Felicity carefully. "Let's try and get out of this rain, shall we, my lady?" Vera started towards the church.

The doors of the church being locked, Felicity and Vera stood against the mottled granite wall of the spire. The wind's direction meant they were out of the rain. They were also out of earshot but still in sight of the policeman, Alex, and Pip.

"What have you learned about Luca?" asked Vera, blinking nervously.

Felicity lowered her umbrella. She chose her words with care. It wasn't her intention to upset Vera, but it seemed unavoidable. "He knows how to use his charms, does he not?"

"Is that a crime?" Her tone was defensive.

"Do you know where he is?"

The tea rooms' owner sighed heavily. "The police caught him, my lady. He made it to Exeter and attempted to board a train to London. I'll admit, it doesn't give a good impression."

"Forgive me for putting this to you, Vera, but I somehow have received the impression that Mr Carli is something of a fraudster. Is there any possibility I might be right in thinking that?"

There was a stony silence. For the first time, there was an edge of hardness to Vera's bright blue gaze.

"I've arrived at the impression that he uses his charms to take money from people," continued Felicity. "From women, more precisely."

"Like I said, my lady, the police know everything."

So it was true. And Vera had known all along.

Felicity felt suddenly rather stupid. Her cheeks grew hot with exasperation. What else had Vera not told her? Had Felicity been dashing around the village trying to uncover something that was plain for everyone but her to see?

A sudden gust of wind whipped a blast of stinging rain around the church tower.

"I came to Ippleford to help investigate a crime against your business." Felicity couldn't withhold the edge in her voice. "Yet you didn't consider it necessary to inform me of this?"

"Luca had told me he was done with it." Vera shook her head. She, too, looked annoyed. "We've all done things we wished we hadn't, my lady. Done things we'd rather forget." Vera's empathy for the downtrodden was admirable but also, apparently, dangerous.

"I've undoubtedly led a life of privilege," said Felicity delicately, "with protection from the worst of what life might throw at a person. But you've had an honourable life, Vera. We're all faced with choices. You took the correct and moral path, did you not?"

The tea rooms owner smiled darkly, her frizzy yellow hair blowing about her cheeks. "Not always, my lady. Not always."

Vera's reaction frightened Felicity. "What do you mean?"

"I'm sorry to disappoint you, but I'm no angel." Her blue gaze was steely. "My husband didn't die in the war, my lady. I never had a husband. I hardly knew Zoe's father."

Felicity drew back her chin. She tried not to look shocked, but it was perhaps too late.

Vera sighed. "There. It's out in the open. I suppose you think differently of me now, my lady."

The admission rather altered Felicity's perception of her grandmother's favourite lady's maid. Didn't it? "I'll be honest with you, Vera," said Felicity, haltingly. "I don't know quite what to think."

The tea rooms' owner let out an odd little laugh. "I suppose you'll tell Lady Henrietta, and I shall lose her support. But it's better than dealing in secrets, isn't it? From the beginning, I should have been more open with you, my lady. I see that now. I've made an absolute mess of things, haven't I?"

"I shan't tell my grandmother," said Felicity. "It's not my secret to tell. I—" She paused. This wasn't at all how she'd expected the conversation to go.

Felicity attempted to focus her spinning thoughts on the original reason for speaking to Vera, but if the police already knew Luca was up to something nefarious, then what useful information did Felicity have to share with them?

"Vera, will you permit me to ask you something frank?"

"Of course, my lady. I'm thankful you still want to speak to me after what I just told you."

Again, wind gusted around the church tower, spattering Felicity and Vera with rain.

"Do you believe Frances committed suicide?"

A softness returned to Vera's gaze. "I don't want to believe it, my lady, only it looks that way, doesn't it?" She put a hand to her cheek. "Oh, I've made a real mess of things, haven't I?" Tears fell from her eyes.

"You've done your best, Vera," said Felicity, unsure she could say anything helpful. "No one can be considered perfect."

The door to the church hall opened. Detective Inspector Daniels and Sergeant Hewitt strode across the gravel, their collars turned up against the rain.

"Sergeant! Detective Inspector!" Alex launched himself from under the yew to intercept them, his notebook at the ready.

Confused by the sudden activity, Pip darted towards Felicity, yapping as he bounded through the rain. Felicity empathised with the little dog's bewilderment. Moments ago, the path ahead had seemed clear. Now she was on the back foot, unsure of almost everything. Why hadn't she followed Alex's lead? He'd stayed focused on the reporting, diligently trailing the police's investigation, and now he would get the scoop.

As Felicity bent down to collect Pip from the ground, her nose tickled. Upon straightening, she did her best to hold it in, but she was powerless. Felicity sneezed.

"Oh, my lady," said Vera, her mothering instincts offering at least some distraction from her inner turmoil. "This weather's doing none of us any good." She reached into her bag and pulled out a handkerchief.

"Thank y—" began Felicity, extending a hand to accept it, but something else came out of Vera's bag with the handkerchief.

Shiny and red, and with an elegant curve to it, the item flew a short distance through the air and rolled onto the gravel, landing in the path of Detective Inspector Daniels and Sergeant Hewitt.

The two policemen stopped to watch the curious item roll to a stop in the rain. Alex watched, too, his eyes slowly widening.

The silence was broken by the crunch of gravel. Footsteps were approaching from the other side of the church hall.

Sergeant Hewitt crouched, shook a handkerchief from his pocket, and used it to lift the item from the ground.

"Well," began the sergeant. "I must say. This rather puts a new angle on things."

"Mrs Monroe," said the detective. "It seems you haven't been entirely truthful with us."

Vera was as white as a ghost, her mouth gaping, her lips quivering. The dread on her face prompted Felicity to realise what the item was.

It was the missing handle from the teapot that had been used to kill Mrs Norrington.

"Ah, Vera, my dear. At last."

Lady Henrietta rounded the church hall in a high-necked, floor-length black coat, the Quick family's driver, Finnegan, close behind her, holding an umbrella above the dainty hat balanced atop her grey chignon.

"And Felicity," she continued. "My darling granddaughter."

Vera turned to Lady Henrietta with pleading eyes. "Oh, my lady. Please. You mustn't see this."

Detective Inspector Daniels stepped towards Vera. "I'm afraid, Mrs Monroe, I have no choice but to arrest you in connection with the death of Mrs Prudence Norrington."

"Arrest?" Lady Henrietta came to an abrupt halt and frowned. "Arrest?" She looked at Vera. "Surely there must be some mistake?" Felicity's grandmother looked at her beseechingly, but Felicity was frozen to the spot, her heart pounding, powerless to do anything.

Sergeant Hewitt passed the teapot handle to the detective and produced a set of handcuffs. Vera stood limply as the sergeant fixed the cuffs around her wrists.

"But... But..." Lady Henrietta stumbled a little. Finnegan deftly put a hand to her elbow.

*Paff!* A magnesium flash went off. Alex had fetched his camera and was recording the moment of Vera's arrest.

"But I didn't do it," said Vera weakly, looking down helplessly at the handcuffs, rain pouring off her hat with its ruined silk rose. "Really, I didn't."

Everything had gone wrong. So terribly and utterly wrong.

## Chapter Twenty-Nine

Where else was there to go but the tea rooms?

Rain continued to batter the windows, and the acrid whiff of Lady Henrietta's smelling salts still hung in the air, having been administered by the ever-reliable Finnegan. Not even Pip's presence could distract little Zoe from her crying, and she continued to grizzle on Katherine's lap, the little girl's arms tight around her aunt's neck.

May's hands shook as she brought a tray of tea to the table around which everyone was seated. Finnegan kept a watchful distance from the cake counter, and Alex was goodness knows where, doing his usual excellent work following the latest twist in the story for the newspaper rather than his own personal curiosity.

Vera was being transported to police headquarters in Exeter. Between bouts of feeling rather queer, Lady Henrietta had made arrangements for the finest of Devon's solicitors to be there for Vera. Still, the mood in the tea rooms was exceedingly sombre. It was becoming difficult to imagine the establishment ever having been filled with vibrant chatter and happy customers.

Felicity had a headache coming on, but she suppressed even the thought of it. Out of everyone, she had the least right to feel hard done by. In fact, she'd let everyone down quite spectacularly, not least her own grandmother, who'd already moved from despair at the situation to outrage. There was also absolutely no chance she and Alex would make the interview with Judge Hawkins.

It was the worst of all outcomes. And Felicity could do nothing to change things.

"I blame myself," said Katherine, shaking her head and speaking to no one in particular, unable to hide her sadness from her niece.

Felicity barely had the energy to say thank you to May as the waitress set down a trembling cup of tea before her. Neither had she the gumption to enquire after Katherine's feelings of guilt. Felicity felt guilty, herself. Had she not accosted Vera in the churchyard, she wouldn't have been arrested.

"Someone must have framed her," thundered Lady Henrietta. "Vera is obviously not a murderess. If she were, then why would she have the teapot handle in her handbag, ready to let it drop to the floor at a moment's notice? And in front of the police, no less. Why would Vera want to ruin her own business? It's absolute balderdash."

Exactly the same considerations had already occurred to Felicity. Unlike Lady Henrietta, Felicity had also heard Vera's confessions. *I've made an absolute mess of things*, she'd said. The situation was indeed a dreadful mess.

Having served everyone with tea, May attempted to comfort Zoe, but her advances were ignored as the little girl continued to sob at her aunt's neck. The waitress took a seat next to Felicity. She had on her black-and-white uniform without the headdress. Over it she wore a brown cardigan that had been mended with patches. She hugged herself and shivered.

"Would you like to look after Pip for a while, Miss Pettigrew?" suggested Felicity.

May blinked hopefully. "Really, your ladyship?"

Felicity lifted the half-asleep Yorkie onto May's lap. "I believe he'll be more comfortable with you. I still need to dry off from the rain." Tweed was, on the whole, weather resistant. Once damp, however, it was difficult to dry.

The waitress smiled meekly at Felicity and stroked the Yorkie's tufted ears, a gesture Pip rarely tolerated from strangers, but given the circumstances, he knew better than to object.

Felicity took a sip of the hot, milky tea May had prepared. It was weaker than she would have liked, but its warmth was revitalising. "I'm incredibly sorry about how things have developed," she said to the waitress, remembering the faith May had misplaced in her sleuthing abilities.

"Oh, your ladyship," returned May, "it's not anything like your fault. Life just isn't fair. I'm quite used to it by now, although that doesn't make it less upsetting."

Felicity swallowed. Vera had found May in an orphanage, had she not? It was a grim statement for someone so young to make.

"Well, we shan't sit down and take it." Lady Henrietta spoke even more rousingly than she did at Lower Diddleton Plant and Floral Society meetings. "We'll fight until our Vera is free. She mustn't take the blame for something she didn't do. We simply can't allow it."

Who Lady Henrietta meant by *we* wasn't entirely clear. Felicity had done what she could and failed. Katherine and May were still dealing with the shock and were in no state to mount a campaign of resistance.

There came a sudden pounding on the tea rooms' door. It made everyone jump.

"Goodness me," said Lady Henrietta, bringing a gloved hand to the ruffled chest of her grey dress. "Who could that be? Who dares so rudely disturb a stricken household?"

"Shall I open it, my lady?" Finnegan asked this of Lady Henrietta.

"I'll see who it is." Felicity rose from her seat before her grandmother could answer. It didn't seem quite right to allow Lady Henrietta to take control of the situation, given her belligerent mood. The least Felicity could do was to protect the peace of the tea rooms, for little Zoe's sake if for no one else's.

Through the rain-spattered window, it was difficult to see who it was. A policeman, perhaps? But upon opening the door, Felicity instantly regretted doing so.

Mr Viner marched into the tea rooms, his corduroys dripping

onto the floorboards. He turned and thrust an accusatory finger in Felicity's direction. "You said you were here for Vera. Got a funny way of fixing things, haven't you?"

The red Collie sat obediently in the tea rooms doorway as cold air swept in from outside. Finnegan stepped forward, tugging at the wrists of his leather chauffeur's gloves, as if readying himself for some physical altercation.

Felicity gave him a sign to stand back. "Wait, Finnegan. Please."

"I knew you couldn't be trusted!" Mr Viner practically shouted this at Felicity.

Zoe had stopped crying, and Katherine snapped her hands over the little girl's ears to defend her from whatever the angry gardener would say next. May clung to Pip, and Lady Henrietta, who was not at all accustomed to people raising their voices above her own, appeared too shocked to react.

"Shall I ask the gentleman to leave, my lady?" suggested Finnegan to Felicity in a way that continued to imply the involvement of physical persuasion.

"Not yet, Finnegan." Felicity folded her arms over her chest and looked up at Mr Viner. Zoe, May, Katherine, and Lady Henrietta all had their eyes on her. "You're right. I've let Vera down. I've let rather a lot of people down, actually. But you're wrong to say I can't be trusted. I was dedicated to Vera's cause the whole time." Felicity hesitated. "I still am."

Mr Viner breathed heavily through his nose and narrowed his eyes at Felicity. "Then why aren't you out there fighting to prove her innocence?"

"Whoa, there." Alex arrived at a jogging pace in the tea rooms doorway, pausing only slightly before stepping carefully past the watchful Collie. "What's going on here?" He eyed Mr Viner as he took off his rain-soaked hat. "You're the fellow I could hear shouting in the street, are you?"

Mr Viner shook his head angrily. "If you won't do anything," he said to Felicity, "there's only one thing for it. I'm going to hand myself in."

"Upon my soul," said Katherine, her hands momentarily falling from Zoe's ears before clamping back around the little girl's head.

May looked both puzzled and frightened. Thankfully, Pip was doing an excellent job of submitting himself to her nervous caresses.

Lady Henrietta stood up, shaking on her feet. "So, it was you." She lifted a dramatic finger in the gardener's direction, her face dark with enmity.

Alex let his hands fall to his sides as he looked between Felicity and Mr Viner. Little pools of water gathered under his overcoat. "Must I call in another edit for our story?"

Felicity seemed to be the only person in the room who knew what was really going on. "And what good would that do, Mr Viner? I very much doubt the police would believe you. Because you didn't do it, did you?"

He held her gaze and spoke through gritted teeth. "Of course, I blooming well didn't, but I won't let them hurt a hair on Vera's head."

Mr Viner's dedication to Vera was now fully apparent. And Felicity was thinking clearly again.

Alex's shoulders slumped with relief. "Good, because I believe the police have quite enough to handle without random declarations of insanity." He shrugged off his soaking wet coat and hung it up by the door. "I just got off the line with a contact up at police headquarters. They've got both Vera Monroe and Luca Carli in custody. Although the two of them are denying any involvement in either death, the police expect one of them to break soon. Then it's just a case of playing off one against the other."

Zoe knocked her aunt's hands away from her ears. She'd stopped crying, her little forehead creased with focus.

"Why the blazes do they think my sister is in league with that scoundrel?" Katherine didn't even try to hide her indignation.

Alex shrugged. "Since the appearance of the teapot handle, they've had to rethink the whole suicide angle. The pressure has rather increased. It's now a double murder."

"How can we know the two deaths are even linked?" asked Lady Henrietta.

"Murder can become a habit." Felicity had learned this not just from the detective fiction she read. She had some tragic real-life experiences to draw upon. "The chance of one murderer with his own set of motives in Ippleford is slim enough. What would be the chances of two?"

Mr Viner shook his head. "It can't be Vera," he growled. "I won't let it be Vera."

"We know Luca couldn't have done for Mrs Norrington because he was in London." Katherine spoke animatedly. Zoe watched her with curiosity from her lap. "But why would Vera do away with her own customer in the tea rooms? And then do for poor Frances? Vera loved the girl like a daughter. It makes no sense whatever."

May shook her head and stroked Pip for comfort. "Does it have to make sense? Aren't all murderers mad?"

It was at that moment, with everyone looking at one another in confusion and pain, that a calm lucidity descended upon Felicity.

With Pip watching her carefully, Felicity went to the Green Ginger's front door and ushered Mr Viner's Collie gently inside. Closing the door, she caught Alex's gaze. A slight narrowing of his eyes told her he knew she was working on something, and he was right. Felicity had come to Ippleford with the goal of finding out the truth, and she wasn't finished yet.

"There's still a chance to get to the bottom of things," she said, standing with her back to the door, addressing the room. "If you're able to place your trust in me?"

"Of course," said Alex, without hesitation.

"We trust you, your ladyship," said May.

Lady Henrietta frowned. "What a queer question. How could I not trust my own granddaughter?"

Katherine nodded her assent. Zoe blinked expectantly at Felicity.

Felicity looked at the gardener. "Mr Viner?"

He sighed. "What choice do we have?"

It was good enough. "I've a plan," said Felicity, "but I believe I shall need some help."

## Chapter Thirty

The next day was cool, bright, and breezy, the pale blue sky showing no sign of rain. It started with a meeting at Felicity's cottage, at which Felicity, Pip, Alex, and Lady Henrietta — who had returned to Bradley Court for the night — were in attendance.

Over tea and hot buttered crumpets, and following solemn promises that not a word would be said to Jasper unless something went wrong and he actually had cause to worry, Felicity explained her plan.

Central to the plan was the spreading of rumours.

"The impression should be given that I've happened upon the solution to the fiendishly tricky mystery over which the police continue to puzzle," said Felicity, sitting on the edge of her fireside seat, dressed in a fresh set of tweeds with a hint of spring green in them, brought from Bradley Court by Finnegan. "People should know that I'm giving the police a day — today — to catch up with my thinking. After that, I'll publish my findings in the Western Daily News."

Alex frowned. He leaned in the kitchen doorway, an emptied plate in his hand. "Without first informing the police?"

"That's the impression I should like to give," confirmed Felicity.

"And do you know who's behind it all?" he asked, somewhat hopefully. "That would make quite the splash on the front page."

"Do you not recognise a ruse when you see one?" Felicity smiled and patted Pip on the head as the little dog stretched out on her lap, enjoying the fire's heat. "If I actually knew, I'd naturally bring my evidence to the police."

"It all sounds like a frightfully clever plan, my dear." Lady Henrietta was seated opposite Felicity. In a staid purple frock with lace trimmings, the dowager wasn't altogether at ease with the cramped and informal conditions of the cottage. She had, however, enjoyed her crumpets, which Felicity had grilled successfully, despite it being her first ever attempt.

"You are an extremely talented young woman, Felicity," continued Lady Henrietta, "but may I ask what you hope to achieve with this?"

"My purpose," said Felicity, "is to draw our culprit into the open."

"Are you certain it'll work?" asked Lady Henrietta.

"By no means, but I should like to try."

Alex looked thoughtful. "What if the guilty party is already in police custody?"

Lady Henrietta looked decidedly unhappy with the suggestion. Vera had spent the night in the holding cells.

"Then I won't have disrupted anything." Felicity stroked Pip. "The police can continue to investigate and draw their own conclusions. I shan't stop them."

Alex continued to look thoughtful but said nothing further.

The practicalities of the plan were then discussed. Lady Henrietta would infiltrate Ippleford's Women's Association to spread the rumour of Felicity's brilliance. While Felicity wasn't keen on her grandmother being directly involved, Lady Henrietta was determined to help, and it was better to guide her efforts than allow her free rein.

"They've a meeting this morning about a memorial bench for Mrs Norrington," said the dowager. "The meeting starts soon at a location known as Gallica Cottage. Are you aware of it? That's what the vicar's wife at Star Torrington told me when I telephoned to her yesterday evening. She's a keen fuchsia grower, you see, and we meet at competitions occasionally."

"You'll be careful, won't you?" Her grandmother visiting the home of the unpredictable Miss Waverley wasn't a thought Felicity relished.

"Please don't worry, dear. I shall keep Finnegan close by, although why anyone should want to harm me, I simply cannot fathom."

Felicity smiled. It was an interesting experience to be worried about someone else's safety.

Lady Henrietta having promptly departed for the Women's Association meeting, Alex went to the little sitting room's window and looked out at the high street, his hands in his pockets. He'd agreed to take the rumour to the journalists. Was he having second thoughts?

Felicity rose and approached him. "It's not too late to change your mind if you'd rather not be involved. It's not exactly newspaper business."

Alex kept his gaze on the high street, his jaw tense. "I want to help."

Felicity's stomach tightened. "I feel quite awful about the interview with Judge Hawkins." There was no chance they'd make it now.

Alex turned towards Felicity, blinking. "What is it I need to tell the fellows at the inn? Remind me again."

Felicity reminded him of the messaging. She was tremendously grateful for Alex's support and promised herself she would make it up to him. She just wasn't yet sure how.

Alex quirked a dark blond eyebrow. "And what will you be doing while the rumour mill gets grinding?"

"Keeping a low profile," said Felicity. "If anyone challenges me about what I know, things could get awkward."

Alex smiled faintly. "You're getting better."

"At what?"

"Being dishonest."

Before Felicity could decide if she was offended, Alex departed for the inn, leaving Felicity alone with Pip. She took the Yorkie for a brief stroll in the sunshine before the rumours had a chance to spread, then holed herself up in her cottage and waited.

Was Felicity's plan dishonest? She put the thought out of her mind. It was too late to go back now.

To pass the time, she read for a while, but quickly became restless. She sat at her typewriter. Without thinking about it too much, she began typing up a diary of her experiences in Ippleford, from when she'd arrived at the Green Ginger, expecting to solve a case of sugar swapped for salt, to where she was now, embroiled in the investigation into a double murder.

Her words were perhaps not fit for newspaper publication, as she shared many of her own quite personal observations. The writing kept her busy, at least.

The first knock at the door came towards lunchtime.

In her grass-green topcoat, Katherine stood on the doorstep in the bright chilly air, a wicker basket on her arm. Zoe stood beside her, her little hand clasped in her aunt's, her wide, curious eyes blinking up at Felicity. Pip, who was in Felicity's arms, stretched his neck towards the basket and sniffed.

"Brought you something for lunch," said Katherine, handing over the basket. "May and I made currant buns. Nothing fancy, I'm afraid, but Zoe helped. Didn't you, darling?"

The little girl nodded shyly.

"Thank you," said Felicity, gladly accepting the basket. The warm fragrance of freshly baked buns was mouth-watering. "They smell glorious."

"Baking took our minds off things for a little while. They won't be as good as Vera's, of course," added Katherine, sadly.

On the high street beyond, passers-by cast curious gazes in their direction. Was Felicity's plan working? Were the rumours already spreading?

"How is everything?" From her eager tone, the sharing of buns was likely not Katherine's only reason for visiting the cottage. "With your plan, I mean?"

"It's a little too early to tell." Felicity was honest but also reticent. There'd been no report from either Alex or Lady Henrietta, but the plan wasn't to be shared with anyone else. Katherine and May weren't necessarily untrustworthy. Felicity simply knew for certain Alex and her grandmother could be relied upon in any sort of situation.

"Have you heard anything from your sister?" Felicity asked, moving the conversation on.

Katherine shook her head. "I went to the telephone box and called police headquarters, but they wouldn't let me speak to Vera. They said she was in good health and good spirits, all things considered." Katherine looked at the ground for a moment. "Well, we're all very grateful for your efforts, whatever they are, exactly." She tugged gently on her niece's hand. "Aren't we, Zoe?"

The little girl nodded slowly, but her attention was on Pip. The Yorkie licked his lips and continued to stare at the basket of baked goods.

Left alone with Pip and her typewriter, Felicity had a lunch comprising currant buns — which were lightly spiced and completely delicious — a juicy, slightly sour red-and-green apple, and a block of tangy, crumbly cheddar that had been stowed in the basket under the buns.

Felicity was still taking bites of lunch while working the typewriter with a single hand when there was another knock on the door.

Detective Inspector Daniels stood in the sunshine on the cottage's doorstep, a look of displeasure on his thinly moustached face. A short distance away, gazing up and down the quiet high street with watchful alertness, was Sergeant Hewitt. He looked even less happy than the detective.

Felicity swept Pip under her arm to prevent the Yorkie having a good sniff of the policeman's shoes, which would no doubt only displease him more. "Can I help you, Detective Inspector?"

The detective squinted at Felicity. "Is there anything you'd like to tell us, your ladyship?"

Felicity blinked. "Why, no. I don't believe so." It wasn't a lie. There was, as yet, nothing to share that would help the investigation. "Why do you ask?" she added innocently. Which of her two rumour-spreaders had got word to the investigating officers first?

The detective grunted with dissatisfaction. "We'd like to be sure, your ladyship," he said, unwilling to delve further into what must have appeared to be spurious gossip.

Was it dishonest to not inform the police of her ruse? In a sense, but as long as they didn't ask about it directly, then Felicity wasn't exactly lying.

"If the situation changes," she said, "I'll be certain to let you know." The plan wasn't entirely dishonest. It would have been utterly irresponsible to publish something of importance to the case before informing the police. "May I ask, if you're here, Detective Inspector, who's interviewing Mrs Monroe and Mr Carli?"

The suggestion of a smile passed under Detective Inspector Daniels' moustache. "Your friend Chief Inspector Luscombe is likely in an interview room with one of the suspects right now."

"Are they both under suspicion for the murders?" continued Felicity. "Do you believe Mrs Monroe and Mr Carli to have been working together?"

The barrage of questions prompted the detective to mumble excuses and vacate Felicity's doorstep. She returned to her typewriter and finished her lunch. With the sun slanting in through the cottage windows and Pip curled before the fire, it was oddly peaceful. To be taking action, albeit through Alex and Lady Henrietta, was satisfying.

Still, one crucial question remained. Would the ruse work?

---

Not long after lunch, there was another knock at the cottage door.

Alex was on the doorstep, grinning with satisfaction. "Story's spreading like wildfire. And I only had to tell one chap. Reporters are a gossipy lot."

"It's clearly doing the trick," said Felicity, trying not to sound too gleeful. "The police came by to speak to me."

Unusually, Pip didn't inspect Alex's shoes. He sat at Felicity's feet and whined. Felicity peered down at the Yorkie. "I quite understand. Perhaps Mr Cooper will take you for a walk?"

Pip gave a bark of agreement and wagged his tail.

Alex raised his eyebrows at the little dog. "Might your mistress do us the honour of accompanying us?"

"Very well," said Felicity. "But we must be careful. I don't want to be challenged for what I know when I in fact know nothing at all. It's lucky the police were so polite."

In the sunshine of the high street, the trees now quite bare of leaves because of the rain and wind, Felicity, Alex, and Pip quickly turned down a side street. The castle loomed above the thatched roofs. Even with the sun out, the ruins were no less ominous.

Pip trotted ahead, sniffing a rough, fern-strewn wall.

Alex put his hands in the pockets of his suit jacket. "It's not quite true to say you know nothing at all. Is it?"

"Suspecting is one thing. Knowing is quite something else." Felicity had learned this the hard way, on more than one occasion.

"You believe the guilty party to still be here in the village, do you not?"

"It's a possibility."

Alex went quiet for a moment. "By drawing the culprit into the open, what exactly do you have in mind?"

As they strolled past rows of back gardens, Felicity enjoyed the warmth of the sun on her shoulders. "The culprit, I believe, is impulsive. He or she used whatever was to hand for the murders. A blow to the head with an item found nearby. A shove at the top of the tower. There's some calculation, of course, like with the teapot handle in Mrs Monroe's bag—"

Alex raised his eyebrows. "Assuming she's innocent."

Felicity deliberately ignored the interruption. She didn't want to imagine Vera being sentenced to the gallows. "—but I wonder how much the guilty party will be able to control him- or herself in the face of our rumours."

They waited while Pip sniffed a tree, the little dog treading carefully through wet leaves still sodden from yesterday's downpour.

The sun made Alex's dark blond hair appear lighter, but uneasiness creased his scarred brow. "I know you don't enjoy being mollycoddled, but this scheme of yours rather puts you at risk, wouldn't you say?"

Felicity had already given the prospect some consideration. "I'll admit it's not entirely without risk."

Alex pushed his hands deeper into his pockets. "What if the murderer comes after you?"

Felicity nodded. "Then that person will expose themselves, and they will be caught and arrested."

Alex frowned. "And what if you get harmed in the process?"

Pip looked up, a paw lifted.

Felicity had considered this as well. Quite seriously, in fact. "Actually, there's something I was hoping to ask you."

# Chapter Thirty-One

It was towards dinner time, the light outside fading, when Lady Henrietta reported to Felicity at the cottage. Felicity had typed up a dozen pages of her story, Alex had returned diligently to his work following the police's enquiry, and Pip lay snoring by the fire.

"What a day," said Lady Henrietta, easing into one of the sitting room's high-backed chairs. "After the meeting at Gallica Cottage, we went across to Star Torrington and met with the Women's Association there. It transpired they needed advice on the management of rhododendrons. And as you're aware, my dear, I have much experience in that arena."

Felicity smiled politely. "Was there any opportunity to spread our rumour, or was the discussion focused solely on gardening advice?"

"I played my role," said the dowager a little haughtily. "Naturally, I did."

"Did you notice anyone paying particular attention to the information?"

"The women all found the story of your brilliance quite captivating, but the topic of the day was actually concern for the future of the tea rooms. That's extremely encouraging for poor Vera, of course, but there was an astonishing amount of interest in the chef's fate. Mr Carli, is it? A Swiss fellow, or so I've heard. Seems he's rather popular. An astonishingly accomplished *pâtissier*, by all accounts."

Felicity raised her eyebrows. How many women in the village were victims of his scheming? Did they even realise they'd been duped? "It wouldn't be at all surprising if Mr Carli had something to do with this whole mess."

Lady Henrietta sighed. "Well. The ladies of the Women's Association would be rather disappointed if that were the case."

Felicity would have liked to have witnessed the reactions of the Ippleford women, Mrs Waverley and her curious daughter, Mrs Biggs from the inn, Mrs Stanton from the post office. They would all be spreading the rumour. Felicity just had to wait.

The fire snapped in the grate. Pip rolled over, giving a small groan of satisfaction.

Felicity's grandmother watched the flames. "I do hope poor Vera is all right. I offered to visit her, but the solicitor said it's better to stay away for now."

Felicity was impressed. That the solicitor could persuade Lady Henrietta to adapt her plans confirmed he was highly skilled. "I'm sure Vera has all the advice and support she needs for now."

There was trepidation in the dowager's lavender-blue eyes. "What exactly do you hope will happen as a result of your ruse?"

Felicity looked towards the fire. She'd expected this question. "If the rumour reaches the culprit, I expect action will be taken. We'll have to see what happens in the morning."

"And if something happens sooner than that?"

"In the night, you mean?"

Lady Henrietta nodded.

"I've taken precautions."

Lady Henrietta let out a sigh. "Very well. I ought to be going. It won't do to have Jasper asking too many questions over dinner." Felicity's grandmother stood up from her chair. "What they say about the younger generation doesn't quite ring true for you, dear girl. You're selfless to a fault, rather like your mother. Just please remember how deeply your brother and I care for you."

"I will," said Felicity, her heart warmed by her grandmother's delicate way of expressing her concern but also her love. "Arrangements are in place."

---

It was completely dark outside when the gentle tap came on the kitchen door. The sound made Felicity's heart skip, even though she'd been expecting it. With the oil lamp turned down, she opened the door to find Alex standing in the darkness, his hat pulled low and his collar turned up, looking not unlike some sort of dashing secret agent.

As he stepped inside, he brought with him a surge of cool night air and the fresh scent of meadows he somehow always had about him. The tiny kitchen felt even smaller with Alex in it. There was no choice but to stand rather near to one another.

Felicity closed the door quietly. "Did anyone see you?"

Alex looked down at Pip as the little dog proceeded with a customary sniffing of his shoes. "I don't think so. It's not my first go at this." He smiled.

Was Alex referring to their time together in Lower Diddleton? Possibly. Perhaps he was recalling an occasion during the Great War when he'd crawled through the mud in the dark in fear for his life. He could choose to smile about it if he wanted to. It was less appropriate for Felicity to do so.

"Right," said Alex, removing his hat and shrugging out of his overcoat. "How do we go about this?"

"The most important thing is that you're not seen," said Felicity, lighting the stove for the kettle. Making her own refreshments had become a soothing and enjoyable ritual.

"The most important thing is that you come to no harm," corrected Alex. "If your ruse has roused the killer to the extent that they come looking for you tonight—"

"There's not only me to think about," said Felicity, frowning. "An innocent woman could be sent to the gallows."

Alex lifted his thick eyebrows in protest but said nothing. He continued to have his doubts about Vera, but now wasn't a time for arguments. There was a plan to execute.

"I'm here for your safety," he said. "That's all that matters tonight."

Felicity cleared her throat as she spooned tea leaves into a teapot. "I have a suggestion, but it's a little... Unusual."

Alex seemed amused. "I'm not sure what usual even is when it comes to working with you."

By now accustomed to Alex not taking her seriously, Felicity pressed on. "There's a large wardrobe in the bedroom. We can pad it out with pillows—"

"I'm sorry." Alex brought a hand to the back of his head. "A wardrobe?"

Felicity had had all day to consider the details. If the killer was to be drawn out of hiding and successfully apprehended, he or she would need to be caught in the act. It was risky, of course, but Felicity had been in risky situations before. She also knew Alex could be counted on.

"I shall go to bed as usual, and everything will seem quite ordinary," she explained as she poured steaming water into the pot, "except you'll be in the wardrobe, and you'll have the poker from the fire with you. I realise it won't be comfortable—"

Alex held up a hand. "I've spent nights in less comfortable situations than a wardrobe stuffed with pillows. However, I've not spent the night in the bedroom of an earl's sister before."

Felicity blinked. She'd been so obsessed with formulating the perfect plan, she'd apparently forgotten the rules of decency. A flush of embarrassment raced up her neck. "Forgive me. How silly of me. Um..." As the redness reached her cheeks, Felicity turned to fetch cups and a jug of milk. "You can spend the night in a chair in the sitting room instead."

"Now, wait. It's not my intention to scupper your plans. I'm just concerned about your honour. If word gets out I spent the night in your room..." Alex trailed off. Was there a flush in his cheeks, too?

Felicity tried to think rationally, but it was a struggle against the queer uneasiness her *faux pas* had created in the kitchen. Pip whined and stretched up on his hind legs to paw at the kitchen table, upon which a basket of food still lay.

"Well," began Felicity, willing her embarrassment to recede as she put some morsels of ham on a small plate for the Yorkie. "We're colleagues, are we not? That makes a difference, doesn't it?"

Alex smiled. "I can't admit to ever having shared a bedroom with a male colleague, either."

Felicity was feeling foolish. How could she not have anticipated this? She had clearly somehow become too comfortable with Alex. "Let's look at it another way." She took a deep breath. "If nothing happens overnight, then you'll sneak away unseen just before daylight. And if something happens, we can say you were passing the cottage to check on me."

It wasn't exactly a convincing argument for the wardrobe rather than the sitting room chair, but the awkwardness of the situation had to be dissolved somehow.

"It's not my reputation on the line here." Alex's dark blue eyes were sincere. "Whatever you're comfortable with, I'm fine with as well."

Felicity weighed up her reputation for a moment. The war had created a dearth of suitors. While life as a spinster would never be a goal in itself, it was a possibility one couldn't ignore. Even her grandmother had given up pestering about marriage.

She poured two cups of tea. "I'll fetch the extra pillows for the wardrobe."

---

Felicity and Alex enjoyed the pot of tea with the remaining currant buns, and after turfing Pip out of the make-shift bed in the wardrobe several times, Alex settled in position, the door ajar.

"I sincerely hope this is an unnecessary precaution," he mumbled as he pressed the heavy iron poker into the bank of pillows beside him.

Felicity slipped under the patchwork quilt on the single bed, still fully clothed with only her shoes and tweed jacket removed. As Pip jumped on her bed and curled by her ankles, Felicity turned down the oil lamp until the flame went out. A shaft of pale moonlight fell across the small bedroom where the curtains at the window weren't quite drawn. It put a silvery shine on the bedroom door's brass knob.

"Goodnight," whispered Felicity into the dark.

"Goodnight," said Alex softly. "Sweet dreams."

The sarcasm made Felicity smile as she stared at the ceiling, her stomach churning with turbulent excitement. Part of her hoped nothing would happen. Another part of her hoped their efforts would count for something. Either way, she was unlikely to sleep.

What was Alex thinking? Was he, like Felicity, torn in his hopes for the outcome? She dared not ask and break the tense silence of the tiny cottage bedroom. Whatever happened, there was no going back now.

## Chapter Thirty-Two

Pip growled quietly, his little chest rumbling at the bottom of the bed.

Had Felicity been asleep?

The strip of moonlight across the cottage bedroom had moved. It now fell upon the bedside table, where Felicity's notebook lay next to the oil lamp.

The Yorkie growled again, louder this time. Had Pip's growling woken her up? Was Alex awake too? Felicity blinked into the darkness. Where the wardrobe door had been ajar, it now seemed to be closed.

*Tap. Tap. Tap.*

There were footsteps on the sitting room floor.

Again, the little dog growled.

Perhaps Alex had got up to fetch himself a glass of water. He and Pip weren't exactly the best of friends, although it would be unusual for Pip to growl at him. It was unusual for Pip to growl at anyone.

The footsteps in the sitting room stopped. The knob on the bedroom door rattled.

Felicity's heart rate quickened. *Steady on*, she told herself. *It's likely Alex. In any case, he's here on watch. No matter what happens, you're safe.*

As the bedroom door opened, Pip's growling intensified.

Something wasn't quite right.

Felicity threw back the patchwork quilt, grabbed Pip, and jumped up so that the bed stood between her and whoever was coming through the bedroom door.

*Let it be Alex. Please, let it be Alex.*

The shadowy outline standing in the bedroom doorway was certainly not her colleague. It was time to face the consequences of her own ruse. The very worst of consequences.

The figure was that of a large-framed woman. She moved slowly, inching into the bedroom. The silvery moonlight highlighted curled hair and a fur-collared coat.

It was the inn's landlady, Mrs Biggs.

Was this the murderer drawn into the open?

Upon seeing the bed was empty, the landlady's gaze searched the darkness before settling on Felicity, who stood in the shadows on the other side of the bed, a still-growling Pip clasped to her chest.

Before Felicity could gather her wits and issue a challenge to the intruder, Mrs Biggs spoke first, holding up her hands.

"I know what this must look like, Lady Felicity, especially with everything that's happened. But I'm not here to hurt you. I'll be perfectly honest with you. I'm here for your notebook."

Felicity blinked and glanced at the wardrobe. At what point would Alex intervene? It was perhaps a mistake they hadn't discussed such details over tea and currant buns.

"My notebook?" enquired Felicity, unable to stop her eyes darting momentarily to where it lay on the bedside table.

"I heard the rumour, your ladyship. The one going through the whole village. Your own grandmother — a remarkable woman, I must say, having met her only for the first time today — she was boasting to the Women's Association ladies that you'd cracked the case. Said you've solved murders before and that you know who it was killed Mrs Prudence Norrington and that poor little waitress."

It was an odd moment to feel pride for Lady Henrietta, but Felicity felt it regardless. The dowager had done her work well.

Felicity stood a little straighter. "The rumour may well be true. However, I still don't see what you want with my notebook, and, dare I say, how you explain such a brazen move as breaking into my cottage in the middle of the night to retrieve it. I believe I locked both doors. That's hardly an invitation to come in."

There was a shade of outrage in Felicity's tone, but she was careful not to overdo it. She was curious to hear what Mrs Biggs would say and would take no unnecessary risks until she knew Alex was alert. He was hopefully not a deep sleeper.

"Oh, your ladyship, you're right. It's bad of me, I know." Mrs Biggs spoke as though she and Felicity had just happened upon one another on the high street. "I didn't break anything. Cottage door latches are so easy to meddle with once you know how. But my thinking was: why wait? If you know who it is, let's get it out in the open and have the whole gruesome matter resolved."

"If you wanted to know the results of my deductions," asked Felicity warily, "why not knock on the cottage door and ask me? Why come here in the middle of the night like... Like... Some kind of criminal?"

Although breaking into the cottage was extremely unorthodox, the landlady hadn't yet said or done anything to incriminate herself directly in the murders of Mrs Norrington or Frances. Might Felicity be able to prompt a useful reaction from Mrs Biggs before Alex stepped in? Which he, at some point, really ought to.

"Oh, your ladyship." Mrs Biggs chuckled softly. "If I'd knocked on your door after supper and asked you who the murderer was, you wouldn't have told me, would you?"

The landlady was right. It would rather have spoiled the ruse to dish out what she knew to anyone who asked. There was also the fact Felicity didn't actually know who the murderer was, although she was beginning to have a strong idea.

Pip renewed his growling with gusto.

"How do you imagine this looks, Mrs Biggs? Creeping around in the dead of night, fiddling with door latches. When the police hear about this—"

"I'm not the only one, though, am I?" The landlady's interruption was rather sharp.

"Well." Felicity's heart pounded. Did the landlady know Alex was waiting in the wardrobe? "Who else is there?"

"Prudence Norrington wasn't at home when they found her, was she? Nor was Frances Lee."

"You're quite right, Mrs Biggs. And Mrs Norrington and Frances Lee both died in rather violent circumstances. I would therefore recommend you return home forthwith." Felicity sighed loudly, as though bored. "I shall make my announcement tomorrow, so you'll have the information you seek then."

Mrs Biggs' hands went to her broad hips. "What if I can't wait till then?" she said with a hint of menace.

"Well," said Felicity, quickly changing course. "As long as you promise not to tell anyone else ahead of my announcement."

"Oh, I won't," said Mrs Biggs, the charm almost entirely dropped from her manner.

Felicity took a risk. "It was Mr Carli."

"Luca?" spat the landlady. "He was in London the night Mrs Norrington died. How could it have been him?"

"Oh, no," corrected Felicity. "That was Miss Lee. She did away with Mrs Norrington. Then Mr Carli did away with Miss Lee. Do you see? Some kind of quarrel arising from affairs of the heart, as I understand it."

"Affairs of the heart?" Mrs Biggs' voice was raised. "Affairs of the..." She snorted. "I've not heard anything so ridiculous in all my life. They weren't lovers."

Felicity drew a steadying breath. Mrs Biggs' emotions were high. Alex could surely not be sleeping through this, could he? Yet Felicity wanted to hear more.

"Oh, is that so?" she said with an air of nonchalance. "And how might you know that? Mr Carli certainly had interests in multiple women. That's an undisputed fact."

"Multiple women?" spat Mrs Biggs. "I came down here expecting you had the answers, and you're spouting this tommyrot at me?"

It had taken little to anger Mrs Biggs. The situation was on the edge of danger, but Felicity needed more. "I fail to see what about my deductions could be classed as tommyrot, Mrs Biggs."

"Luca wasn't interested in that little rat of a waitress," thundered the landlady. "She thought she was so special, getting that role in the play. She was a dirty little blackmailer, and she deserved what she got."

Blackmail. There it was. It had cost Frances her life, but the pieces were coming together.

"And Prudence?" Mrs Biggs let out a laugh. "Where to start with Prudence?"

Felicity gripped Pip tightly as he continued to growl. "My understanding," she said carefully, "is that Mrs Norrington and Mr Carli were involved in some kind of tryst. Do I not have that correct, then?"

"A tryst? Where the blazes did you get that from? Luca wasn't interested in that shrivelled old shrew."

"Who was he interested in, then?" Felicity posed the question innocently, but she was already shuddering in anticipation of the dreadful reply.

"Me," confirmed Mrs Biggs. "Luca has eyes only for me. He and I have plans. Just you wait and see. He's extremely talented, and I'll see to it he goes places. Not just some silly little tea rooms or even the old inn. No. He's worth more than that."

Felicity took a deep breath. Alex was welcome to interrupt at any moment, and she prayed silently that he would do just that. Still, not everything had been explained.

"I appreciate your telling me this, Mrs Biggs," said Felicity. "Clearly, I got a few of my facts wrong, and I'm now left wondering about Miss Lee. Would it be correct to assume you were the subject of her blackmail?"

"Why you—" The landlady snatched up the oil lamp from the bedside table. "I've had enough of you."

As Mrs Biggs hurled the lamp across the bed, the doors to the wardrobe flew open.

# Chapter Thirty-Three

Dawn arrived slowly, the golden light bringing with it another clear-skied chilly day. Felicity stood on the doorstep of the cottage with a blanket around the shoulders of her tweed jacket, watching the pale-yellow sunshine spread behind the castle ruins on the hill, her breath visible in white, the rose hips swaying on their trellis in the breeze.

She was still a little unsteady on her feet, but despite the hubbub of police, journalists, and curious onlookers around her, Felicity was at peace.

Inside the cottage, officers were still gathering evidence from Mrs Biggs' break-in and subsequent flight. They'd captured her near Star Torrington station, presumably intending to take the first train to Exeter and onto who knows where after that.

Now in custody, the landlady admitted nothing, denying even having been in Felicity's cottage, so the police were careful to collect as much evidence as possible, taking fingerprints from the shattered fragments of the lamp Mrs Biggs had thrown at the wall just above where Felicity had ducked, curling her body over Pip to protect him.

Alex had charged out of the wardrobe as the lamp had gone flying. Stunned by the ambush, Mrs Biggs took flight, but Alex didn't chase her.

First, he checked on Felicity — she was quite shaken but not harmed — then he dashed to alert the police staying at the inn, and they quickly mounted a search, pursuing Mrs Biggs down lanes and across fields until finally she was caught.

Katherine approached from the direction of the tea rooms, her stylish grass-green topcoat a contrast to the humble tray she carried, upon which wobbled a teapot complete with a woollen cosy, a jug of milk, and a teacup and saucer.

"Thought you might appreciate a hot drink."

"How incredibly kind," said Felicity, as Katherine balanced the tray on a nearby plant pot and poured out a steaming cup.

"It's the least I can do." Katherine looked fresh-faced and hopeful. After handing Felicity her tea, something caught her eye, and she waved.

May and Zoe were returning along the high street from a walk to the churchyard with Pip. The little Yorkie behaved as though nothing had happened, but Felicity had had to hold him tightly to prevent him from chasing after Mrs Biggs when she took flight. He'd been awfully brave.

Zoe was skipping and tugging on May's hand. Even May smiled in greeting Felicity.

The investigation wasn't over yet. The police were questioning Mrs Biggs, and Luca was still in custody. Exactly why two women had been murdered in Ippleford had yet to be fully explained. But Vera was no longer a suspect in the case. She was on her way home.

Felicity smiled as May and Zoe approached. She hadn't the energy to raise a hand and wave. She was so tired she hadn't argued when Detective Inspector Daniels and Sergeant Hewitt accused her of recklessness. The risks had been clear, the appropriate precautions had been in place, and the outcome was rather satisfactory. What more was there to say on the matter?

Alex had wriggled free from the police's questions and hastened to his typewriter at the inn, even though the Blue Lady was something of a crime scene now, with Mr Biggs also taken in for questioning and the Biggs' living quarters being searched. An exclusive account of the night's events would be delivered for the early edition of the Western Morning News, which would no doubt send circulation figures through the roof.

Felicity had offered to help write the story. Alex had insisted she rested, and Felicity didn't have the energy to object. She was doing her bit by being there for Vera's family as they awaited the tea rooms' owner's return.

Katherine hugged Zoe tightly. "There you are, my precious girl. Your mummy shall be here soon. What do you think about that?"

The sun glinting in her bright blonde hair, Zoe went shy, eyeing Felicity with a timid smile. It was obvious the little girl couldn't wait to be reunited with her mother.

"We can't thank you enough, your ladyship," said May, her eyes bright and her once-sallow cheeks flushed pink from the cold. "It's wonderful Mrs Monroe is coming back to us. And perhaps Mr Carli will be back soon, too."

A flicker of disgust passed over Katherine's face. "Now, May, I wouldn't be too sure of that. The police have plenty to discuss with Luca. What do you think, Lady Felicity?"

Whether the patisserie chef had been directly involved in the deaths of Frances and Mrs Norrington wasn't yet evident. What was clear, however, was that Luca was a manipulator with an interest in money and there had been — and still were — women in Ippleford susceptible to his charms.

"I think we'd best wait for the police to inform us of their findings," said Felicity between sips of hot, reviving tea.

The women stood aside as Sergeant Hewitt exited the cottage with two uniformed police officers carrying boxes of items tagged with labels. As the sergeant passed Felicity, he gave her an uneasy look, somewhere between dislike and begrudging respect. "Your ladyship." He touched his policeman's helmet.

"Sergeant," replied Felicity, with no hint of gloating.

The familiar purr of the Quick family's Rolls approached.

Onlookers stepped aside as the elegant motor came gently to a stop before the cottage. Finnegan held the door open for Lady Henrietta as she alighted, pressing the point of a folded black umbrella into the ground to steady herself.

To Felicity's relief, there was no sign of Jasper. She hadn't yet the energy to deal with her brother.

"Where is she?" said Lady Henrietta, looking about her. "Where is my dear Vera?"

As soon as the post office opened, Felicity had sent a telegram to Bradley Court, sparsely relaying the developments in the Ippleford case, including the police's decision to release Vera.

"She's on her way to us, your ladyship," said May, a big grin on her face.

"Thanks to your granddaughter," added Katherine, hugging Zoe to her side.

"Do you know," said Lady Henrietta a little haughtily, approaching the cottage with a swing of her folded umbrella, "I never had a doubt in my mind. I knew my Felicity would get to the bottom of things. She always does. Her father — my son, the late Earl of Denbury — was a newspaperman, just like his father before him. Naturally, it fell to Felicity's brother to oversee the business, but Felicity inherited her fair share of sharpness of intellect."

Felicity smiled. Lady Henrietta had come a long way in her acceptance of Felicity's career choices.

"Then of course there's the natural talents of her mother, who was incredibly astute when it came to people. Very emotionally sensitive." Lady Henrietta looked proudly at Felicity. "With such a combination, you have a rather formidable sleuth on your hands, I would say. It's no wonder the police can't keep up with her."

Katherine, May, and Zoe looked at Felicity in slack-jawed awe. It was heart-warming but also a trifle embarrassing.

Felicity raised her eyebrows. "I'm a reporter, Grandmama. Not a detective."

The comment went almost unheard as a familiar figure appeared on the high street. Zoe dashed away from Katherine's side.

"Mummy!"

"Oh, my darling." Vera pulled the little girl into a strong, warm hug. "I'm so sorry I left you on your own."

"I wasn't alone," said Zoe, a huge smile on her face. "Aunt Katherine and Auntie May were with me. And Mr Pip." She pointed at the Yorkie, who had indeed spent the entire morning being rather attentive towards the little girl, watching her even as he snuffled around the front of the cottage.

Vera approached Felicity. She looked fatigued, but the sparkle in her cornflower-blue eyes was back. "I can't thank you enough, my lady." She looked at Felicity's grandmother. "And Lady Henrietta, of course."

"Not at all, Vera, not at all." The dowager waved a dismissive hand. "One should be able to depend on one's friends, even in the most desperate of situations."

Felicity didn't mind her grandmother taking control of the conversation. Without Lady Henrietta's influence, Felicity would never have come to Ippleford, and despite feeling extraordinarily tired, Felicity's mind still hummed with perplexities. At the root of the mystery was the sabotage of the tea rooms. If Mrs Norrington had been the guilty party, what had been her motive?

A low growl from Pip snapped Felicity out of her thoughts.

Tall, wiry, and full of purpose, Mr Viner strode towards the cottage, his red Border Collie at his side, his angry stare fixed on Vera.

"I do beg your pardon—" began Lady Henrietta, ready to accost the gardener before he'd even spoken.

"It's all right, my lady," said Vera gently, and she stepped forward to meet Mr Viner.

"You're back, are you?" The gardener towered over Vera, his dog coming to a stop at his side.

Vera hadn't an ounce of fear. "Thanks to Lady Felicity, I am, yes."

The gardener glanced at Felicity in a manner full of suspicion. However, given Mr Viner's rather limited range of expression, the glance could equally have been an acknowledgement of gratitude.

"I should have done a better job of protecting you," said Mr Viner. "I shan't let anything happen to you again."

Vera sighed. "Lewis," she whispered. "We've been through this before."

"Mrs Monroe. Mrs Monroe!"

It was Mrs Waverley from Rose Cottages, waving her walking stick in the air to attract Vera's attention. With her was her daughter in her misshapen tweeds, her face sourer than usual. Miss Waverley eyed Mr Viner and Vera as she and her mother drew closer to the cottage, busy policemen stepping aside as Mrs Waverley's advance was, despite her diminutive size, as unstoppable as that of a tank.

Mr Viner straightened his back and kept a watchful eye on Vera.

"Mrs Waverley," said Vera politely but with an edge of fatigue. "I can only apologise that the tea rooms aren't yet reopened. We'll be rectifying the situation as soon as possible."

"Oh, it's not that," said Mrs Waverley, fluttering her hand in a banishing motion. "It's not that at all. We heard the news. We heard about everything that happened. And I'm afraid my daughter has something to say to you."

An uncertain silence fell upon the gathering outside the cottage.

Mrs Waverley gestured for Miss Waverley to step forward. "Go ahead, Millicent. Tell it just as you told me. You've kept things to yourself for long enough, and it has helped no one."

Miss Waverley scowled, deeply uncomfortable. She advanced reluctantly towards Vera. "I'm sorry," she mumbled.

Vera looked at Miss Waverley, then at the woman's mother. "I don't quite follow."

*I do*, thought Felicity.

"The sabotage at the Green Ginger," said Miss Waverley. "It was stupid and spiteful. I didn't see that at the time. I hope you'll forgive me, but I perhaps don't deserve it."

Vera's mouth fell open. Lady Henrietta looked stunned.

"You?" said Katherine in disbelief.

"Have you informed the police that you were in the tea rooms the night Mrs Norrington died?" enquired Felicity calmly.

Miss Waverley's wide and frightened eyes snapped to Felicity. "But I didn't see her. I didn't see anyone else. I didn't kill anyone. And I stopped after she... After she..." Miss Waverley looked at her mother.

"I will not tell it for you, Millicent." Mrs Waverley shook her head. "Although I suppose I must blame myself. They warned me you weren't completely well when I took you home from the hospital."

Miss Waverley looked back at Vera. "I'm sorry. I really am so awfully sorry." She gazed up at Mr Viner. Tears rolled down her gaunt cheeks.

"My goodness," said Lady Henrietta, fanning herself with a gloved hand.

Detective Inspector Daniels had been approaching the cottage but stopped a short distance away. He'd heard Miss Waverley's confession.

Vera looked shaken.

"Why'd you do it?" The question was Mr Viner's.

Miss Waverley blinked back her tears. "I was jealous. I was angry. You followed her around like a dog, and she never treated you well. She kept you hanging on, always pushing you away. You deserve to be treated better than that."

Vera's face creased with disbelief. Mr Viner took a step backwards. Evidently, neither of them had been aware someone had been paying such close attention to their fraught interactions.

The Collie twitched his ears and let out a quiet whine.

Detective Inspector Daniels stepped forward. "Are you ready to come with me, Miss Waverley?"

Miss Waverley looked at Mr Viner. "I'm sorry." And then to Vera. "I am truly sorry."

"Come now, Millie," said Mrs Waverley. "Perhaps we can get you the help you actually need."

Accompanied by the detective and a uniformed police officer, Miss Waverley and her mother began moving towards the church hall, where the work of the police continued in full swing.

Mr Viner and Vera looked awkwardly at one another.

"At least the mystery of the sabotage is now solved," said Felicity, gripping her teacup to warm her hands. "I'm only sorry I wasn't able to solve it for you."

"Please, my lady," said Vera. "Don't apologise. If the sabotage and the murders are as unrelated as Miss Waverley says, then I'm glad her actions brought you to our village. Otherwise, I might still be under suspicion."

Accepting compliments wasn't Felicity's strong point. "I'm certain the police would have arrived at the correct conclusions eventually."

"What about a cooked breakfast at the tea rooms?" Katherine looked at May and Vera.

Zoe nodded enthusiastically. "Can Mr Pip come, too?"

The little Yorkie was already sitting to attention. His ability to understand words like *breakfast* was astonishing when basic commands like *sit* and *heel* never caught his attention.

"Will you be joining us, Mr Viner?" enquired Katherine, blinking innocently.

Mr Viner looked at Vera. Beyond his grim frown was a questioning look.

Vera nodded. "If you'd like to, Mr Viner, you're more than welcome."

"Lady Henrietta and Lady Felicity?" enquired Katherine.

But it was time for another interruption.

Alex came jogging up the high street. His energy and stamina were awe-inspiring.

Felicity had initially been mildly aggrieved by how long it had taken him to emerge from the wardrobe. When she'd learned he'd been alert and waiting for precisely the right moment, knowing that Felicity would have been even more vexed had he revealed his presence too quickly, she had melted with gratitude towards him.

"Awfully sorry to interrupt," Alex said a little breathlessly, "but I was about to telephone in our story when I heard you'd returned, Mrs Monroe. Could I get a short quote from you? We can do a thorough interview later, when you're ready for it."

"It's the very least I can do for you, Mr Cooper." Vera looked enquiringly at Felicity. "But there's another element to the story now, isn't there? As we just heard from Miss Waverley."

Felicity stood up straighter. "Yes, of course. The mystery of the sabotage has been solved. It's... It's..." She sneezed in such a tremendous and uncontrollable fashion that she spilt some of her tea.

"It's time for us to return to Bradley Court," filled in Lady Henrietta. "Mr Cooper, considering all you've done, I'm sure Vera and Mr Viner won't mind relaying to you what they heard just now about the identity of our saboteur. I shall return forthwith to Lower Diddleton with my granddaughter, who, as I'm sure you're all aware by now, is well on her way to getting a cold, if not something worse."

"I'm fine, Grandmama, really, I—" Felicity sneezed again. She was fooling no one, including herself. She was, indeed, ill.

Allowing herself to be guided by Lady Henrietta to the Rolls, Felicity was showered with praise and thanks from Vera, Katherine, May, and even little Zoe. Mr Viner nodded at Felicity, which was by far the friendliest gesture she'd received from him so far.

After fetching a checked blanket to cover her knees, Finnegan lifted Pip onto Felicity's lap. It felt unusually good to be sitting down.

Alex came to the motor's window wearing a commiserating yet slightly amused smile. "Thanks for another adventure. And another scoop."

"Do you not need my help to finish the article?" Felicity said, but her voice was weak.

"Listen to your grandmother." Alex's tone was stern. "You need to rest."

"But I heard Miss Waverley's confession, word for word. Might I just write up that part?"

Lady Henrietta joined Felicity in the back of the Rolls. She tapped the back of her granddaughter's hand. "It's time to get you home, dear."

"This won't be our last chance to work together," said Alex. "Far from it."

Finnegan climbed into the driver's seat.

"We're a good team, aren't we?" Sitting down made Felicity feel drowsy. She was perhaps saying things she wouldn't normally have done.

"Yes," said Alex. "We jolly well are."

The Rolls glided up the hill beside the castle, and Felicity watched as everyone waved.

## Chapter Thirty-Four

### MANY WEEKS LATER...

The scone was the perfect balance of melt-in-the-mouth and crumbly, the clotted cream was deliciously unctuous, and the warming ginger jam was a most wonderful foil.

"I don't think I've ever had a better cream tea in my life," said Felicity, allowing a few crumbs to fall 'accidentally' towards Pip, who was seated, as usual, on her lap.

"Nor in mine," agreed Lady Henrietta, dusting her fingertips on a bright white napkin. "And it's been a long life, as I'm sure you're aware, my dear."

Felicity and Lady Henrietta were sitting at the same table as when Felicity had first arrived in Ippleford to investigate a case of sabotage. Time had flown by, and it was now January, which usually meant awful weather and a distinct lack of tourists. Yet the tables at the Green Ginger were full.

Vera approached with a beaming smile. Her cheeks glowed pink, and her hair shone like gold. "Lady Henrietta, Lady Felicity. I'm so sorry I couldn't welcome you properly when you arrived. We're so busy, it's quite unexpected, but I can't tell you how happy I am to see you both. Is everything all right with your cream teas?"

"Absolutely splendid, Vera, my dear," gushed Lady Henrietta.

"And no need to apologise. We're thrilled to see you so busy and simply delighted you invited us."

"It's the very least I could do, my lady," said Vera with a faint curtsey, an echo of the employer-servant relationship that was still so dear to the two women. "How was your break, Lady Felicity? Are you back to good health?"

After leaving Ippleford, Felicity had come down with a terrible cold, owing no doubt to the time she'd spent wearing damp tweeds in the rain. Her cold had developed into a rather nasty cough, and owing to her family's experience with Spanish flu, which had been the tragic and unexpected cause of Felicity's father's death just a few years earlier, no chances were taken. The family doctor ordered full rest until she was completely recovered.

While Felicity regained her energy and appetite quickly, her cough had been rather persistent, which meant Christmas had been a cosy affair spent entirely at Bradley Court. The family home was also where they saw in 1922 in a quiet, firework-less fashion. The height of the season's excitement had been a light sprinkling of snow on New Year's Day, which melted rapidly in the sun.

"I'm back to full strength, thank you, Vera," said Felicity with a faltering smile, for while it was rather marvellous to venture further afield than Lower Diddleton again, she had reason to be nervous.

"Will Mr Cooper be here soon?" Vera squinted out of the window at Ippleford's high street. "We're looking forward to giving him the royal treatment as well, of course."

The last time Felicity had seen Alex was the last time she'd been in Ippleford.

Naturally, Alex had continued to work while Felicity rested. She kept up with his exploits through her daily reading of the Western Daily News. He'd clearly been given permission to report on whatever he chose in her absence and had scored many scoops and countless front-page headlines in doing so.

While Felicity and Alex had been through much together, it was doubtful he'd want to return to working as a team. That made the prospect of being reunited with him rather fraught. On one hand, it would be splendid to see him again. On the other, it would likely be the occasion to wish one another well and say cheerio, for other than their work together for the Western Daily News, they had no reason to spend time together.

Felicity put on a brave face. "I'm sure he'll—"

*Bang!*

Everyone in the tea rooms jumped at the noise.

Mr Viner had slammed a tray of tea cakes onto the cake counter in a rather ungraceful manner. He grunted — which was perhaps his way of apologising — then disappeared through the kitchen's glossy green swing doors.

Immediately, Katherine pushed through the same doors, an apron around her waist, looking hot and bothered and sprinkled with flour. Zoe quickly appeared at her side, also dusted with flour.

Katherine put a hand on her niece's shoulder. "We're ever so sorry," she announced to the tea rooms. "I'd like to say it won't happen again," she added quietly to her niece, who had spotted Felicity and Lady Henrietta and was waving at them. Katherine smiled and waved too, before she and Zoe disappeared back through the swing doors.

It was a charming vision of family togetherness. "Are you training your daughter to take over the tea rooms?" enquired Felicity with a smile.

"I never force her, my lady," said Vera. "But she loves baking with her Aunt Kathy. It's a struggle to keep the two of them out of the kitchen."

"Are you still in need of staff?" asked Lady Henrietta.

"Yes, my lady. I'm being more careful about the selection this time, of course. I'm thankful my sister has decided to stay in Ippleford, and Lewis is doing whatever he can, although he refuses to work with the customers directly."

*Sensible chap, Mr Viner,* thought Felicity. *Clearly aware of the limits of his capabilities.*

"There are also his duties up at the castle," added Vera with a hint of pride.

"Oh, yes," said Lady Henrietta, her eyes sparkling. "The ruins have been acquired by one of those government agencies responsible for preserving our nation's heritage, have they not?"

Vera gave a satisfied smile and nodded. "Lewis is responsible for the upkeep, making sure the paths are safe and that sort of thing." Her relationship with the gardener had improved since Felicity was last in Ippleford. "Zoe often accompanies him on his walks up there. She adores that handsome dog of his. And he always makes sure there's a bunch of flowers for poor Frances up there. I realise not everything she did was right, but none of us are perfect."

May approached the table, looking extremely neat and standing taller than ever in her crisp black-and-white maid's uniform. "I'm so sorry to interrupt. How lovely to see you again, Lady Henrietta and Lady Felicity." She spoke somewhat formally and added a curtsey, but her shyness seemed to have left her.

"A pleasure to see you too, Miss Pettigrew," said Lady Henrietta. "Are you well?"

"I am, yes, thank you, your ladyship. We're very busy, especially with the inn still closed, but we should have some new girls soon, and I'll be the one to train them." May glowed with self-confidence.

"How wonderful," said Felicity. May's progress was genuinely pleasing.

The waitress looked at Vera. "If I may ask you something about the tea cakes, Mrs Monroe."

"Certainly," said Vera. "Please excuse me," she said to Felicity and Lady Henrietta. "I'll be back over as soon as I can."

Felicity and her grandmother had barely topped up their teas and taken another bite of their scones before they were again interrupted.

Ernestine and Philip Heard had spotted Felicity in the tea rooms' window and come in from the high street, the bell above the door tinkling.

The actors were in high spirits, with plans for a new, much lighter play. Lady Henrietta smiled politely and listened intently, but Felicity could tell her grandmother didn't give a fig about local theatre productions and was rather keen to continue enjoying her scones.

"We've decided to stay away from the old legends," said Ernestine. "I still feel we stirred things up by dragging out those old stories and traipsing around the castle."

Philip adjusted his spectacles. "Ernie. Please."

"It's how I feel, Philip. I can't help how I feel."

"Any news on Colonel Norrington?" interjected Felicity.

"Sold up," said Philip. "Gone to live with his nephew on the Isle of Wight. Breeds Dachshunds, apparently, so even that poor little dog should have a happier time of it. And would you believe? A pair of musicians have bought his cottage."

Felicity spared a thought for Doctor Grant and his desire for nothing but a quiet life.

"We're considering a musical for the summer," added Ernestine, bubbling with enthusiasm. "We do so hope that the Western Daily News will be there to review it."

"I'm certain someone from the newspaper will attend," reassured Felicity, although she wasn't sure it would be her. "Any news on the Waverleys?"

"Miss Waverley's at a sanatorium in the Cotswolds," said Philip. "Her mother is still at the cottage and still busy with Women's Association affairs, although her garden isn't looking half as attractive since her daughter left."

"I do hope Millicent gets the help she needs," said Ernestine with a sigh. "I realise sabotaging the tea rooms wasn't right, but nervous conditions can be so tricky."

"Am I interrupting?"

Felicity hadn't noticed Alex's approach. Her heart gave a little leap.

## Chapter Thirty-Five

Two months hadn't been enough to change him. Alex had the same swept back dark blond hair, the same calm blue eyes, and the same faintly amused smile as when Felicity had seen him last.

As the Heards said their goodbyes and left the tea rooms, Pip eyed Alex and sniffed the fresh, cool scent he'd brought inside with him.

Alex took off his hat and shrugged out of his coat. "Terribly sorry I'm so late."

Lady Henrietta waved a hand. "Please, my boy, don't mention it. I only hope you don't mind that we started without you." She gestured to the cream teas on the table.

"Certainly not," said Alex, taking a seat. "It's no excuse for my tardiness, but I was just with Judge Hawkins."

"You finally got to meet him." Felicity smiled wistfully. The original plan had been to interview him together, but that was now ancient history.

"I can't say it was the most thrilling encounter of my career." Alex picked up a menu without really looking at it. "But it seems I'll be working closely with the courts from now on." It was quite the achievement, and Alex was playing it down, most likely for Felicity's benefit.

"I'm happy for you," she said, and she meant it.

May approached the table to take Alex's order. At the waitress' recommendation, he ordered a slice of Devon apple cake and a pot of Ceylon.

"I must say, I'm rather pleased that Swiss fellow's gone," said Lady Henrietta. "Awful how he conned those poor women out of their savings. It's more fitting that Vera focuses on local delicacies."

Eventually, Luca admitted to the police he'd been collecting what he called 'investments in his career'. The money had apparently been given to him freely by women around Ippleford, including by Mrs Norrington and Mrs Biggs. The patisserie chef had told them he was saving to start his own business. There was, however, little evidence of any business plan.

When captured at Exeter's main train station, Luca had his tips box with him. It was stuffed with bank notes totalling a sizeable sum of money. He'd encouraged his female admirers to leave their 'investments' in there for him.

Alex frowned. "I never got to try the fellow's cakes, but I gather the whole thing was rather a sordid affair."

Some of Luca's admirers would sneak into the tea rooms after opening hours to leave money without being seen as they tried to outdo one another, each of the women believing herself to have a special relationship with the chef. Jealousy over Luca's attentions had ostensibly triggered the deadly events that began at the tea rooms.

Although her account of the night remained inconsistent, it seemed Mrs Biggs had ended Mrs Norrington's life in a fit of envious rage when the two of them happened upon one another attempting to leave love notes and money for Luca at the tea rooms.

Mrs Norrington's murder had nothing to do with the acts of sabotage carried out by Miss Waverley, although jealousy was at the root there, too. She'd wished to punish Vera for her perceived mistreatment of Mr Viner, a man Miss Waverley herself very much admired.

The overlap of the two affairs was uncanny. It was also utterly bizarre what people would do for love. Or what they believed to be love.

"The treacherous fellow had tried it all before, of course." Lady Henrietta sniffed. "I shall ensure Vera is much more circumspect when next hiring staff."

With both Mrs Biggs and Luca refusing to tell the full story — and with no other women from the village coming forward to talk about the patisserie chef's scheme, most likely out of shame at having been duped — it had been difficult for the police to piece everything together. Things had fallen into place when detectives from Switzerland came to Devon.

Apparently, Luca had tried much the same system in his home country. Rather than becoming rivals, the women there came together to report the patisserie chef to the police, at which point he fled for England.

Felicity stroked Pip. She had, of course, read all the details of the case in the Western Daily News. Alex had been the chief reporter and had done an excellent job of writing up the twists and complications.

Lady Henrietta had also become a dedicated newspaper reader. "Mr Cooper, I've been wanting to ask you something. I'm interested in your opinion on Mr Biggs."

"The landlord?" Alex rubbed his jaw. "Well, he admitted to giving the false alibi for his wife the night of Mrs Norrington's death, which he said he did on his wife's advice. Beyond that, there's no proof of any wrongdoing. I believe he was in the dark about his wife's obsession with Carli. He even told the police how Mrs Biggs talked about leaving the inn and going to do something else. It started the day Mrs Norrington was found murdered. She was quite pushy about the idea, apparently. Mr Biggs was even warming to it. He says he still hadn't made the link himself."

Lady Henrietta's eyes sparkled. "If my dear granddaughter hadn't set up her ruse, that awful Mrs Biggs might have escaped?"

Alex smiled with satisfaction at Felicity. "The account Mrs Biggs gave to Felicity is expected to play an important role in getting a conviction for the murder of Frances Lee. As you know, the landlady's been rather tight-lipped while in custody."

Mrs Biggs' connection to the death of Mrs Norrington had been confirmed thanks to a single fingerprint found on the teapot handle — which was, of course, completely clear of Vera's prints — and a blood-spattered teal dress found at the inn, which Mrs Biggs had tried to insist was from working with sausage meat in the Blue Lady's kitchen.

For Frances' murder, the evidence against Mrs Biggs was less clear cut. There were boot prints at the castle that matched a pair of wellingtons belonging to Mrs Biggs, but it wasn't strong enough, especially as Mrs Biggs had, like most ladies in Ippleford's Women's Association, spent some time supporting the play.

"I believe we can be extremely proud of our dear Felicity." Lady Henrietta tapped her granddaughter's hand.

Felicity smiled, but she didn't feel particularly proud.

From what Mrs Biggs had told Felicity, Frances knew or at least suspected Mrs Biggs' involvement in the murder and had attempted to blackmail her. Exactly what Frances knew and how she found out wasn't clear, nor were the details of their fateful meeting at the castle.

Felicity would give evidence when the case came to trial, but while Mrs Biggs' fate was sealed concerning the death of Mrs Norrington, a conviction for Frances' wasn't guaranteed.

The whole situation was deeply tragic. Had Frances gone to the police with what she knew instead of to the murderess, she might still have been alive.

Felicity stroked Pip's silky back. "As long as Mrs Biggs refuses to talk to the police, the details will never be fully clear."

Alex raised his eyebrows. "They'd be even less clear if you hadn't set your trap and got her talking."

"I couldn't have done it without you." A note of sadness crept into Felicity's voice, and she silently chastised herself for being melodramatic.

"Speaking of working together, and now that Felicity is feeling a good deal better…" Lady Henrietta looked enquiringly from Felicity to Alex. "Have you chosen your next case?"

Felicity was grateful for how far her grandmother had come in acknowledging her work as a reporter. Lady Henrietta's trust in her powers as a sleuth was, however, less convincing. And she certainly had one thing wrong.

"I'm afraid, Grandmama, that Alex and I are a team no longer."

Alex looked confused. "Why ever not?"

Felicity returned a look of confusion. Was it not obvious to him as well? "You've proved to Jasper you can cover crime stories without me."

Alex almost laughed. "Were my abilities as a reporter ever in question?"

"I'll have you know," began Lady Henrietta, a little aloofly, "Jasper has frequently remarked that you're a perfect team. It's the combination of your approaches. Mr Cooper's methodical detail and hard questioning, and Felicity's emotional connection with the people at the heart of the story. You've won the paper a vast number of new readers." The dowager gave a little cough and raised her thin, grey eyebrows. "But I'm not talking about newspaper business."

Felicity and Alex exchanged looks of bewilderment.

"If you don't mind me asking, your ladyship," began Alex, "just what is it you're talking about exactly?"

"Telegram for Quick!" A young messenger boy came dashing into the tea rooms, his cap in one hand and a folded paper in the other.

Felicity waved a hand in the boy's direction. "Over here, please." It wasn't unusual for Jasper to receive telegrams wherever he was, but for the Quick ladies it was rare. "Are you expecting news, Grandmama?"

"Thank you, young man," said Lady Henrietta, slipping a coin into the boy's fist as she took the paper from him. "Let's see." She fished a pince-nez out of the pouch on her lap. "Aha." Her eyes brightened. "It's not for me, my dear." She refolded the message and handed it to Felicity.

Felicity glanced doubtfully at Alex, who watched with rapt

attention as she slowly unfolded the telegram and read, Pip lifting his head to sniff the missive.

When she'd finished, she refolded the sheet and handed it to Alex. Felicity waited while he read it. Then they looked at each other.

It was apparent their thoughts on the matter were aligned.

"Well, Grandmama." The corners of Felicity's lips twitched upwards. "I believe we've found our next case."

Claim your free Lady Felicity Quick ebook!

Sign up for my email newsletter and you'll get **Murder at Afternoon Tea** absolutely free.

This exclusive story isn't available anywhere else.

As a newsletter subscriber, you'll also receive writing updates, special offers, and peeks behind the scenes...

Use this link to sign up and claim your copy today:
https://BookHip.com/XMGPNZC

Read the next in the series...

**Murder at the Ball**

A Lady Felicity Quick 1920s Cozy Mystery
Book 4

**The party at Grimstow House promises tremendous fun, with cocktails, games, costumes ... and a killer on the loose!**

England, 1922. Lady Felicity Quick's success as a sleuth has upended her reporting career, yet she simply must answer a relative's plea for help. Sinister letters are threatening her cousin's reputation — but who's the sender?

Posing as an innocent party guest at a remote country manor, Felicity investigates her cousin's clique for hints of guilt. Amid raucous games, free-flowing champagne, and some ghastly squabbles amongst supposed friends, Felicity finds a trail of revealing clues.

But when a body is discovered, a dangerous web of intrigue is revealed, and a new deadly game begins...

Can Felicity unravel the tangle of motives and alibis to identify the killer and avert another slaying? Or will the party finish with the wrong kind of bang?

If you love puzzling country house murders set in the old-fashioned elegance of 1920s England, then you will love this cozy mystery series! For fans of Agatha Christie, Downton Abbey, Magda Alexander and T E Kinsey.

## The Lady Felicity Quick Mystery Series

**Murder at Afternoon Tea**

(Novella | Exclusive for Newsletter Subscribers)

**Murder on the Village Green**

(Book 1 | Available Now)

**Murder at a Country House**

(Book 2 | Available Now)

**Murder at the Tea Rooms**

(Book 3 | Available Now)

**Murder at the Ball**

(Book 4 | Available Now)

**Murder on the Coast**

(Book 5 | Available Now)

**Murder at a Boarding School**

(Book 6 | Available Now)

**Murder at a Flower Show**

(Book 7 | Coming Soon)

# About the Author

Rosie Hunt is a British author of cozy mysteries both puzzling and historical. Her books include the Lady Felicity Quick mystery series set in the green and pleasant countryside of southwest England in the 1920s.

A history addict and former journalist, Rosie grew up immersed in the worlds of Poirot and Miss Marple. This early exposure to baffling murder mysteries rather coloured her outlook on life, and it was only a matter of time before she began writing her own.

Rosie loves clotted cream, knitting, and Golden Age crime fiction, and she'll never miss an opportunity to visit a National Trust property. She lives with her husband and their four-pawed overlord on a river in Northern Europe.

**Join Rosie's mailing list:**
bookhip.com/XMGPNZC

**Follow Rosie on Facebook:**
facebook.com/RosieHuntAuthor

Printed in Great Britain
by Amazon

47322290R00148